ex libris

For additional information, please contact:
A-Girl Studio
P.O. Box 213, Burbank, CA 91503 U.S.A.
www.a-girlstudio.com

ISBN: 978-1-936622-27-6

First paperback edition, 2017

Cover model is Faestock, http://faestock.deviantart.com/

POISON
GARDEN

An Elle Black Penny Dread
Volume Two

By
Elizabeth Watasin

A-GIRL STUDIO

Kind hearts are the gardens,
kind thoughts are the roots,
kind words are the flowers,
kind deeds are the fruits.

–Henry Wadsworth Longfellow

CHAPTER ONE

In hazy, noisome London, across Regent's Canal and a tree-lined path, simple Camden Town lay. Women worked in the cottages and vegetable gardens where spring rain, insubstantial and brief, sprinkled the roofs and earth. A row of two storey red-brick villas stood before one of the few paved streets, and in the very centre, a home sat with a red door and a gleaming, black iron knocker. Twin sphinx statues lounged on either side of the entrance, gazed past the black iron fence that separated the house from the walk, and smiled.

A gangly postman marched down the row, fading raindrops spotting his hat and coat's shoulders. He turned for the red door, raised his hat to the sphinxes, bent down to stuff envelopes through the brass mail slot, and then departed. But the door opened and a silver-haired woman emerged, waving. In her hand, she bore an envelope.

"Mr Topps!" she called.

"Good day, Mrs Haggins," the postman said, returning. He raised his hat. "Looks like more rain, won't you say?"

"If you can call those pitiful drops 'rain,' Mr Topps!" she exclaimed, handing him the envelope. "We may have clouds, but nothing worthwhile showers down. A terrible period of unnatural dryness, I say. And with such few breezes, the air keeps growing thicker and thicker!"

Mr Topps shook his head. "And tempers grow shorter and shorter—everywhere in London! With this noxious air and the 'orrible, diseased murders, I'm blessed to have the Camden Town route as the Defiler's evil hasn't touched 'ere. But come what may, nothing can stop rain, Mrs Haggins."

Mrs Haggins bade him good day and closed the door.

Inside, she gathered the envelopes on the floor, noted the continued sound of the mechanical washer churning in the scullery, and then entered the warm parlour with its bay windows facing the street. A woman in a deep blue Polonaise draped over gold and white underskirts sat reading a newspaper. Tall, blonde, and blue-eyed, with a straight nose, full lips, and tapered chin, Mrs Faedra White-Black sat in her armchair near the windows and scanned the pages with keen interest. The *Times'* headline read: Defiler's Disease Monstrofies More! 5th of April, 1880.

Mrs Haggins laid the mail on Faedra's side table, laden with catalogues, magazines, and a patchwork knitting bag. Faedra smiled, revealing dimples.

"How relieved I am you're home, Mrs White-Black," Mrs Haggins said. She went to the fireplace and stirred the low fire with a poker. "Can't help but worry with those attacks happening near your work, corrupting people into monstrosities!"

"The attacks no longer remain in the East End, Mrs Haggins." Faedra's voice carried an American inflection. "Victims are manifesting as far as Westminster. The Defiler has spread his zymotic taint, as he wrote the papers he would."

Mrs Haggins shook her head and tutted. She straightened the daguerreotypes and tintypes on the mantle and carefully moved a framed cabinet card to the fore. In it, a smiling Faedra stood, arm in arm with a smaller, dark-haired woman whose large and frank eyes were lined with kohl. It read: MARRIED, 22nd of June, 1878.

"Those supernatural agents of His Royal Highness should hurry and catch this brute," Mrs Haggins said. The washer in the scullery ceased churning, and Mrs Haggins excused herself, leaving for the kitchen.

The red velvet mantle clock ticked. A petite woman brandishing a feather duster entered the parlour from the adjacent drawing room. Ignoring Faedra, she dusted the photographs and clock, then moved the MARRIED cabinet card to the mantle's centre, displaying it prominently.

Mrs Elle Black, aged twenty-four, dusted the terracotta Egyptian sphinx figurine and sandstone statuette of Bastet on the mantle, and then picked up the poker to stir the fire. With swept-up hair dyed blood-red using henna and cloves, hazel eyes lined with kohl, and lips touched with rouge, she wore earring drops of lapis lazuli and a bullet-pierced penny as a pendant necklace. White lace edged the three-quarter sleeves of her black house dress, and black velvet bows dotted the circumference of her skirt's hem while another large bow draped over her modestly sized bustle. Her black bodice bore a white, ruffled front with large black buttons running down her chest.

She turned to a display cabinet and dusted Faedra's tennis and archery trophy cups, markswoman medals, and the framed photograph of her wife's girlhood cricket team. She then dusted Faedra's hung bow and quiver.

Hours earlier, she'd risen before Faedra, opened all curtains, cleaned all grates, refilled the oil in the lamps, ran her mechanical sweeper on the hall carpets, and swept the front porch. Then she'd entered the garden wearing a smock, hat, and gloves to water her rows and strawberry hotbed with Faedra's latest gift, a mechanised precipitation pump. She picked a few tomatoes from the vine and some sea kale from its forcing jar, then returned to the kitchen to prepare a breakfast of fried eggs, braised sea kale, jugged kippers, fried tomatoes, fried mushrooms, bacon, blood sausage, toast, and ham. While Mrs Haggins laid the breakfast table, Elle went upstairs to scrub Faedra's back as she sat in her morning bath, filled from their bedroom stove's hot water spigot.

Though her morning's labour was done, Elle's cheeks were still flushed from activity. She moved from object to object with her duster, like a bee needing to visit every flower. Then she heard Faedra's paper rustle. Feeling that the noise was made deliberately, Elle turned around.

Faedra looked over her newspaper with an arched brow and patted her lap. Elle smiled and turned back to the trophy cabinet.

"I believe one of your cups needs polishing," Elle said.

"The cup may have your company, then." Faedra's tone sounded hurt, and she returned to reading. "And I shall sit here, alone, while absorbing the latest ghastly crimes to assail London."

Elle stored her duster behind the display cabinet and went to the chair by the windows, facing Faedra. Sitting, she noticed the mail and her knitting but attended to neither, twining her fingers in her lap.

"I feel I must keep busy," Elle said.

Faedra moved her paper again to gaze with sympathy.

"I am nervous about our impending visitor as well, Elle. Especially after what we've learned about him."

"That we now know my former spouse is some...vampyre, does not disturb me as much as other questions needing answers. Questions that, five years after his supposed death, I wish had not come to me."

"My poor dear! Won't you sit with me?"

"I cannot, or else I would need to reapply my rouge."

"Cheeky kit. Perhaps you're keeping your lips pristine for that certain former spouse."

"Oh, Faedy!" Elle rose and sat in Faedra's lap. She kissed her.

When their lips parted, Elle pulled her handkerchief from her sleeve to wipe Faedra's smiling mouth of rouge.

"You're a silly goose," Elle said. "I only want to look my best. For such a long time I'd kept myself less so while mourning Valentin. Had I known the truth, I would have married you straight away after you rescued me from the asylum! I'm done suffering for that false spectre."

"I hope this meeting will further ease your heart. Darling, you were mourning your parents and brother as well. It was only proper you made me wait three years. During that time you were, and are, beautiful." Faedra looked up in adoration.

Elle smiled. "I'm grateful you're here and not rent-collecting. How did you manage time away?"

"The ghastly deaths are to blame, Elle. My Whitechapel warrens have been segregated by the Public Disinfectors." She opened the paper to indicate the story, and Elle took it from her hands to read more.

"How dreadful! Are the Secret Commission agents any closer to capturing this madman? With an agent dead and another stricken, I hope Artifice suffers no harm in securing his capture."

"But darling, resurrected criminals are put into service for just this purpose," Faedra said gently. "To fight what we cannot. I know the artificial ghost is your favourite. Here's a thought: when she triumphs over this monster, we shall visit Artifice's lair at that notorious club, the Vesta. Then we can congratulate Artifice ourselves."

"Oh!" Elle said in delight.

"But until then," Faedra continued. She took the paper from Elle's hands and folded it. "Our most dependable journalist, Lady Helia Skycourt, writes of no gains by our valiant agents, only of the fearful madness gripping London. The editorial letters are replete with hysteria, outlandish accusations, and the most hateful commentary. I've never seen the like." She tossed the paper aside and placed her hands at Elle's waist.

"The Defiler's taunting letters have inspired people's darker sensibilities," Elle said, thoughtful. "But thanks to such rancour, Miss Skycourt's Sundark story has been overlooked."

"Much to our relief. Your fellow psychics hadn't opportunity to voice their opinions regarding your last case. And with your methodology very much at odds with theirs, dear, they're certain to say dreadful things once your anomalous perturbationist skills become further known."

"I prefer the descriptive, 'remote influencer,'" Elle said. "Oh, let them make noise. We'll ignore them. But Miss Skycourt's stories must be read. Having met her, I believe she is the authority on the supernatural the *Times* makes her to be."

"Yet I've heard that Lady Helia is a madwoman, Elle." Faedra frowned.

"But I'm a madwoman too, Faedy."

"Darling." Faedra kissed Elle's bosom. "Formerly mad! Never mind that you are most specially gifted. I've no tolerance for other mad women. But since you're fond of Lady Helia, I will reserve judgement."

"She's far more odd than myself," Elle said.

"Such words do not help me keep an even-tempered mind."

Elle kissed Faedra on the forehead, wiped away the rouge mark, and rose from her lap. She walked away in thought.

"I granted Miss Skycourt sole right to the Sundark story in exchange for her expertise, and it proved most valuable," Elle said. "I wish you had been here when she explained the nature of vampyres. There were many aspects, just as the fantastic stories say, but some qualities do not explain Valentin."

"How so?"

"Truly, such creatures are revenants. A vampyre's heart, she had said, does not beat. Yet I know Valentin's does."

"Perhaps he'd woven some enchantment to give you such an impression?"

"Valentin was more a man of action, not of mental arts. I will ask him why his heart beats."

An approaching carriage rumbled in the street, and Elle turned and walked towards the windows. She reached for Faedra's hand while her wife remained seated, and they looked out together.

A hansom cab rolled into view and halted. A dark-haired gentleman with a pencil moustache exited the cab to pay the driver. Tall, slim, and broad-shouldered, his skin was toned like one tanned, and his hair glistened with pomade. He carried no hat or gloves. He wore a long, fitted grey coat with black lapels over black trousers. When he turned for their door, she saw his pearl-white, double-breasted waistcoat beneath and the grey tie and folded collar points at his throat. She looked at his sculpted cheekbones and jaw. His sleepy-lidded gaze beneath arched brows hid the grey-green eyes she knew well. His eyes slanted slightly, like a feline's.

Elle felt Faedra's reassuring squeeze on her hand.

"It really is him," Faedra said softly. "I nearly thought we collectively dreamt his strange, nighttime appearance to our bedroom."

"He is making an effort to appear demure," Elle remarked as the doorknocker sounded. "And therefore, without threat. Grey is not his preferred colour; he'd always found it dreary. Nor is he wearing any sort of jewellery. Not even a jewelled pin for his tie."

"Mrs Black, Mrs White-Black," Mrs Haggins called from the hallway.

"Yes, Mrs Haggins?" they answered in unison. Mrs Haggins entered with a card in hand, her expression cautious.

"The gentleman you're expecting, ma'ams. Mr Valentin... Black." She handed the card to Faedra.

"Won't you show him in, Mrs Haggins," Elle requested. She moved to stand beside Faedra's chair and rested a hand along the back.

Valentin stepped past Mrs Haggins and into the room.

Though he was very fit, with broad back and shoulders, he was not a burly man. His figure tapered to a slim waist and hips, which Elle had always thought gave him the perfect lines so suitable to fitted dress. He had the long legs and muscular calves that could drive noblewomen to fling aside their carefully chosen doorsmen, coveted for their shapely, stockinged legs. Yet she suspected that her formerly dead husband had never had to serve or labour as such men did. She wondered how many young heiresses he'd married, rendered destitute, and then made widows of, beside herself.

They stared at each other. Valentin's heavy-lidded gaze, though sensual, was impassively composed. The mantle clock ticked.

"I'm very angry with you," Elle ejected.

She felt Faedra look up in surprise, and Valentin's gaze dropped, his lips pursed. She was certain he was suppressing a smile.

While she fumed and silently counted backwards, his gaze remained on the floor, as if patiently waiting for her mood to end.

"Well," she said. "Let us have tea." She motioned for Valentin to take the chair across from Faedra, its back to the fireplace.

"Elle," Valentin said. "Please seat yourself fir—"

"This is my house," Elle said.

He looked at her, his gaze tolerant, and then sat down. Mrs Haggins departed with a wary look at the trio.

"This is a most...unique situation." Faedra looked up at Elle again, who continued to stand. "And yet it's one where we can learn more fully what has happened to you since your 'death.'"

"I will do my best to answer," Valentin said.

"Then perhaps you should introduce yourself properly to my wife?" Elle's tone was cool. "We now know that you are one of those creatures, a vampyre. Therefore, anything I know about you must be from having been beguiled."

"The only times I beguiled you were when you came too close

to suspecting the truth, Elle. You are very clever."

"That sounds like a great many times," she said.

Again, she thought he hid a smile. But when he rose from his chair, it was with a solemn, formal air. He bowed to Faedra.

"I am Valentin Black. And I shall give you and Elle the facts of my past. At least those safe for you to know. As a young man I was an officer. I'd told Elle that, and it was true. I will not say what rank I held or what uniform I wore. What country I was born in does not matter. But as is the nature of creatures like myself, we live a long time, and in that time I began to value the frivolous society of well-to-do women rather than the manoeuvres of military life."

"And you accept the money of such women," Faedra said. "Like a courtesan would from men."

"I was...am, such a companion to women."

"Oh, Valentin, sit. And how many did you marry?" Elle asked.

"Only you, Elle." He gave her his steady gaze.

Elle's jaw clenched. She felt a retort come to her lips. Faedra touched Elle's hand resting on the chair back and squeezed it as Valentin took his seat again. He moved slowly as he did so, watching her all the while.

Oh yes, stare. So that I may not feel dismissed, and that I might develop the absurd impression that you still care.

"Valentin, did you marry me for my money?"

"I did." He held her gaze, but his eyes seemed sad.

"Do not look so contrite," she said.

Mrs Haggins entered the room with the ladened tea tray. She set it down on the table and silently made her exit.

"You state that Elle is the only one you married for her fortune." Faedra's tone was solemn. "After you duelled with Elle's brother, Hector, where you had killed him and he, you, Elle had to bury you both. And in the midst of such grief she discovered that Hector's accusation against you was true; you had taken all of her money and left her penniless."

Valentin's gaze dropped. He stared at the carpet, his brow dark.

"For some reason, you became greedy." Faedra's tone turned sceptical. "I work with a great many working-class families, Mr Black. They are happy to do as they do until something drastically changes their lives. That is when unfortunate decisions are made."

"I had need of the money," he said.

"You were a rake and you had your expenses," Elle said. "But I knew you to be indifferent to gambling. I wouldn't have married you had you been a wastrel. What need had you for my entire fortune?"

When Valentin set his jaw and said nothing, she huffed.

"You are protecting another," she said.

He looked at her in surprise, then grinned, his teeth perfect and white. She was taken aback, having forgotten how brilliant his smiles were and how they lit his face, much like Faedra's did.

"Your intuition had always impressed me, Elle." He seemed pleased.

"It's not so much intuition as a most bothersome imagination," she said. "Then you will not disclose the entirety of your swindle? The very reason behind it?"

"I cannot."

"We could only summon you here by placing an ad in the paper," she continued. "Did this attention compromise your... family?"

He grinned again and sat forwards in his chair.

"Dear Elle. I was confident you would remarry. You are a perfect little wife. True, you had mental abilities that might perturb another man, but they were so harmless back then. Mere sensations, flutters of the air. Blossoms, leaves, and paper wrappers that you caused to drift. Now I've learned from this Sundark affair that your gifts have matured. You can move even more with your mind! And you've found another who is not threatened by such queer powers. Your woman takes good care of you. Certainly you are happy?"

"I am. But Valentin, when you and Hector died, I went mad. My talents manifested, wreaking havoc. I was committed to an asylum. I would be there still if Faedra had not come for me."

Valentin's smile faded, and his face stilled. His gaze turned bleak.

"You did not know." Elle's tone was bitter.

"All that I've done to you is unforgivable."

"It is. Especially shooting Hector! But worst of all, Valentin, you were my husband. My love. I saw and felt you die, your wound bleeding like a burst dam beneath my hands. I've since learned that bullets can't kill creatures like you. Yet I felt you leave. You were gone."

Her voice quavered. Faedra rose, and Valentin did as well. Faedra coaxed Elle to sit in her armchair, then knelt and grasped her hand. Valentin approached and knelt beside her, holding Elle's tremulous gaze.

"I did die," he said softly. "I've died many times. In that way, I am unlike other vampyres."

"You had to leave," Elle said. "You could not stay with me."

He reached for her free hand as her tears fell, and she allowed him to take it in both of his. His clasp was warm and firm.

"When I'm dying, I can control nothing," he said.

☠

After she dabbed her tears away, Elle calmed. She reassured both Faedra and Valentin that she was well, rose, and seated herself by the windows to serve tea. She served Faedra first, surprising her wife with the overt slight to their guest, then gave a cup to Valentin.

She anticipated that Faedra would wish to bring their meeting back to more even-tempered and practical matters, and her wife did so.

"It has been five years since you had stolen Elle's fortune," she said. "Will you be returning any of it?"

"I would, but it is entirely gone," Valentin said. "Which is why, when we recognised each other at Regent St, I came here to offer her my help should she ever need it." He glanced at Elle. "Now that she is endangering herself more with this psychic detective business, I wish to aid, all I can."

"Please. You came at night and entered our bedroom balcony to offer that 'aid,'" Elle scoffed, "at a most inconvenient time. That was hardly helpful."

"I was affirming whether I'd the correct house."

"You were being rude. Like a naughty schoolboy," Elle muttered.

"That night you showed Elle your fangs," Faedra recalled. "And I thought them impressive."

"Thank you," Valentine said.

"Yet, as I look, your canines appear the same as any man's. Why can't we see them now?"

"They appear when I awaken my true nature."

"I'm truly confused as to your 'nature,'" Faedra said. "You can die. And as we now know, can return to life. Therefore you must succumb to poisons and manmade weapons."

"I do. You know a little, perhaps, of the conventional vampyre of lore? The one that is of the revenants? I am the other sort. Warm and breathing, born a vampyre from a living woman."

"A living woman?" Faedra repeated. She glanced at Elle. "Your...father was a vampyre?"

"Both my parents are living vampyres."

"That would explain his beating heart, Elle," Faedra said.

"It certainly does." Elle sipped from her cup.

Valentin took that moment to change the subject of conversation to Faedra. He learned then that she was indeed, Elle's beloved schoolgirl friend who was four years older and then left England after coming of age. When Elle ceased to answer Faedra's letters, Faedra returned to England only to find Elle in an asylum.

Valentin queried as to Faedra's accent, and she affirmed that on her father's side, she was part American.

"I told you everything about Faedy when you and I were married, Valentin," Elle said. "You did not listen."

"I did listen," he replied, unruffled. "But it is a pleasure to affirm what you had told me with the woman you loved then, and now." A smirk touched his mouth.

Charmer, Elle thought with resentment.

He then indicated the silver cups and medals on display.

"Surely these winnings are yours?" he said to Faedra. "I've never known Elle to take interest in any sports. Not even fishing."

"That is a pastime I'm encouraging her to pursue with me." Faedra smiled at Elle.

"I'm perfectly happy just cooking the fish," Elle said.

She said no more when Valentin looked at her, expectant, as if pleased to hear her make a light remark. In the following silence, he returned his attention to Faedra.

While the two conversed, Elle watched them take the other's measure. Though Faedra had confessed to her that she'd never found men of romantic interest, she was then looking at Valentin with curiosity, perhaps in wonderment of what Elle had found to love in him. But Valentin was perfectly behaved and charming, and such was enough to lower Faedra's guard and allow her to express the bright sociableness that was her natural demeanour.

Elle recalled when Valentin would hold himself aloof at functions, confident that women would flock just from his beauty alone. He found the majority of such women dull and made little effort to keep their company. But with Faedra he was accommodating and quick to please. Perhaps he did so knowing Elle watched him, but she suspected more that he was genuinely engaged.

Valentin had a bold gaze when it came to admiring the female sex, and he only allowed that scrutiny to spark with very interesting women. It did not matter what shape or age, or even if some, by certain standards, were not terribly attractive. Intelligence, complexity, maturity, or a mysterious nature intrigued him. Regarding herself, Elle thought it had been her queer way of seeing the world that caught his attention, for she had grown up in her father's archaeological digs and once back in England, had never quite understood proper society. That, and she had often amused him. In light of his deceit, she then knew better. But Valentin was still Valentin. Right then, he was running that especial, bold gaze down Faedra's figure as she leaned to add more sugar to her cup.

He is surely recalling how he'd seen her nude during that nighttime visit, Elle thought. She hardly found such impropriety and possible lustful recollection an affront. Had he no desire for her beautiful wife she would have thought him somehow rendered a eunuch during their time apart.

"That would be fitting," she said to herself.

"Elle?" Faedra queried. Both she and Valentin regarded her with curiosity.

Elle set her cup down. Dread welled within as she recalled her chief reason for the meeting.

She looked at Faedra. Whatever was in her expression made Faedra move forwards in her chair, her face worried.

"I nearly enjoy this," Elle said. "I almost would like it to continue. Yet I haven't the good sense to let a matter lie."

"What is it, darling?" Faedra asked.

Elle gazed at Valentin. She thought he looked concerned and he too, moved forwards.

"Elle," he said.

"Had you not the good fortune of being shot, how would you have left me?" she demanded.

The room's warmth fled. Valentin seemed to withdraw and fold in upon himself, his face stark and solemn. Shadows grew and clung to him, compressing him where he sat.

"I have to know," she said.

"Elle. Don't—"

"Answer me, Valentin."

"I would have taken a trip across a lake," he said, abrupt. "Had a boating accident, and been assumed drowned. My body would not have been found."

The china on the tea tray began to tremble. The objects on the shelves and on the mantle also began to shake. Faedra set her cup down and quickly rose. She coaxed Elle to her feet.

"You must not be present when we return," Faedra said to Valentin.

She walked Elle out the parlour as Valentin stood and watched them go.

☠

Faedra hurried Elle through the kitchen where hung pots and pans began to clank around a bewildered Mrs Haggins preparing a jelly mould. They entered the garden and Elle's plants fluttered in their rows. The garden gate flew open with a bang. Faedra urged Elle through and down the alley, past their neighbours' gardens. Trees shook and Lt Montague's alarmed chickens flew up in the air as if tossed. Once Elle and Faedra passed the row and cottages, they climbed a footbridge arcing over the canal. At the apex, Elle gripped the railing to bring Faedra to a stop. The water below began to roil.

"*How I hate you!*" she cried. Water rose below her, a miniature tsunami, and crashed, sending waves away from the bridge. Quacking ducks flapped up, flew ahead of the sudden burst of water, and then came down to settle again. They bobbed as the waves traveled into the distance.

Faedra clasped Elle to her.

"I don't mean it, I really don't," Elle sobbed into her shoulder. "But oh, he's shown me what a fool I am still."

Faedra held her as she wept. Children appeared on the opposite bank, jostled each other, and stared.

"That coward!" Elle ejected tearfully. "Thief! May his penis fall off!"

"Elle," Faedra said, dismayed. She soothed Elle's back. "Breathe, dear. I know it's upsetting, but please think no more bad thoughts! You know what they say of those who speak ill."

"That I should end up in hell?" Elle's tone was shaky.

"Those you've sent there, and deservedly, will have long memories."

Elle stepped back in Faedra's arms to fumble for her handkerchief. But once in hand, she clenched it in fury.

"If I find myself in hell and without you, I'll take my revenge again and again upon such enemies. I'll do more than piss on Abigail Sundark. Why, I'd seize a Circle for my own and pile up the piteous damned to heaven, for surely that's where you'll be. The first in that pile would be Valentin."

"Dear," Faedra said, concerned.

"Doesn't matter that he comes to life again," Elle said sharply. "Each time he dies he must end up there. I'd build a tottering corpse tower right on top of him to reach you, and set the firmament on fire with my rage."

Faedra clasped her close. "My poor Elle."

"Oh Faedy, why can't I simply forgive him? He's not worth more of my suffering. But such animosity consumes me! This is who I am, then? Immature, unfit in temperance? I've said worse in the asylum!"

Faedra took Elle's hands in both her own.

"No, I'd heard your mad ranting. This is not like you at all. There's a poison in London's air, Elle! I truly believe there is, turning good natures into violent souls just like the Defiler's corruptive taint. Several letters in the *Times* had mentioned our insalubrious atmosphere. It's not only you losing temper— everyone in London is! I didn't share the whole of my situation's circumstance, but those of us maintaining Whitechapel warrens are instructed to stay away for a week. Given this rare chance, we should leave."

"Leave?" Elle gulped, forestalling further tears.

Faedra smiled. "This was my surprise for you, darling. How would you like to visit Peaseflower?"

"Peaseflower Manor?" Elle gaped. "And its extraordinary gardens?"

Faedra led Elle down from the bridge. The children clamoured up to the vacated spot, waved their arms at the water below and made "whooshing" sounds.

"I knew you would like the idea," Faedra said as Elle drew shaky breaths and wiped away the last of her tears. Faedra slipped her arm into hers. "Peasy has written me. And do not worry. She will pay all travel expenses. Our old school friend has need of our assistance. I'll explain once we're back home and I've her correspondence in hand. It's an odd letter, but I'm certain what she writes of is nothing you can't solve."

"Peasy was never very fond of me, Faedy, only of you. And you know I'm not fond of her. Though we're married, she may not welcome my aiding you in this plea of hers."

"Welcomed or not, my reply stated that my wife, clearly named as you, must accompany me if I come." Faedra squeezed Elle's arm in assurance. "Her response should be in the mail just arrived."

"And that response is certain to be in the positive. Even the prospect of myself darkening her doorstep will not deter her from seeking your company. Oh, what nonsense has she gotten into now?"

"Elle," Faedra said with patience.

"I apologise, dear. This vulgar discontent has its grip on me again. Yes, let us go, Faedy. In Peaseflower's legendary gardens I might find my temperance again. The countryside air will be invigorating!"

"That is exactly why I think we should leave."

"Yet you don't seem affected at all by this supposed tainted air, Faedy. Insalubrious, you say, but I'd always found London's atmosphere to be so."

"Bucolic wench! Perhaps I'm not as sensitive as you." Faedra smiled. "With your esemplastic abilities. I've had a great urge for marathon rounds of glass ball shooting, however."

"Your loud and imposing instrument you affectionately named 'Miss Sharps' will not be traveling with us," Elle said with severity. "And Peasy was and likely still is, an avowed vegetarian. I'm quite certain no birds are bagged at her estate. Your shotgun shall remain at home."

"Spoil my fun. The only time we enjoy wild game is when my markswoman reputation earns us an invitation to a hunting party, and that's been a while!" They reached their garden's gate. Faedra glanced at their home then at Elle.

"Why don't you see to your water starved blossoms, darling? I'd like to speak to Mrs Haggins, then I'll fetch you."

Elle doubted Valentin still remained inside and nearly said so. Instead, she brought Faedra head down to kiss her.

"You are my treasure." She didn't bother to wipe the rouge from Faedra's lips.

Elle dabbed more at her eyes when Faedra disappeared within and noted with dismay that her eye cosmetics had smudged, making her resemble an American raccoon. She distracted herself with examining her rows, window herbarium, and then her small clay pots, hanging from nails hammered into the cement of their brick home. In those pots, she tended to seedlings awaiting their transfer to a ready row. One was a pea seedling, grown tall enough to curl tiny tendrils around a small stick. It looked to have pulled itself out of the soil a fourth of an inch since yesterday.

Though Faedra loved to gift her with the latest domestic devises like the mechanised precipitation pump, Elle thought nothing could replace gardening needing the delicate touch of a hand. She picked up her smallest watering can and gave the plant a brief shower.

"Peaseflower," she mused. "How fortunate we are to have this opportunity."

When she turned for the doorway, she spied a piece of paper stuck in the frame that Faedra had, in her haste to enter, apparently missed. Elle went to retrieve it. She unfolded it, a page torn from a small notebook. The penciled words were in Valentin's hand. She read:

To summon me—
L'Eglise de l'Hôpital
59 Brick Lane
Spitalfields

"You live in a Huguenot chapel, truly?" she exclaimed.

She crumpled the paper into a tiny ball, her anger returning. Then she thought of Faedra, who would, in practicality, advise that they keep it.

She put it in her dress pocket, leaving it crumpled.

CHAPTER TWO

Dear Faedy,

How remiss I've been, neglecting our correspondence for this long! Often, you were in my thoughts, yet somehow life became a whirlwind and before I knew it, two years had gone. You'd changed residences in that time, but I recalled your employer's name of business and hope that through their hands this letter reaches yours and that it finds you happy and well.

I wish I were writing under better circumstance. Peaseflower is well, the business is very well, and since Mother and I are free of the management of Bunkley Teas, she oversees the estate while I toil on the gardens, having taken over Papa's botanic passion with vigour and furthered it with my own vision. It has required all my energies, for I believe I am creating one of the most significant conservatories known to present man. I boast, but it's true! Dear cousin Cherish continues her plant hunting in the Malay Archipelago and sends back rare specimens that I add to my conservatorial domain. I've successfully propagated a recent acquisition, which—thanks to a cataclysm of nature— would have never seen its like on this Earth again. Conservation *is rewarding work, and I am happy; I should be happy!*

But are we well, Mother and I? That is the question. Since Papa's passing over two years ago, Mother fell ill, and as I'm all she has, I stayed and shunned London. I love our land, and I never cared for meeting suitors any more than you did, Faedy! Unless they should be very pretty women like you, but any possibility of that happening here, in the countryside, is quashed by Mother's sudden reclusiveness, and now the resulting isolation is such that I've only my plants for companions.

Yes, Faedy, Mother has become—dare I write it? Queer. She had looked forward to recovery and trips abroad once more, and after two years of mourning, I welcomed such possibilities. But suddenly such intentions disappeared, as if she'd never considered them and somehow never desired them.

It was such a drastic change; one day she was as I knew her, the next, she was a stranger. I thought her behaviour a temporary affectation, perhaps brought on by sombre news she'd not shared with me, and when she did not recover, a mania of the spirit. She never eats and dully exists, a ghost in this house. I tried to summon doctors, but she would not see them. She dismissed all my scientists except for Polly, and nearly all my conservatory staff and gardeners! I don't know why this has happened! Questioning Mother is useless, and I worry how this will affect the hamlets within our purview, for we employed many on Fairditch's former land.

Mother has also rebuffed neighbours and driven away concerned visitors. We've been rendered invisible to our society thanks to such rudeness, and now—well, I feel as if what has made Mother so queer has spread throughout the household!

Somehow, I've lost Mother, and a shade has taken her place. Please do not consider my suspicion some fancy borne of boredom or evidence of a weak mind (or evil indulgence!) I would be happy to ignore all such queerness and continue focus on my latest acquisition, but my unease grows, my distrust of those around me as well, and my cousin being so far away and unreachable—Faedy, I hope you might come, look at Mother, look at everyone, and tell me I am wrong. Or agree, that yes, something is terribly amiss, and then help me. I need help, please come.

A rail passage awaits you—
Your grateful friend,
Peasy Bunkley

Elle laid the letter aside and picked up the letter just arrived. She was seated at her bedroom writing table while Faedra puttered with her stored sports equipment in the sewing room. Dinner had long been served and cleared. Elle read:

Dear Faedy,

How wonderful to hear you are coming! And to learn that Elle—goodness, funny Elle!—is your spouse in truth! How is that possible? No, do not write to explain, you will tell me all when you arrive. And of course Elle must come with you! I've not seen her since we were schoolgirls. I believe we'll have such good times. How eager I am to show you all the delights and distractions of Peaseflower!

Our London agent has his instructions. Do nothing more than pack your most fetching frocks!

I await you with impatience,
Love,
Your devoted Peasy

"'Most fetching frocks?'" Elle said with a raised brow. She looked at the envelopes' postmarks, noting the amount of days between their arrivals.

"Her post is only a day's train delivery from North East England. Despite the urgency of her first letter, she allowed several days to pass before answering Faedra's reply."

She laid the letters side by side and studied the penmanship, vaguely hearing Faedra exclaim and trip over something.

"A rather light tone to her last letter, don't you think?" Elle said when Faedra walked in with her wrapped fishing pole. She had concluded that the same hand wrote both letters.

"It is a queer change from the worries of the first. Perhaps Mrs Bunkley was observing Peasy write?" Faedra suggested. "Therefore she would not want to reiterate her concerns." She pulled the fastenings of her fishing pole's long, cloth case and inspected the rod and line.

"Perhaps," Elle said in thought. "Do you know who Polly is, dear?"

"I do not," Faedra admitted. "But I assume she is one of Peasy's botanists."

While Faedra rewrapped her pole, Elle put the letters away in her carpetbag, and then went to the armoire to look through Faedra's clothing. Peasy's agent had delivered first class rail passages that very evening, for departure the following morning when a carriage would pick them up. Elle had sighed at the haste but she knew Mrs Haggins could easily take care of their home and garden while they were gone. Portable lunches were not needed either, since meals were included with the extravagantly priced tickets. Just as Peasy had instructed, they only had to pack.

Once Faedra brought out their suitcases, Elle pulled Faedra's handsomest street attire from the armoire and made certain none were frilly, overly decorative, or revealed any skin.

"What of your detecting suitcase, dear?" Faedra queried, opening the case in question. The interior of the halves revealed leather straps, casings, and pouches that held the items and tools Elle might have need for: her policeman's lantern, candles, coffee press, compact microscope, portable stove, a ball of string, self-heating cans for coffee and tea, a first aid kit, a package of sea salt, and a bright, red paper parcel tied with red string that Faedra had labelled: "Especial Surprises". Chinese letters were also written on the surface.

"Yes, let's bring it, Faedy. I shall add biscuits and jerked meat."

Faedra grinned. "I love your dehydrated experiments with the parabolic mirror-concentration cooker! But surely we can endure the exoticism of vegetarian dishes for a few days?"

Elle paused, thinking of an entire day without any sustenance derived from an animal. She grabbed Faedra's arm with a dramatic air.

"You must catch us many trout," she demanded.

☠

Elle rose early at the crow of Lt Montague's rooster. While Faedra dozed more, Elle donned her black dress with red piping that ran along the scalloped high collar, down the black-buttoned front, the edges of the bodice, and the folded cuffs. Folds in the layered skirts hid peeping red panels. Since giving up the aspect of mourning for a husband who hadn't been dead after all, Elle decided to experiment with more colour. She carefully applied kohl to her eyes, and then retrieved her brass chatelaine, which Faedra called her "detecting equipage."

Items like a brass doll's mirror, a notebook with telescoping pencil, a compact spyglass, a magnifying lorgnette, a match safe, and a petite, brass holder of retractable tools dangled from chains attached to the curling snakes of a large Medusa-head medallion and clip. The longest chain was of three feet with a weighted fob of brass and crystal, and this Elle wound around her small waist. Freshly repaired and returned from the jewellers after its Sundark adventure, Faedra had added one more tool to the chatelaine: a mother-of-pearl inlaid pocketknife, shaped like a woman's leg and ending in her booted foot.

It was a very naughty little novelty tool, no doubt intended for the chain of some dandy or rapscallion, but its presence made Elle smile.

She descended to prepare breakfast and found Faedra's tennis racket, golf clubs, quiver and bow, cricket bat, and Elle's own modestly sized (and seldom used) fishing pole wrapped for transport and added to their luggage. When Faedra joined her, Elle firmly informed that since she did not pack Faedra's very fetching tennis dress, the racket would not accompany them. She did, however, pack her wife's riding habit and hat. The bow and quiver, Elle's fishing pole, and the cricket bat were also removed. Elle argued that Faedra could not possibly find a women's cricket team in the countryside to play with, much less two teams for a suitable game.

"And these will surely not accompany us," Elle finally said, and hefted two three-pound Indian clubs away from their bags.

"But Elle, it's for the exercise of your—" Faedra pointed at her temple.

"My mental abilities shall take a deserved rest as much as my emotional condition, Faedy. I adore that you are overseeing the strengthening of my remote influencing skills, but I will resume lifting these weights upon our return."

Thus, when the carriage arrived to take them to King's Cross Station, Faedra still had her fishing pole and golf clubs but was cheered by the prospect that she might ride at Peaseflower.

"Mrs Black," Mrs Haggins said, while Faedra saw to the loading of their luggage and Elle, in her black bonnet and cloak, bade goodbye to the sphinxes. "No need to worry, I've everything in hand. But what should I do if that...Mr Black should visit again?"

"Oh, Mrs Haggins, I doubt he'll call by conventional means. But if he should do so, you may tell him Mrs White-Black and I are presently in a bedroom elsewhere," Elle said.

Mrs Haggins smiled, uncertain, and nodded.

Half an hour later, Elle and Faedra boarded their express train for the 254-mile journey to North East England. They'd a first class compartment all to themselves, with buttoned, black leather seat cushions, curtains, and carpet. Faedra placed Elle's carpet bag on a seat, her own valise in the rack above, sat down, and promptly opened the *Times* newspaper she'd purchased at the station's newsstand. While Faedra read, Elle remained standing and slowly stared around their spacious compartment.

She retrieved the brass doll's mirror on her chatelaine to inspect the air's reflection for any spectral impressions, whether violent, sexual, grief-stricken, or merely of death, and then deemed the compartment free of lingering manifestations. She sat in the seat opposite, took out her knitting from her carpetbag, placed the ball of yarn in her skirt pocket, and began work on a baby blanket for the foundlings' hospital.

When the locomotive whistled and slowly advanced down the track, Elle heaved a sigh she didn't know needed releasing. The weight of certain concerns were finally left behind, one being Valentin, the other the Defiler crimes, which had occurred too close to her wife's rent collecting territory. Faedra was even then reading more news about his defilements.

"Another woman outraged and dead," Elle said in a sober tone, noting the news on the front page. She'd lost enjoyment in following the activities of her favourite agent, Artifice, when it became clear how the Defiler's victims were attacked and infected.

"It may be little comfort, but these latest infections may have been caused by conveyance from victim to victim rather than direct outrage by that fiend," Faedra said as she lowered the paper. "It is only a matter of time. He is certain to be captured soon."

"I dearly hope so. Such crimes need an understanding of science rather than of the unseen and are therefore far above my amateurish expertise."

"Amateurish, you say, yet who was it that defeated a possessed, mechanical house?" Faedra said, smiling. "But as you've mentioned science, I must wonder if the condition of Peasy's mother may be due to something mundane, though no less damaging: apoplexy."

"A brain attack?" Elle's needles clicked. "From the little described, it certainly sounds like it. But Peasy, though socially obtuse, is hardly slow. She could have surmised that herself and forced her mother to accept the attention of doctors. Yet she did not, for whatever she suspects not only unnerves her but is something she can't quite believe, else she would not ask a trusted friend to come witness."

"It is as you say, dear. Which is why you must look too, Elle, with your 'truth-knowing' eyes, as Miss Dufish would describe." Faedra smiled.

Elle smiled as well, fondly recalling the strong-willed, Jamaican secretary who had summoned her to investigate the haunted mechanical hotel, the Sundark.

"Did you bring your Smith & Wesson?" she suddenly enquired.

Faedra did not answer, but only batted her eyelashes.

"You naughty girl." Elle smiled as she knitted. "Well, at least it's smaller than Miss Sharps."

"We are leaving London," Faedra then remarked. Elle glanced out the window and saw that it was so. The tenements, work yards, and well-to-do suburbs gave way to scattered cottages, estates, and stretches of fields. Elle breathed deeply and knitted.

☠

Though Elle's family had been relatively wealthy, theirs had been a frugal household. Her half-English and Tunisian mother had been an impoverished language interpreter before meeting the antiquities hunter Edgar Dunny, Elle's father. Hayat Dunny had preferred to make the family's clothes, cook, and spend modestly on travel. Second rail passage was perfectly acceptable, and she had made it an adventure for the children by introducing them to new people and things. Secluded as Elle and Faedra presently were in first class, while factory towns and rural villages rolled past their picture window, Elle was surprisingly not bored. With the corridor blinds drawn and the door firmly latched, the privacy and comfort of their compartment was inspiring her to certain fantasies, fuelled more by the fact that Faedra was engrossed in a magazine that published women's intimate confessions.

She watched Faedra read her latest copy of *The Englishwoman's Friend* and slowly raised her foot for the one Faedra dangled from her crossed legs. Before she could caress the ankle, Faedra abruptly lowered her magazine, startling her.

"I believe it's time for luncheon," she announced with an eager grin and reached for her pocket watch. Elle lowered her foot and sighed.

For the relaxation of first class passengers, a parlour carriage was present as well as an upper deck solarium lounge and observation carriage, accessible by stairs. There, Elle and Faedra enjoyed a midday dining experience beneath a glassed rooftop and picture windows. But the sensation of being served ham and pea soup in the swaying car while the sun heated their heads and the scenery barrelled past made Elle a bit queasy.

"Is this not like riding full bore in the hunting saddle, dear, whilst eating a shooter's sandwich?" she said, valiantly ignoring the sky and land trundling by as she buttered her bread. Her wife gifted her with a brilliant smile, blonde brow arched, and leaned towards her.

"Yours I eat when taking a stand," Faedra whispered, "all the more to savour it."

Elle missed the butter dish and stabbed the tablecloth instead.

"For that appreciation, you deserve a proper 'tipping' when we return to our accommodations," she said.

Faedra's cheeks reddened, and she glanced aside as if to see if other diners had overheard. Elle thought them married long enough for her wife to cease self-consciousness at Elle's use of vulgarisms, yet Faedra still blushed, and Elle found it both endearing and titillating. Before she could initiate foot-play again, Faedra indicated their soup.

"What a coincidence that we should be enjoying pea soup, Elle. Do you recall—?"

"Oh darling, please." Elle's passion deflated. She thought it just as well. The tablecloths in the observation car did not drape low enough to hide flirtatious foot activity.

"'Am I not an English girl?'" Faedra quoted with a smile, stirring her spoon.

"'For I am as English as our pea,'" Elle replied, smiling in reluctance at their shared schoolgirl memory. "That Peasy. Using pea soup of all things to confront those rude girls for slurring her Chinese origins. It took her long enough."

"I had admired the passion of it, her extending the hand of friendship."

"A hand ignored, Faedy. Malice needs challenging, not understanding. Despite Peasy's wishes, I am glad you resolved the matter with your fists." Elle's tone was pleased.

"And who arranged that confrontation?" Faedra accused. "Peasy refused my help, believing I'd be ejected. What she didn't know was that you survived Miss Head's School For Girls with your own gift for speech: hyperbole." Her eyes widened in humour as she added more pepper to her soup.

"I might have exaggerated when I said you'd break their noses," Elle said, "and render them unsuitable for marriage. But embellishing your rough, American reputation was necessary. Those vicious things insulted my mother when I'd arrived. Then when you came, they disparaged your accent. I had to protect you—despite you're being so much older."

"So much?" Faedra repeated.

"The next winter, Peasy came," Elle recalled. "What a trio we were, you, Peasy, and I."

"Peasy was so eloquent," Faedra mused. "Where your words bit, hers impressed. Such earnest heart she showed when she gave that speech. I was happy to apply my rough American reputation to keep Peasy from further harm. She was so slight, and even smaller than you, Elle, for a girl of ten. Just like her fairy namesake, Peaseblossom."

Faedra return her attention to her soup, and Elle reached over to touch her wife's resting hand.

"Once we arrive at Peaseflower, I will look at everyone and everything there," she assured with gentle firmness. "Whatever assails Peasy, we shall put to rest."

☠

Faedra might consider Peasy someone needing caring, and perhaps Peasy had that need when first arriving at their school, but Elle saw in Peasy a difficult and complicated girl. She was both too intelligent and societally inept; Peasy might expound with insight and clarity upon some recent scientific discovery (to another ten year old like Elle, it had seemed insightful), and then be at an utter loss when angering a girl for remarking that her nose was too big. Peasy knew how to speak on a great many things but didn't understand when spoken to, especially when told she wasn't to speak. At times, Elle wondered if Peasy was merely putting on an affect.

"Peasy, pay attention, those awful girls mean to make an example of you again," she had warned her once.

"What girls? Do you mean the ones who are always rude to you, Elle?"

"Not just to myself, Peasy!" Elle had snapped.

And perhaps Peasy had needed to cause such confusion—such deflection—because she was the only Chinese in an English school. She looked different but spoke, thought, and acted like any girl, as English as she'd claimed at that infamous pea soup dinner. Always, schoolmates and adults asked how she came to be adopted by the founder of Bunkley Teas. Peasy would patiently recount, in a matter-of-fact tone unlike her usual enthusiasm, how a much-beloved female servant in the Bunkley's Shanghai home died giving birth to a baby girl (namely, Peasy) and Mr and Mrs Bunkley had vowed to call the child their own. She always recited the story with the preface, "I was told", and from that objective tone, young Elle knew that Peasy was as aware as she was of the two kinds of information adults shared: one was given to children, while the other was spoken only between adults.

Such was the case, Elle believed, of her and her brother Hector's situation. Having always accompanied their travelling and excavating parents, the siblings never understood why they had been abruptly exiled into English boarding schools. It was an abandonment seemingly hasty, and explained away by mother as her and papa giving the children the time to familiarise themselves once more with England.

"But we are always in England at least part of the year!" Elle had cried. "Why are you leaving us now and returning to Egypt?" She had a mother who could be warm, lively. But when mother's face was not alight and free of worry, she was wrapped in solemnity and intensity, as if always watching for the unforeseen. It was her way, but it also meant her face informed more than she wished. Father portrayed the sudden arrangement as a holiday for the children, his robust jolliness quashing suspicions—until Elle looked to her mother. Elle had wished at their parting that Mother had learned to be facetious, like Englishwomen could be.

"I love you," Mother had said when Elle, ready to unravel, boarded her train. Mother's gaze seemed to grip Elle's soul. "You and Hector will do well by this experience, and we will reunite soon."

Then why did you cry? she had wanted to shout to Mother, who still wore kohl even when in England. She had seen Mother's face as it grew smaller and smaller on the train platform. *Why did you allow your beautiful, fierce eyes to shed tears?*

"Something must have happened to our Indian tea plantations if mother and father can't have me with them," Peasy would say when she first came to the school, which was quite a practical thing to say, rather than her entertaining fanciful excuses to ease a ten year old child's lonely and frightened heart.

"Peasy," Elle had said. "Those girls. Can't you be civil to them for a day? When you ignore them, they—"

"No!" Peasy had cried and covered her ears. "No-no-no!" She then lowered her hands and gazed with a resolve Elle didn't know possible in another girl's face. "Elle, I must pay attention to what is happening in India."

Then Peasy chatted with teachers in hopes of acquiring a newspaper with empire news. After that, Elle felt silly placing importance on the society of cruel girls and her own indulgence in comforting fantasies; of her parents secretly battling living mummies, or saving the empire from some mad desert prince, thus requiring that they regretfully leave their children on England's safe shores.

When Faedra came of age and left Miss Head's School for Girls, Elle's parents returned, and fortunately for Peasy, hers did too. Elle and Hector accepted the story of their mother and father having spent their time at a dangerous dig, while Peasy's parents had indeed been wrestling with plantation affairs. Later in their marriage, Faedra confided the true story of Peasy's adoption, told to Peasy when she came of age. Peasy had been taken in by the Bunkleys in memory of her mother, that part had been true, but out of keen remorse for accidentally running over and killing the woman, a Chinese peasant unknown to them.

Elle followed Faedra down the narrow, carriage corridor for their compartment, her hand pressed to her wife's back as she reminisced. When Faedra stopped at their door, Elle laid her cheek against her shoulder.

"Elle?" Faedra said as she slid open the door.

Elle reached around and grasped Faedra's breasts through her bodice. She felt Faedra shiver in her touch.

"Inside, please," Elle ordered, and when Faedra stepped in, she followed, using her mental abilities to slide the compartment door shut and activate the latch behind them.

☠

Elle disembarked the train at Durham station with Faedra, whose cheeks were pink and whose step was lively as she set foot on the platform. Working the stiffness from her neck, Elle smiled, smug. A young couple passed, their heads close as they walked arm in arm, reminding her of when she and Valentin had disembarked at Brighton, newly wed.

Faedra and I must have that seaside holiday, she thought, thinking again how they'd never had the honeymoon due them. She followed Faedra and the porter as they exited the station.

Blue skies streaked with clouds greeted them. The station stood on a hill overlooking Durham, the city marked by a distinct cathedral and castle. The small town rose above the River Wear, with verdant woods and cleared fields lining the banks. Elle smiled at the sight and breathed deeply.

"Rain will come," she said, and turned for Faedra. A pale-faced driver with sandy hair stood on the walk with a horseless buggy near. His expression emotionless, he held up a sign reading: *The Mrs Blacks.*

Elle felt pride stir; Peasy had instructed the driver to not use Faedra's maiden name but her married one, and she thought that a considerate gesture.

"Elle," Faedra exclaimed as they and the porter neared the man, who simply touched the brim of his hat in acknowledgement. "Our transport is a Charvolant—a kite carriage!"

Elle looked on, confused. The large-wheeled, open-air buggy had neither horse readied nor a harness attached. When she bent to peer beneath, it possessed no electric battery, unlike the horseless vehicles Faedra enthused over, illustrated in the *Strand.* Instead, two large spools of sturdy string were mounted on the carriage's front, the two lines paid out and suspended taut in the air. When she looked up and followed the strings to their terminations, she spied giant kites flying in the higher reaches of the sky.

"By the size of our propellants, Elle, I'd say they're kites meant for man-lifting!" Faedra pointed.

"No doubt for the sole use of propelling vehicles," Elle added, hoping to forestall notions of Faedra lifting herself with such kites.

The driver and porter loaded their luggage in the back of the springy vehicle while Faedra helped Elle board.

Elle thought the pretty buggy light; with massive wheels spread for balance, it was built for speed. She secured her bonnet, set her black parasol aside, and studied the driver's seat before them. The two taut lines ran through horizontal bars suspended in the air above the spools: steering bars. A long-handled brake lever by the driver's seat was pulled firmly back. Faedra seated herself next to Elle.

"How fortunate for the kites that no great buildings or trestles are near. Truly, we are in the countryside now, Elle."

"Nothing but greenery shall greet us," Elle assured.

The silent driver returned to his seat and took hold of the steering bars, pulling them down. When he released the brake, Elle held Faedra's hand and the rail next to her. The buggy departed rapidly from the station.

They ran down the hill and to a road that circumvented the sparkling River Wear, and though Elle regretted not being able to experience the picturesque city across the river, she thought it just as well that their horseless buggy and its precariously hovering lines avoided any traffic encounters. Faedra pointed out the grey towers of Durham Cathedral and the Norman keep of Durham Castle, rising above the city's dense high street. Then their sightseeing ended as they gained a road flanked by the flowing water on one side and the English countryside on the other, the city of Durham fast becoming a speck behind them.

"Elle, what a sensation. Not one hoof sound." Faedra held

her hat to her head as their buggy sped along. Sunlight flashed through the trees, and the wind upon their faces smelled of earth and meadows.

"It rather agrees with Peasy's vegetarianism to use horseless transport. I wonder what pulls the ploughs on her farmlands? More kites? Oh, darling, it's possible she keeps no horses at all, even for riding."

Faedra's face fell so quickly, Elle chastised herself for speaking without forethought. She let go of the rail to take both of Faedra's hands and immediately regretted her next words.

"But dear, perhaps she'll let you drive one of these Charvolants."

When Faedra's face lit again, Elle hadn't the heart to voice additional cautions about the dangers of Charvolant driving.

Their buggy deftly passed carts, pedestrians, and other carriages as they sped. They spotted the occasional rowboat or leisure sail boat, one of which sported fishing lines. Faedra pointed out a narrow craft with a large, spinning wheel in the centre. Two women sat with parasols in front while a man and boy pedalled in back.

"Aquatic picnickers," she exclaimed. "That's quite a splendid water velocipede, Elle."

"It floats rather low, Faedy." Elle watched the valiant pedal pushers forge through the water. She hoped Peasy didn't possess such a contraption.

Faedra then indicated a hot air balloon floating in the blue sky above. A woman gaily waving her handkerchief and Faedra raised her parasol to wave in response. Elle peered at the balloon with the compact spyglass on her chatelaine.

"Such pastimes in the countryside, Elle," Faedra enthused, her eyes above.

Elle lowered her glass and noted a colliery with its smokestack as they sped past. Coal women trudged down the road leading away from its coal pit, perhaps departing at shift's end. Elle glanced back to take in their weary disposition and blackened faces.

"We are fortunate," she said.

After a while of viewing meadows, cow pastures, farm fields, and orchards, a formidable blackthorn hedgerow then appeared, towering twelve feet above and blooming with small white flowers. The Charvolant ran alongside until it reached a gate to a winding drive. The driver pulled back on his brake and the buggy slowed. Beyond the gate, the drive cut through a vast lawn of rolling grass and disappeared behind windbreaker trees in the distance, behind which the manor lay. Elle looked to the river and to the grass continuing down towards it, interrupted in its smooth progression only by the road and the blackthorn hedgerow.

Faedra held up the open face of her pocket watch for Elle to see.

"Remarkable," Elle murmured when she saw the time.

In forty minutes, their extraordinary buggy had covered twenty miles. In that time, their driver had remained silent and merely operated his steering bars and kite ropes. A man emerged from the gatehouse and pulled the gate open. As the buggy advanced, Elle looked at his impassive face and sandy hair.

He's the very image of our driver, she thought, surprised.

The driver in question released the brake more and sped their Charvolant down the drive for Peaseflower Manor.

CHAPTER THREE

Peaseflower, Elle recalled from one of Peasy's often-repeated stories at school, was an estate purchased from an old noble family, the Fairditches, and renamed Peaseflower by Mr Bunkley. Old Fairditch Manor had in its possession acres of farms and forest (Elle had no memory of the number, for she pointedly ignored Peasy's penchant for reciting exact figures), and a local village or two. When schoolmates asked Peasy what she hoped to enjoy at Peaseflower, she did not express interest in a stable full of fat ponies, a playhouse castle, or even a mechanical circus. She fancied having a train.

"The gardens will be 160 acres, and should you come visit—for all the world should come visit such delights—you will need to ride a train," Peasy had stated.

As their Charvolant passed the brace of tall windbreakers and approached the sprawling red brick, Jacobean manor, Elle spied the great dome of the glass conservatory's main building, far behind the house. Ivy crawled over the manor's red face, nearly choking windows, and below, sweet pea climbed the trellises, the ruffled blossoms pink, azure blue, and magenta. Their seductive scent, beguiling and sweet, struck Elle, and she grasped Faedra's hand.

"Our wedding corsages," Faedra said, her tone soft.

"Yes, I made them so." Elle belatedly realised that the sweet pea, present at both her marital unions, served to remind her of her first marriage too. A raven-haired figure fluttered about in pure white silk chiffon before the entrance, her white limbs and face as slight as a baby bird's: Peasy.

The Charvolant came to a stop, and Faedra alighted first. Before she could turn and help Elle down, Peasy ran into her arms.

"Oh, Faedy, *oh!*" Peasy held tight. Faedra laughed and looked at Elle in surprise.

"Dear Peasy, I have missed you too," she said.

Elle disembarked with the driver's help, amused. As an adult woman, Peasy had not managed to grow taller than Elle, nor put much flesh on her bird-bones. Peasy finally let Faedra go and stood back.

"Bascomb." Her butler, a pleasant-faced man with silver and grey hair, stepped forwards with a silver serving tray carrying crystal glasses filled with a fruity-red liquid.

"My friends, please enjoy this refreshment after your journey," Peasy bade. Elle recognised the beverage and delighted, picked up a glass. She inhaled its sweet fragrance, and then sipped.

"Hibiscus tea," Elle sighed, revelling in the cool, sensual taste. Faedra made a sound of appreciation as she drank hers.

"Wonderful," Faedra said.

"Our latest import from Egypt." Peasy smiled. "Is it as you remember, Elle?"

"The refreshing fruitfulness transports me once more to magical Aswan and its Nile shores. Thank you, Peasy." Peasy then opened her arms, and Elle accepted her hug. When they parted, Peasy's gaze searched them both.

"To see you after so long, I feel nothing has changed! Elle, you are the very image of your henna-haired mother. Such eyes!

I'd forgotten how their portentous, black-rimmed gaze gave me pause."

Elle quickly swallowed the tea in her mouth while Faedra suppressed her laugh with a hand.

"Elle has that effect, if not that power," Faedra then said.

"Mysticism." Peasy waved her hand, dismissive. "Faedy wrote that you are now a mental sleuth, Elle?"

"A psychic detective, Peasy," Elle corrected.

"How intriguing. But you are both to rest your psyches whilst here. Peaseflower is at your disposal for rest, relaxation, and rejuvenation."

"But what of your—" Faedra began.

"Please! I want nothing to detract from this joyous reunion, Faedy, and especially from enjoyment of your beauty and company." Peasy grasped Faedra's hand with a breath of happiness. "There is so much I want to share with you—I've croquet erected, and bowling; there's a ladies' putting green, and my tennis court, and the river, where we may row. I even have a water velocipede! All of outdoors is at our disposal!"

Elle took Faedra's other hand. "We will refresh posthaste, so that Faedra may rejoin you with her golf clubs."

☠

The manor stood a mere three storeys when including the gables and turrets, but it stretched the length of one small street block, and Elle thought it far too large for a single daughter and her ailing mother. As they walked the entrance hall to the grand staircase, Peasy narrated the house's architectural achievements, such as the dimensional and ornamental carvings of the structural framework. In the Jacobean manner, it was intricate with floral and plant themes, mixed with playfully grotesque beasts and demons, from floor to ceiling paneling. Before mounting the ornate staircase, Elle noted the bannister's sculpted posts and its mother-of-pearl eyes peeping from jungle leaves. Whether the eyes were of animals hidden within the foliage or belonged to the plants themselves, she could not tell.

"I am relieved that the Fairditches' forebears refrained from painting all this wonderful wood black, to imitate Chinese lacquer," Peasy said as they mounted the staircase.

"The natural wood does lend warmth to the beautiful strapwork," Faedra said.

"And the fanciful allegories lend your home droll humour," Elle remarked, spotting a demon's face with lolling tongue. *Though I think it more mockery.* When they reached the second floor landing, they followed the footmen carrying their luggage down the hall.

"Look at the size of this place," she said. "I remember, Peasy, when we were little girls, you would tell us that you thought Peaseflower would make a very successful hotel."

"I recall that as well, Peasy," Faedra said. "What a wonderful vision you had! And the grounds would be a public park, staffed by hundreds, with a rolling-railway, and merry-go-round—"

"Open Peaseflower to outsiders? No, that was a silly, girlish fantasy." Peasy sniffed. "I prefer it the way it is, myself and my staff. Here is your room, dear friends." The footmen entered a large bedroom suite and placed their luggage within. A round-faced maid with a blonde fringe promptly hefted their main suitcase on to the bed, unlatched it, and began packing a dresser's opened drawers with the contents. Peasy touched Elle's arm.

"And my chamber is just beyond the stairs' gallery, only a door away." She pointed. The double doors of a master suite sat at hall's end, beyond where Peasy indicated. Sunlight leaked from beneath the doors.

Mrs Bunkley's chamber, Elle thought.

A footman tripped over Faedra's fishing pole, upsetting the golf bag. Her clubs spilt to the floor.

"Oh! Hold on." Faedra entered to help him. Elle noticed the

footman's blank reaction, as if he were in a stupor. The maid ignored all and continued to pack the dresser with efficiency.

"You must wonder about my letter," Peasy said, low, and Elle turned.

"My, your eyes." Peasy's voice was hushed as she returned Elle's stare. "Eyes that might see everything. I've hidden something for you to read. In a dresser's third drawer, on the left side and beneath the intimates." She suddenly smiled. "I look forward to what your detecting mind makes of it. I will await you both downstairs!"

She then leapt away and ran for the stairs. Her laughter echoed as she descended.

Elle raised a brow.

"Was that Peasy?" Faedra's expression held surprise as she returned to Elle.

"Yes, Faedy, it was Peasy. Having an eccentric moment, I believe." The footmen left the bedroom, and the maid followed as well. Elle's detecting suitcase sat unlocked and opened on the bed.

"The maid would have unpacked everything had I not dissuaded her." They entered the suite. "Elle, Peasy has said nothing about Mrs Bunkley and we've yet to greet her." Faedra frowned. "I am at a loss by this slight." Elle took her hand in reassurance.

"Worry not. I will take care of it. I do want you to preoccupy Peasy in the meantime."

"Elle?"

Elle leaned in to speak into her wife's ear.

"When you rejoin her below, you must plead my need for rest. Then I may pry."

"Tea should be in only a few hours' time," Faedra said, low. "Please rejoin us then."

"I will. And with your usual charm, see if you can't wheedle Peasy's strange concerns out of her. If she denies you that information, at least harm her pride by winning many games." She straightened and gave Faedra a smack on the bustle. "Now go distract our besotted hostess with your beauty and company."

☠

Peasy had gifted her with a clue, but Elle chose not to be guided by gifts. She liked her impressions on a case to be informed first by independent observations. Thus, after discarding bonnet and cloak, she went out on the bedroom's balcony and looked around at what she might see.

A vast lawn rolled down to a brace of trees and a hedgerow she thought as high as her middle, the hedge opening to a rose garden and a small, glass half-dome attached to the main conservatory. Tall trees blocked the main structure, but the great dome was evident above the treetops, reflecting bright sunlight off its glass. Farther away, birds rose into the sky, and Elle retrieved her spyglass on her chatelaine. She focused the glass beyond the rose garden's hedges and the gardens interconnecting with it, spying the woods' far treetops. Training her glass across hedged gardens, vast flowerbeds, and small orchards, she noted the surrounding forest. Something niggled.

She was being observed.

Elle dropped her glass to view the lawn. Spotting nothing, she raised her glass for the rose garden again. There, beneath the shade of an exotic ornamental tree hung with orange trumpet blossoms pointing downwards, a large black dog with long face and tan muzzle stood, its gaze in her direction: a Gordon Setter.

"A black and tan, in a flower garden?" Elle said, incredulous. Despite the presence of the big dog, the garden appeared unmolested. A broom moved below. Elle lowered her glass and leaned over the balcony rail. A maid swept the terrace beneath, her motions slow and methodical. Elle raised her spyglass again.

Beneath the tree of trumpets, the dog still stood, motionless and seemingly staring into her glass, a shaggy black presence among the sunlit greenery and red, orange, and pink roses.

Elle looked about for its owner, and spied no one. When she withdrew into her room, the dog still watched from beneath the tree.

☠

After walking the ground floor of Peaseflower and standing within each room—the library, music room, drawing rooms, and Mrs Bunkley's study—which Elle took the liberty of unlocking with her mind in order to enter, not wishing to overlook an important location—she came to the conclusion that nothing supernatural lurked within its carved walls. She felt nothing, and her mirror revealed nothing. To her senses, the manor was simply a house.

"Character it may have, but this house possesses no presence of its own." *Despite the watching, mother-of-pearl eyes.* She went in search of the household's heart: its kitchen.

She followed the servants' access from the dining room. When she stepped into the vast kitchen, it was empty. Pots brewed on the hot stove, washed produce filled the sinks, and the cutting boards held vegetables, partially chopped or diced.

"House boy, footman, scullery maid?" Elle did not bother raising her voice as she expected no answer. She inspected one of the stove's pots, simmering with vegetable stock, and then exited the open scullery door. In the bright sunlight, she promptly tripped over shoes.

She stumbled on to the grass and trod on more abandoned shoes, all women's wear and in perfect shape. She discarded her thought that a dropped charity box had strewn them. Shielding her gaze, she looked for the owners.

Down the lawn and by a ten-foot tall hedgerow, maids in aprons and caps stood in the grass, facing this way and that, random pegs on an uneven board. Still and silent, the only movement came from the light breeze disturbing strands of their hair.

They seemed to be sunning themselves; the impropriety of such an act while on duty aside, Elle did not believe their loitering was simply that. The manner of their stance reminded her of fresh shoots, emerging from grass.

A shuttlecock sailed through the air beyond the tall hedge. A racket's blow sounded.

"Got it!" Peasy cried in glee, her voice faint. Another whack rang, and Elle was certain by the strike's solid forcefulness that the returning serve was Faedra's. The maids stirred.

They scattered, and then converged towards the scullery door. As they passed Elle, the maids neither nodded nor looked upon her. Faces pleasant and gazes calm, they picked up their shoes, pulled and laced them over bare feet, and filed into the kitchen. The activity of preparation and cooking resume, and when Elle peered in, the kitchen and scullery maids were busy at their tasks, their movements slow and methodical. The cook, an older woman, stood over the kitchen table and consulted her open cookbook.

"The kitchen staff doesn't care to wear stockings, does it?" Elle said to the dark-haired scullery maid intent on her washing. She had a narrow nose and face.

"Yes ma'am," she said. Elle waited, but the maid said nothing more. No one spoke in the kitchen, not even the cook, who went about the supervision of her assistants in silence.

Elle turned in thought. She walked down the lawn, hearing Peasy's distant laughter, and sought the area the maids had sunned in. She stood herself in the sunlight and gazed around for anything worth noting. House, lawn, treetops, more hedges, and a laundry line; the reading of her chatelaine's compass revealed nothing of distinction from the cardinal directions.

She sighed and went to her hands and knees. Her magnifying lorgnette also could discern nothing more than simple earth and grass. She regained her feet and wandered down the lawn to the laundry line. Laundry maids had emerged from the house to pin wash up, and as Elle neared, she noted that they worked in silence as well, engaging in no chatter. Among them, the round-faced maid with the blonde fringe laboured.

Both chamber maid and laundry maid? Well, Peasy did say her staff was severely reduced.

And if there was a housekeeper still, the woman was too strict, imposing silence upon the staff—especially when Elle needed them to talk and relax. She stepped closer to their group and smiled.

"How beautiful the day is," Elle enthused. "And that birdsong! Truly, this day is like the song, 'Pleasant and Delightful'. Surely you girls know it?" Elle sang:

It was pleasant and delightful on a midsummer's morn
And the green fields and the meadows were all covered in corn.

She paused in singing, expectant. The maids had stopped working to regard her and one maid parted her lips. Elle nodded, encouraging. In unison, the maids sang:

It was pleasant and delightful on a midsummer's morn
And the green fields and the meadows were all covered in corn;
the blackbirds and thrushes sang on every green spray,
and the larks they sang melodious at the dawning of the day.

Elle rejoined their pitch perfect voices on the refrain, watching as they sang, and she walked among them. They stood about, not bothering to sing to her or to each other. Her own voice faded when she recognised the narrow-faced scullery maid, her hand on the line.

Elle glanced at the scullery entrance, than back to the maid. The scullery maid seemed to look over Elle's shoulder with a distant regard as she sang. When the refrain began again, Elle joined her:

I must go and leave you Nancy; you're the girl that I adore.
I must go and leave you Nancy,
I must go and leave you Nancy,
I must go and leave you Nancy; you're the girl that I adore.

Elle ceased singing once more, the woman's dispassionate gaze and voice inspiring a similar coolness within her. The beauty of the day flattened, its sunlight too brittle and bright and its air cloying from the overwhelming scent of sweet pea blossoms. Elle did not even care right then that William was leaving Nancy. She glanced up.

A brown-haired woman moved out of sight from a second floor window.

Elle picked up her skirts and hurried for the house. The song ended behind her on the last chorus, the tune not fading but stopping as suddenly as it had begun. When she glanced back, the then silent maids had turned and resumed pinning up the wet laundry.

☠

Elle ran up the servant stairs, and upon reaching the second floor, opened the door a crack, peeping. No one stood in the hallway. She emerged, held her chatelaine's brass tools still, crept past her and Faedra's room, and then by the gallery overlooking the grand staircase. The room Peasy had indicated as hers had its door ajar. Someone searched within.

That person paused once Elle came abreast of the open door. Peering in, she spied the young woman who had been at the window, staring intently within a large, black journal with leather cover and the initials, PCB, stamped in gold. Elle cleared her throat.

The woman dropped the book onto others piled on a writing

table. She stared at Elle with wide-eyed surprise and, Elle thought, with some fear.

"Oh!" Elle exclaimed. "Pardon me, I was looking for my wife."

"Your what?" the woman ejected. Her expression bore both startlement and revulsion.

"And who might you be?" Elle said with the indulgent authority of one elder, though the woman appeared as young as she. She clasped her hands before her. "I am Mrs. Black."

The woman stood a little over Elle's height and was sturdier of build, her dress of middle class and her hands pink though not noticeably roughened by labour. Elle could not see the state of her nails. Her mouse-brown frizz had the fried look of having one too many applications of the curling iron. And her fresh, round face held a fretful timidity, as if she'd been told an awful thing too often and was in danger of hearing it again.

Elle didn't believe it an aggrieved expression—one ready to either dribble tears or give passionate issue for some private wrong held too close to the heart. At least Elle hoped not.

What a sop, Elle thought.

"I am Miss Polly Devereux," the woman answered in a stiff tone.

"Miss Devereux!" Elle exclaimed, recalling Peasy's letter. "How do you do? I am very pleased to meet a female scientist in residence." Elle glanced about the room. "And one held in such high regard, as to be given a room on the same floor as your employer."

"No, I—this is Miss Bunkley's suite, Mrs Black. I was in search of a notebook. So if you'll excuse me, I must return to my work." Polly pushed passed Elle, empty-handed, and walked quickly down the hallway.

"Miss Devereux!" Elle called. Polly stopped with reluctance. "If you should see my wife, Mrs White-Black—tall, blonde, blue-eyed—please let her know I'll join you both for tea."

Polly stared, incredulous. She turned without a word and hurried for the stairs.

Elle entered Peasy's suite and picked up the black notebook. She gave the bedroom a cursory glance, thinking the maids needed to visit, as it appeared either Peasy or Polly had left shoes and clothing scattered. Books and rolled plans piled on the writing table. Sheets lay crumpled into balls.

Elle unfolded one, revealing a map of Peaseflower's estate, renamed *Peaseflower Court* with train tracks and circles drawn. Notes with arrows that Elle assumed were in Peasy's hand read: Rolling-railway, mechanical roundabout, ornamental lake (with question mark,) education centre, vegetarian restaurant, souvenir shoppe, and electric train.

The map's corners were torn. Elle glanced up. Pinholes marked the wallpaper and one pin, a torn paper piece dangling from it, remained.

A very recent desire to crumple up a dream, Peasy.

She turned for Peasy's dresser and opened the third drawer. Lifting Peasy's folded undergarments in the left hand corner, she found nothing hidden.

She searched all of Peasy's drawers, removed them to feel about, then replaced them, looked within Peasy's armoire, bath suite, beneath her bed, and within her bed. After remaking the bed, she retrieved the journal Polly had perused and closed the door behind her.

Once in her own room, Elle wondered if Polly searched for the same clue Peasy had meant for Elle, and had somehow left the room with it. Her gaze fell on the dresser the maid had packed, thinking it of the same design as Peasy's. She then threw up her hands.

"Oh, clever Peasy." Elle pulled open the third drawer. On the left side and beneath her and Faedra's undergarments, two notebooks lay, one brown with a dangling red silk ribbon embroidered *Polly*, and the other of black leather with an envelope stuck in its pages. Elle used the brown notebook to hold the envelope's place as she pulled it out. The letter, bearing a postmark five months old, had been sent by Peasy's cousin Cherish from her ship in the Malay Archipelago.

Elle pulled the bed's service cord. She intended to enjoy another cool glass of hibiscus tea while she read.

CHAPTER FOUR

The people shun the atoll. In such paradise as this, where there is only peace, goodwill, and contentment, almost entirely untouched by the excesses and desires of civilised man, it is hard to conceive of any presence that can be considered evil. Not merely dangerous, for death, injury, and illness will happen in the natural world, but a malevolent intent. This is by my own interpretation, dear Peasy, for the people haven't words or concepts in their language for wrongs like deception or theft. They call the island the Unreal Atoll.

And how do they mean, "unreal?" I took it to mean a place of trickery, and as I've mentioned, of deception. The people tell me that ones like themselves walk on that island, but they are not meant to be. I fear my ability to interpret what they try to convey is inadequate to the task. Do they mean apparitions?

I couldn't stand the thought that some false man or unscrupulous band—perhaps pirates!—was present on that island, hoodwinking and preying on these people. I took men from my ship to Unreal Atoll and investigated, found nothing but what appeared to be evidence of some human presence, several years old. I might guess at four to six years' passing. It seemed an island like any other, though I will confess, Peasy, to

*experiencing an unease whilst there, and the men felt it as well.
For it was too quiet on that soil, amidst the beguiling flora.
Few birds sounded or stayed. I only remained a single day,
obtained one specimen of singular appearance and with an
unusually large corm, having never seen its like, and recorded
but a few observations. You must know that my watercolours
included here and your dormant specimen are all that remain
of Unreal Atoll. A significant earthquake occurred soon after
my expedition there, and the sea swallowed the island whole.*

Elle searched the envelope and found no more leafs: it contained
no watercolours. She settled more against the red pillows of the
bedroom's settee, picked up her glass, and sipped her hibiscus
tea. Then she looked at the first page of the black notebook the
letter had been tucked into; Peasy's name was within, and by the
starting date, she assumed the book was her latest journal. She
turned for the page that the letter had marked and found an entry:

*I have found an exceptional plant explorer, one trained in
university and whose work with propagating specimens from
the Americas gives me the utmost confidence she can oversee
observation of the Unreal specimen's unexpected flowering. I
hope her arrival will also resolve the strange effect the plant's
presence has visited upon my foolish gardeners—an irrational
fear now spreading to my scientific staff! Perhaps as Miss
Devereux has written, the specimen's possible disruptions from
afar (and here, I still laugh at the notion) having upset the
equilibrium of my staff, resemble telæsthesia, for she had read
of similar effects from potions derived from the South American
Banisteriopsis caapi, the talking Vine of the Soul.
I've spent significant time in the Unreal specimen's presence,
and it has not spoken, whispered, or so much as fluttered a
communication to me, no more than our usual exotic resident.
I've decided that too much idling has perpetuated such*

nonsense, and the staff is now working at a pace that disallows time for fanciful stories.

Mother has approved the appointment, Miss Devereux has accepted, and I look forward to her arrival and much needed assistance.

Elle skimmed a week's more of entries, mixed with watercolours of the local river and plant life, until one caught her eye:

Miss Devereux has arrived so ill! And after escaping an unfortunate fire at her previous employer's, the smell of smoke still inhabiting her clothes. However, she exhibits all the symptoms of having dosed herself with a deliriant, and I made jest with her that she ought not conduct such self-poisoning in the midst of travel. But I cannot blame her for taking the opportunity. My scientists and I have also experimented upon ourselves, and the stimuli of an active, outside environment aids in self-observation whilst under chemical influence. She would not say what narcotic she was studying, though I suspect belladonna. She has hidden herself away with the Unreal specimen in the Rare House now, and that is what's needed. I look forward to reading her observations.

Another week of entries, and Elle read:

I thought Miss Devereux might join me in painting watercolours by the river, as she'd expressed such interest in her last letter before coming here. But she continues to decline my invitations. I must assume she has lost interest in sharing natural outings with me. She spends all her time in the Rare House and promises her report on the specimen's successful propagation will be soon. As I've so much to supervise, I must grant her this lenience.

Elle laid the journal aside and picked up Miss Devereux's notebook. The pages audibly crunched. The fore edge of the latest leafs were stiff and warped, having absorbed too much watercolour paint. The tucked, red silk ribbon did not seem to mark pages of note. Elle flipped through the book's beginning, filled with vibrant watercolour studies of wild blossoms, birds' nests, birds' eggs, butterflies, and other small creatures, mixed with precise, analytical botanical illustrations that dissected plants down to their minute parts.

The meticulous paintings showed a sharp and observant eye with greater artistic skill than Peasy's earnest paintings, though Peasy's efforts made up with passion what she lacked in technique. Written on the following pages in Polly's perfect script were detailed and dated accounts of her botanical subjects, all of which looked native to England.

This is her personal journal, recording her nature walks. Her fabled research with propagating exotics perhaps remained with her previous employer.

Elle thumbed closer to the warped leafs; the written records stopped. When she turned to a crumpled page, bombastic colour assailed. Blooms burst, their star-faces exploding seeds and stamen filaments that wound into the darkness. She turned the page to another vision, where long fronds wiggled amid tangles of spiralling, unearthly blossoms, their elongated petals lashing. Four more pages revealed unleashed studies, it seemed, of the unseen in God's grotesque world. But the last painting gave her pause; darkness erupted against a smear of light that acted as barrier or incendiary upon the verdant world. The plants burned, yellow, orange, and of green smoke, and an unsteady hand had scrawled a simple phrase beneath:

I aM UN weLL

No dates for these paintings. She flipped back through the pages, noting that the date on Polly's last precise painting (that of a female emerald damselfly) was over a month ago. Elle closed the book.

"Then she became ill," Elle pondered. "Painting in the frenzy of phantasmagoric fever. Yet, that is a long while to be under the sway of an intoxicant, unless she dosed herself *again* before coming here. Then...."

She picked up Peasy's journal and resumed where she'd left off:

> *It has been barely a week since all the dismissals, and I still don't know why Mother has done this. I've no time to wring my hands, much less weep. Oh, why? No one left to help, and I've specimens dying left and right. The gardeners do the best they can, what's left of their staff that I have. My queer, silent staff. When did this happen to them? What is happening to me?*
>
> *I did not write Faedy the truth. I said I was not under some evil influence, but I believe now, I am. In my haste to save my plants, was I careless in the poison garden? I feel unwell. I feel very unwell. And I can't remember what is happening.*

Elle turned more pages, all blank. That had been Peasy's last entry. Elle put the book down and regarded the black cover of the notebook Polly had been perusing. *PCB*; Peasy's initials. The fore edge revealed crinkled leafs like the last pages in Polly's notebook, the edges soaked with colour.

Elle opened it, finding paintings and drawings done with abandonment, the colours and lines bleeding to the edges. None held the precision of scientific observation or the aesthetics of natural portrayal. Flowers, growths, fruits, root systems, insects, suns, and odd creatures Elle assumed were the sort found wriggling on microscope slides massed on the pages in layers of images; all nearly pictographic and aboriginal in the manner of their telling.

Faedy comes! Peasy wrote on one page, and then the fantastic imagery resumed. But Elle noted a disturbing progression; the drawings and paintings soon became solely blue, with ghost-white occupants stark upon the pages. Plants and creatures dripped, wet and sad.

"Tears," Elle said. She shut the book and sighed.

You and Miss Devereux are no longer under some narcotic's sway, Peasy. But something is still wrong.

She finished her tea. Elle rose and hid the books inside her detecting suitcase, beneath the wrapped parcel of jerked meat.

"Let us see what your mother thinks of all this," Elle said, and left her room.

CHAPTER FIVE

Elle stood outside the master suite's double doors, bright sunlight no longer shining from beneath. She still had time to talk to Mrs Bunkley before joining Faedra and Peasy for tea. If the brusque Miss Polly attended, Elle wouldn't mind making the woman more uncomfortable with a few questions—and perhaps with open displays of affection with Faedra.

When she raised her hand to knock, The scent of soil, moist and mixed with decay, rose. Elle lowered her hand and gazed intently at the door handles.

With a click, the locks disengaged. Elle mentally turned the handles. She pushed, and the doors swung slowly open.

Tiny emerald damselflies darted in a mote-filled suite where large ferns grew in pots and loose, moist black earth piled on the carpet and floor. Dead fronds lay where they fell. In more pots and scattered earth mounds, hardy, weedy plants bloomed. Mrs Bunkley, white-haired and slumped, sat in a rattan wheelchair in the middle of the suite, wrapped in a velvet and brocade dressing gown. The round-faced maid with the blonde fringe stood by the great windows carrying a porcelain water pitcher. She turned her head to regard Elle, and then returned her attention to the outside.

Elle stepped in. Her foot crunched old leaves, and a brown

beetle emerged from beneath and ran across the floor. Elle took a breath and made her way to Mrs Bunkley's chair.

Once near, Elle thought the authoritative, assured woman of her childhood looked far older than her true age, her face worn and tired and her pale eyes cloudy. Mrs Bunkley's gaze was no longer sharp, alert, and inquisitive; the nature of the woman that Elle recalled. She knelt so that Mrs Bunkley could see her, and when the older woman's gaze seemed to acknowledge her presence, the cloudiness briefly lifted.

"Hayat?" Mrs Bunkley softly exclaimed in a tremulous voice. Then she peered with suspicion. "You're not *old*."

"No, Mrs Bunkley," Elle said gently. "Hayat Dunny was my mother. I am Eleanor, her daughter."

"Oh." Mrs Bunkley's suspicion lessened, but she still seemed wary. "I hope you're as *clever* as she." She moved back into her chair, and Elle became overwhelmed with the smell of plant decay. She refrained from covering her nose as the damselflies darted.

"Why am I still here?" Mrs Bunkley's voice quavered. "Haven't I done enough?"

Elle wondered if it was a philosophical question. "I'm not certain, Mrs Bunkley. All I know is that we've a wish to live."

Mrs Bunkley did not answer, her gaze inward, and Elle thought the older woman might be drifting.

"I'm meant to sleep." Mrs Bunkley's tired voice held yearning.

"How may I help you?"

"I'd like some sun."

Elle nodded. The sunbeams from the windows had shortened, and if Mrs Bunkley had been sunning herself, she was then a foot away from its warmth. Elle stood. The maid, who still held her pitcher, simply gazed out the window. Elle moved behind Mrs Bunkley's wheelchair and took hold of the handles. Then she remembered the wheel locks. When she reached down to disengage them, a black millipede wiggled out from beneath the chair, undulating swiftly away. Elle closed her eyes briefly, and then released the locks.

"It's too much. We ought not to have so much," Mrs Bunkley ejected.

"Too much of what, Mrs Bunkley?" Elle attempted to move the chair.

"Water."

Liquid sloshed at Mrs Bunkley's feet and then something splashed Elle's shoes. She looked down in surprise at the chair's footrest. When she carefully pulled the older woman's robe up, a porcelain footbath appeared. Mrs Bunkley's shrivelled feet sat in clean, clear water. Elle glanced at the maid, who was then looking at her, her gaze impassive.

"A cleansing...for too much salt." Mrs Bunkley said.

"Are you on a strict sodium diet, Mrs Bunkley?"

"There." Mrs Bunkley pointed to the sunbeam.

Elle pushed the chair with effort. It slowly squeaked towards the light. Once Mrs Bunkley sat within sunlight, Elle locked the wheels again. She moved to the older woman's side and knelt.

"Mrs Bunkley, I've come to ask...about the dismissals of your staff, and about Miss Devereux."

"No," Mrs Bunkley sighed.

"No?"

"I can't remember. And I've been unwell."

"Your daughter has written the same," Elle said.

"She'll be *me*, soon." Mrs Bunkley grabbed Elle's arm with a strength that surprised her. The old woman stared into her eyes. "You should know, Hayat...first it was the dog, then me."

"First the dog," Elle repeated.

Out of the corner of her eye, Elle saw an emerald damselfly nab a moth out of the air.

"Then me. I do her bidding," Mrs Bunkley whispered.

"Whose, Mrs Bunkley?"

Mrs Bunkley's fingers dug.

"I was picked *too* early," she cried, "and then she turned our minds."

She let Elle go.

Mrs Bunkley's trembling finger pointed to her bed's nightstand. A dust-covered journal lay atop.

Elle went to retrieve the book. When she turned back to Mrs Bunkley, the old woman's eyes were shut.

☠

Elle closed Mrs Bunkley's doors behind her, her mouth grim. She heard the door click open again; the round-face maid stood there.

"You ought to—" Elle began.

"Help us," the maid said.

Elle stared in surprise. The maid's distant and cool regard did not quite return her gaze. She seemed to address Elle's shoulder.

"Of cour—"

The maid went back into the room and shut the door.

"—I will," Elle finished, baffled. She opened the journal. The last pages held writing. Mrs Bunkley's account of her days was ordered and precise, all filled with mundane matters and practical observations. Then Elle read the last entry.

The new botanist has been here nearly two weeks—sufficient time for my suspicions to be confirmed. She should remain no longer. I will discuss the matter with Peasy.

The following pages were blank. Elle closed the journal. A memory of a childhood conversation with her own mother came to the fore.

Elle, Hayat had said. *What do you think of Peasy's mother?*

She's as strict as a general, Elle had quipped. *What do you think, Mother?*

She misses nothing, Hayat had said.

"And now Mrs Bunkley remembers nothing," Elle whispered.

☠

A footman fetched Elle for tea and she followed him across Peaseflower's lawn, passing the trees that hid the conservatory. Sheet clouds skirted the sky. Tea was being served in a little grassy garden with trellises of blooming sweet pea. The garden sat next to the tennis court, high hedges blocking the late afternoon wind from the secluded interior. Bascomb waited within and led Elle to the table, shaded by a pitched umbrella. Faedra sat beneath and rose to welcome Elle with a kiss.

"Thank you for keeping her distracted," Elle whispered.

"Did you discover anything?" Faedra asked in a low voice.

"Faedy," Peasy called from across the garden.

Elle squeezed Faedra's arm. "Later." Peasy ran to them.

"Oh! The work of running Peaseflower is never done, but now my gardeners have their evening assignments. Elle, did you rest well?" Peasy was breathless as Bascomb helped her with her chair.

"I did, Peasy, thank you. And I also heeded your suggestion and did some reading," Elle said as Faedra seated her.

"How delightful, Elle."

Bascomb laid tea out, and Peasy said no more, her gaze on her butler's work. Elle's lips pursed.

"I understand you've recently acquired an exotic—" she began.

"Elle," Peasy interrupted. "Let us enjoy ourselves and not talk of my conservation work! There will be plenty of that tomorrow, when I show you what's within its glass walls. Then may I bore you with the science and labour of it. Oh Elle, here! Have some strawberries."

"Thank you, Peasy. Will it be only the three of us enjoying tea?"

"Why yes, Elle! We three friends. Mother would join us if she were able, but an outing even to this little garden is a bit much for her now."

"We are sorry to hear that, Peasy," Elle said. "We should visit her."

"Yes, we hope our presence will cheer her," Faedra added.

"Thank you, Faedy. I know your presence has already cheered me," Peasy said warmly. She indicated the garden. "This little place was where I read and played after leaving Miss Head's School for Girls. Though I was finally given a governess, it was lonely here. It's a simple little retreat, isn't it? But it refreshes the mind after so much stimulation in the conservatory."

"Well, I asked if another might join us because you'd mentioned a Polly in your letter, Peasy," Elle said. "Who is she?"

"She is our resident botanist, Elle. My assistant, really. Not as sharp as I would like." Peasy leaned in a conspiratorial manner. "But since she's here, she'll do."

The brilliant, university-trained plant hunter? Really. Elle then noticed the laid out tea as Bascomb poured. *Where are the cakes?*

Peasy touched her arm and beamed. "Now you'll experience a real treat; a tea made with not even a pinch of flour."

☠

Elle did not understand how it was possible—or vegetarian for that matter—denying the table any food made of flour. But cakes and biscuits did require milk, butter, and eggs, and perhaps Peasy chose to dismiss flour's use to simplify cook's dilemma. Tea, then, was a strange medley: fresh green figs, fried potato shavings, chutney over fat slices of tomato; cucumber, radish, and watercress sandwiches (without the bread) neatly wrapped in lettuce, slices of lemon-seasoned creamy avocado, dried Norfolk Biffins, baked quince sprinkled with sugar, and all manner of sliced, fresh fruit—apples, melons, peaches, pineapples, strawberries, and—

"Why, are these dehydrated vegetable slices?" Elle examined the turnip chip she held.

"They are, Elle, for anything of fruit, root, stalk, or leaf may be rendered so."

"Yet no salt added, Peasy?" Elle nibbled, and thought of Mrs Bunkley's footbath.

"No, Elle." Peasy's tone was curt.

"These are splendid in their natural state! Though perhaps one could add vinegar," Faedra suggested with a smile.

"Or cayenne pepper," Elle murmured.

"Faedy, vinegar is a wonderful idea!" Peasy laid a hand on Faedra's arm.

"Or a dash of curry powder. How did you produce such a variety in your oven?" *With your odd and silent kitchen staff?* Elle ate a dark red chip that looked like a beet slice.

"Oh, I didn't experiment in the kitchen, Elle. Right by my House of Succulents sits a large concave mirror. I simply fill it with sliced specimens. In this fashion I utilise the sun for dehydration purposes."

"Elle also uses a parabolic mirror-concentration cooker," Faedra said with pride. "She has made jerked meat in it."

"Faedy loves her mechanised advancements." Elle smiled. "Peasy, you are barely eating. Not even a nibble. And you've been engaged with Faedra all day in the sun."

"Indeed, Peasy, are you well?" Faedra said. "We can forego our tennis match so you might rest."

"No, Faedy, I wish to play! I am merely too excited for words, having you here. And Elle, as well. Just you wait, I may defeat you in our match."

Elle thought Peasy could do with a little nap, for her brightness seemed to be waning, in her gaze and in her demeanour.

"Peasy, you work so much," she said. "With your mother ill, why not reverse her decision and call back your dismissed staff? That would also take care of your worry for your hamlets."

"My hamlets? Why should I care about them?"

Before Elle could answer that Peasy had written such concern in her letter, Bascomb approached. He laid down dessert crystals containing dollops of black currant ice sprinkled with powdered sugar.

"Oh!" Delighted, Faedra quickly scooped a portion. Spoon in mouth, her eyes closed as her lips did upon the utensil.

"Mm," she said.

"Faedy loves her ices," Elle said indulgently. Peasy did not comment, her enrapt gaze on Faedra.

"Faedy, how did you manage to legally unite with Elle?" Peasy suddenly asked. "You did send me your wedding announcement, but I mean...well, the proper recognition of it."

"Interestingly enough, it does not take much to gain formal recognition." Faedra smiled. "Marriage is a legal contract uniting two households. Thus, it was a simple matter to create such a contract—one where we made provisions for the other in matters of finances and estate, death, and for the possibility of divorce." She picked up Elle's hand and grasped it. "I insisted on that part only to take care of Elle."

"Faedy had paid particular attention to the companionship issues of the American actress, Charlotte Saunders Cushman, when drawing up the contract," Elle said. "I appreciate such caring consideration, but the very thought of leaving Faedra destroys me."

"I can imagine, Elle," Peasy said, and Faedra lifted Elle's hand and kissed it.

☠

Near tea's end, Peasy excused herself to see to more conservatory matters, but promised to return posthaste, and bade her friends to wait by the tennis court. Peasy ran, a white fluttering wisp racing across the green lawn beyond the high hedge, and Elle thought Peasy headed for the rose garden area: the conservatory. Faedra took Elle's hand.

"I now have a frightening longing for cheese," Elle remarked as they walked to the tennis court. Faedra chuckled. Another table beneath a pitched umbrella awaited them. Faedra seated her, and Elle noticed the centrepiece of red carnations.

"Can she be more obvious?" Elle remarked, peeved. Faedra glanced at the flowers and then at Elle in curiosity. "Dear, recall your flower language. An 'aching heart,' indeed. I don't think this love token is for me. Faedy, did you and Peasy ever meet again since our leaving Miss Head's School for Girls?"

"We had when she was sixteen. She has grown into an interesting woman, hasn't she?"

"Who would have known how she and I would grow, when of age. We already knew you as a woman, Faedy, when Peasy and I were only fourteen. Oh, the sight of you." Elle gulped. "Listen to me! Still affected by the memory of my girlish love for your eighteen-year-old self. And I, the one who ended up married to you."

Faedy smiled warmly, her eyes twinkling.

"But I saw you again when I myself turned eighteen, before I married Valentin. My affections for you could then change; grow. Peasy, however...." She plucked one red carnation from the centrepiece, gave it to Faedra, and then tapped her own bosom, indicating her wife should place it within the buttonhole she indicated. Faedra leaned forwards and did so. "This is the first time she has met you as a fully grown woman herself, and I know exactly how she feels."

Peasy ran from the lawn into the tennis court area. "Oh!" she said, spying the carnation Faedra was placing on Elle. Peasy brought up her tennis racket and brandished it. "Faedy, I am ready! Ready-ready-ready!"

Elle noted Peasy's overly bright eyes and seemingly agitated state, but said nothing. Faedra picked up her racket and obligingly ran to the court's other end to begin the game.

☠

Whack. Whack.

Elle watched the tennis ball fly over the net between the two players. Peasy floated, like one too light to be of meat and bone, to meet the balls Faedra sent, but her returning salvos hadn't great strength, despite the energy of her playing. Faedra stepped to and fro on the court and answered Peasy's strokes with half her usual intensity.

Whack. Whack.

Elle slid her gaze towards the manor. She gave her pocket watch a surreptitious glance. Bascomb had been standing on the lawn near the house for nearly ten minutes, as still as a tin toy soldier.

When she lifted her gaze from her watch, Bascomb entered through the hedge, bearing a silver tray ladened with a crystal pitcher. Elle looked to the house. No Bascomb stood on the lawn.

"Have you a twin, Bascomb?" she asked as Bascomb laid a glass down for her. He poured out cool hibiscus tea. "I believe I saw your—"

Bascomb bowed, then turned to depart back through the hedge.

"No one wants to speak to me today," Elle grated. She consoled herself with sipping the tea.

Whack.

A feeling niggled; once again, she was being observed. Elle glanced to the hedge beside her. Another garden with a lily pond was present through the hedge's opening, and a black Gordon Setter stood silently before the pond, watching her. It was the same dog from the rose garden.

Have you words for me? No? Then go away. She turned her back to it, in time to witness Peasy winning the game as Faedra missed a returned volley. Elle clapped politely, and the two met at the net. While Peasy and Faedra laughed and conversed, Another black dog, in appearance and stance the same as the first, stood at the hedge opening behind Faedra, watching the players. Elle stopped clapping.

"Before your presence should disturb my wife, I suggest you both leave, *now*," Elle said with force to the dog at her side. She grabbed the crystal pitcher and poured out tea for Faedra and Peasy as they returned to the table. Peasy, still addressing Faedra, then pointed in the direction of the conservatory. The two thus occupied, Elle glanced to the side; the dog before the pond was gone. The one that had been watching from Faedra's side of the court had disappeared as well. Elle rose with a smile as Faedra approached. She gave her pink-cheeked wife her tea.

"Oh, how hot I am!" Peasy fanned herself with a hand. She accepted the second glass from Elle, sipped, and put it down. "I must offend, please forgive me."

With the scent of sweet pea filling the area, Elle could not say whether Peasy offended or not. She studied her friend's pale face, which appeared as cool as ever and showed no signs of exertion. Then Peasy bade them a hasty farewell, saying it was necessary she refresh. She promised to meet them at the house and ran in the manor's direction.

"She is always running," Elle mused. "Her stimulant must be quite strong."

"Elle?" Faedra said. Elle poured her another glass and Faedra drank it.

"I refer to Peasy's boundless energy, dear. She may refresh, but I do not mind my sweaty wife at all." Elle retrieved her handkerchief and dabbed at Faedra's perspiration. "Would you like to return to the house?" Faedra shook her head.

"I want to spend time with you. Such an expanse of grass and freedom needs our company. Won't you walk with me?" She offered her arm.

Elle smiled and accepted. They departed from the court and stepped upon the great lawn. Long shadows stretched upon the grass, and the sun sank. The conservatory's dome loomed over the treetops, gleaming.

"I love to watch you play," Elle said.

Faedra took a deep breath, her bosom expanding. She sighed in contentment.

"I noticed that you let her win," Elle added as they walked.

"She is our hostess," Faedra said with quiet gallantry.

"A hostess who has become quite queer in her secluded, paradisal domain, won't you say?"

"Well...I'd always thought Peasy a unique girl, dear. And she has been under duress."

"'Unique' is not quite the word I'd use. In all your playtime today, did she say anything to you relating to the letter?"

"Not a thing, though I tried. I'm afraid we spoke of nothing but reminisces and frivolous matters. She did share something rather unsettling when we spoke after the game. As I'd expressed a wish to take you for a walk, she cautioned me to not approach the conservatory grounds to the far north." Faedra indicated the same direction Peasy had pointed to earlier. "It is a very ways off, isn't it? At the conservatory's other end. We wouldn't make it halfway there before nightfall. But she has a conservatory house there that she's protected with deadly mantraps. Can you believe it, Elle? The place is called the Rare House."

Elle paused their walk. "Did she tell you what was in it?"

"Only that it contains a rare exotic, one very precious to her. I can't imagine what that would be, for her to fear it being stolen, somehow."

"And regarding these traps, she tells you this, but not me? I was the one gallivanting about." Faedra then hugged her.

"You were assumed to be resting, remember darling? But I agree, she should have told us of such danger at our arrival. Had something happened to you, I don't know what I would have done."

"That Peasy," Elle grumbled, and took comfort in her wife's embrace. When they parted, she resumed their walk, linking arms with Faedra. They descended for the tree line near the conservatory.

"And since you're safe here with me and not in some mantrap," Faedra continued, "out with it, my little sleuth, for I've been dying of curiosity all day. What are your thoughts on Peasy's secret dilemma, having now seen the house and its staff?"

"Mm, the staff. I shall withhold my thoughts on them for now. But know that they are as odd as Peasy's letter had suspected. Now, to that letter. It is looking more like an elaborate sham to lure you here. She's burdened with an invalid mother, is overworked, is far too lonely and bored, and wants a more accomplished playmate than that sour Polly Devereux."

"Elle," Faedra admonished. "What you describe sounds like a petulant child."

"Yes, but Peasy had always been that, you never noticed."

"Tut, now I believe your own intolerance is colouring your detecting perceptions."

"My perceptions are perfectly objective. I only tell you what I'm witnessing. What we are shown to see. None of this circumstance fits the letter she sent, Faedy."

"Then you believe the letter, and not Peasy's seeming disregard. Have you witnessed anything supernatural, Elle?"

"I've seen nor felt no spectral presence. There is nothing amiss with the house or within it. How surprising to say that with regret. I suppose preternatural activity would be familiar territory." They strolled by the long line of trees that separated the great lawn from the conservatory proper. Plants and palm trees appeared within the distant glass walls, becoming as dark as the outside world. The silhouettes of gardeners worked within, of men in flat caps and coveralls. They moved at the same even pace as the maids.

"But there is something very wrong still, upon which inhabitants of the Fourth Dimension cannot be blamed," Elle then said, pensive. "That queerness alluded to in the letter; that I can sense, and it is not something solely present in the servants.

I feel that there is something more here, and I cannot say right now whether it means harm or is merely some catalyst for the strangeness present. Whatever it is, it is with us, Faedy, right now, and it is different from anything we know. Look there."

A Gordon Setter stood in the clearing across, watching through the trees. Its face resembled the ones Elle had seen all day.

"Such a beautiful black and tan! Come," Faedra commanded, and slapped her thigh. The dog did not move. "I've never known a hunting dog to not obey. I said, come!" When it still did not respond, she regarded the dog with surprise. "I wonder if it's ill. It doesn't pant, Elle. Even its tail does nothing."

"It has gone odd, Faedy. Just like the servants." Elle picked up a stick, waved it before the animal, and then threw it. The dog merely stared.

Faedra looked at her.

"Elle, are you and I in danger of becoming queer?"

"You mean even more queer than I am?" Elle took a breath. "Peasy and that Polly Devereux, whom I met earlier today, are not affected. I believe we're safe, yet."

"Then we must do all we can to solve this for Peasy," Faedra said, determined. Elle sighed and smiled.

"I thought you'd say that," she said.

☠

When they returned to the house and entered via the drawing room's veranda doors, a maid knelt at the hearth, holding a box of matches as she stared at the logs.

Her again, Elle thought. It was the round-face maid with the blonde fringe. The maid swiped a match across the striking surface of the box, and then held it out. The match head remained unlit. Elle and Faedra exited for the main hallway and Faedra paused, glancing down one end and then the other. Elle tutted.

"You hadn't a chance to see the house properly, much less

spend time in our room."

"Being outdoors without crowds, noise, and London's insalubrious atmosphere was divine pleasure. The only thing missing was you."

"My charmer." Elle smiled. "The main staircase is this way."

But as they approached the stairs, a round-faced maid with a blonde fringe emerged from the door leading to the servant's stairs, carrying linen. She moved away from them and proceeded down the hallway. Faedra paused again.

"Wasn't she," Faedra began.

"In the drawing room we'd just left? She was also our chamber maid, a laundry maid, and the last time I saw her, a nurse."

"That many—? Elle, these are merely hard-working twins. Peasy did say that so many of her staff had been dismissed."

"Yes, of course. And perhaps this estate favours many twins." Elle glanced up at the gallery. A footstep's echo sounded. "Though I was thinking the blonde maids may be quadruplets. Their poor mother." A face peered down at them: Polly. The botanist pulled back out of view.

Another footstep echoed, and Peasy appeared at the top of the stairs. She swiftly descended.

"Oh, my dear friends!" she exclaimed. "Did you enjoy your walk?"

"Your grounds, Peasy, are delightful," Faedra said.

"And to think there will be even more to amaze us when we visit your conservatories," Elle said as Peasy reached the first landing. "And we're to tour them tomorrow?"

"That is my intention, Elle! I will try my best not to make it boring for you, for I'm more prone to discourse on my treasures' botanic virtues rather than their inherent and obvious beauty. This won't be one of those mundane RHS flower shows."

My, what a slight to the Royal Horticultural Society, Elle thought drily. Peasy alighted from the last stair with a ballet-like leap.

"Peaseflower is the repository of our global floristic knowledge, but we do not merely preserve and catalog. There is much to test and discover, for any new exotic has curative potential. And this is why I must leave you. My greatly reduced staff has me burdened with maintaining our remaining experiments. Please forgive my absence tonight—I want you both to have a lovely dinner!"

What? Elle's latest chance to ask about the journals dissipated.

"Oh, Peasy, we will miss you!" Faedra said.

"And I will miss you, dear Faedy! Oh!" Tears glistened in Peasy's eyes, surprising Elle. Peasy turned and hurried down the hall for the entryway.

"Well...good night, Peasy," Elle said, her tone sharper than she intended.

"Good night, Peasy!" Faedra called.

"Adieu, my dear friends!" Peasy stood poised at the doors the footman held open, blew them a kiss, then departed in a flurry of white silk chiffon.

"Flutter-cup," Elle muttered.

"Again, she has said nothing about her mother." Faedra's tone held frustration. "I had been enquiring all day."

"I have seen her," Elle said solemnly.

"Oh, Elle. Is she as the letter described? Should we—?"

Elle shook her head, casting her gaze above again. She spied no Polly. "Let us leave her to her rest, and we will try in the morning." They ascended the staircase.

"Is it a matter of the brain?" Faedra said in a hushed voice.

"Perhaps, though, I wonder. Since we shouldn't expect Mrs Bunkley at dinner, it shall be us and the barely civil Miss Devereux."

☗

When Elle and Faedra had changed and descended for dinner, they did not meet Polly Devereux, though her table place setting remained. Elle assumed from its presence that Bascomb expected the woman to appear. Elle chose the head of the table, where Mrs Bunkley might have sat, and Faedra seated herself to Elle's right.

"I will not sit at the other end," Faedra said. "This is a very long table and I will need you to pepper my dishes."

"I will gladly season anything you desire." Bascomb entered, bearing their first dish. "And now Faedy, let us see what vegetarian surprises await us."

The dishes were varied and plentiful, requiring Bascomb to make many trips. He served them spicy Indian Salado, dressed cucumbers, a potato balls salad (lacking any sour cream, Elle noted with surprise) Jerusalem artichoke soup without a hint of bacon; fat, broiled tomatoes, giant, grilled flat-cap mushrooms lacking their sprinkle of breadcrumbs, a gratin of asparagus (having no butter! Elle thought with dismay) and a lightly flavoured saffron pilaff. She was certain that a medley of boiled vegetables contributed to the pilaff's broth rather than hearty and more savoury bone broth.

Elle had especially noted the absence of tureens of melted butter and white sauce. Nothing had been salted. There was no accompaniment of eggs, hardboiled or poached, nor of fried toast. In observing each dish that arrived, she concluded that not one drop of beef fat had been utilised.

After a discreet inquiry for salt that was met with a brief shake of Bascomb's head, she requested the shaker of ground black pepper and sprinkled it on Faedra's plate liberally.

What is salt's danger, except perhaps to Mrs Bunkley's condition?

"Cook has been most ingenious with her dishes," Elle said, addressing Bascomb as he refilled her drinking glass. "Please convey my compliments for having to work with such strict ingredients."

But before Elle could enquire about the absence of salt, Bascomb, his pleasant gaze distant and fixed, did not respond, not even with a murmured "yes, ma'am". He turned away with the crystal water pitcher as if she'd never spoken. Faedra indicated her ear and raised a brow.

Elle focused on Polly's place setting. With a mental command, she moved the dinner fork off the table. It dropped, clattering to the polished floor and startling Faedra.

The butler turned from the sideboard and walked across the room for the fallen utensil.

Not deaf. Elle smiled to placate her wife.

☠

Dinner done, they chose not to dawdle below and ascended the main staircase. Upon reaching the second floor, Elle spied Polly gripping the handle of Mrs Bunkley's door, as if she'd just emerged and was shutting it. Polly looked startled to see them and pocketed the long, thin black case she held. Elle steered Faedra in Polly's direction.

"Faedra, this is Miss Polly Devereux, the botanist Peasy spoke of."

"Miss Devereux," Faedra greeted holding out her hand. "How do you do? I'm Mrs Faedra White-Black. We did miss you at dinner."

"How do you do." Polly accepted Faedra's hand warily, and Elle smiled.

"And how is Mrs Bunkley?" she asked. "We would like to —"

"She rests now," Polly interrupted, "and shouldn't be disturbed."

"Oh, very well. Then we would like to bid Peasy a final good night, Miss Devereux," Elle said. "Would you know where she might be?"

"Oh, Mrs Black. She's in her laboratory at this time. Your arrival did disturb her work."

"Is she working with the recent acquisition that she mentioned?" Elle asked. "Has there been progress with the plant that has her attention?"

"Scientific work, especially with rare exotics, is held in confidence, Mrs Black." Polly's voice held a note of indignation. "I may not say."

"Of course. I do apologise. I know it is very important work, the Unreal specimen."

Polly stiffened, and her face shuttered.

Elle smiled more. "Good night, Miss Devereux."

"Good night ma—Mrs Black," Polly bade, her tone curt, and quickly passed them for the stairs.

"A rather puffed little partridge, isn't she?" Faedra whispered in humour as they listened to Polly's descent, and Elle giggled. "But what were you referring to, this acquisition?"

"The one mentioned in Peasy's letter," Elle said in a low voice. "And in certain notebooks Peasy has made me aware of."

"Oh? What note—" Faedra stilled, looking down. Elle joined her wife in gazing at their feet.

The pale, yellow legs of a Goldenrod crab spider stuck out from beneath Mrs Bunkley's door. It emerged, a fat body following the menacing forelegs, and then ran passed them, fleeing down the hallway.

Faedra and Elle stared after it.

"That little beast is usually seen in the south," Elle remarked. "And where there's one, others may—" Faedra raised her hand to knock on the door.

"Oh, dear, perhaps you shouldn't." Elle stayed her hand. "Though you've killed many a spider for me, it may upset Mrs Bunkley. She should rest."

"The vegetarian's sanctity for life goes rather far," Faedra softly exclaimed as Elle led her from the door.

"Mrs Bunkley certainly bears more tolerance for our insect creatures than I. She has created a rather interesting natural environment in which to...vegetate."

"Elle, the entire estate may be vegetating. It's very pretty, but as a place itself...have you felt that it might be too quiet, too peaceful, here? Oh, my words are inadequate. It is more than that."

"Peaseflower *is* a conservatory, Fae'. What is peace—to us, a kind of slumbering—but plants merely poking up from the ground, breathing and growing? How bored you were when you accompanied me to Kew Gardens." Elle smiled.

"Was Eden ever thus? Perhaps I would have found myself ejected from Paradise for being too rambunctious. Today felt like Peasy and I were romping puppies, making a mess of nature's serenity." Faedra opened the door to their room. She poked her head in. "Well, no insects in here. That puffed Polly gave you nothing for your questions, dear."

"Oh, but darling, even nothing can tell me something." Elle followed her wife in. "Sometimes that's everything."

☠

Once Faedra shut the bedroom door, she turned to Elle.

"Shall we leave now to investigate?" she whispered, though there was no one else present in their room.

"No, *we* shall not," Elle said, indulgent.

Faedra looked affronted. "I've not once accompanied you on your cases, not even to investigate that pinching ghost, as I was always working," she complained. "And now you'd deny me the experience of sleuthing about?"

Elle kissed Faedra's pouting lip.

"I will, because you are too beautiful and will draw everyone's attention. Even the plants. Which is what you are supposed to do, so that mousy little me may pitter-patter in the shadows, unobserved, fulfilling the stealthy part of sleuthing. However, we'll be doing none of that tonight. I would like to know what Peasy is working on in that lab of hers, but unless we wish to encounter one of her sinister traps in the dark, we'd be best informed of where to poke our noses once we've had our formal tour, tomorrow."

Faedra sighed, crestfallen. She reached beneath the folds of her dress into her bustle and brought out her silver Smith & Wesson, then walked to where she'd hidden its case in their luggage. "I guess sleuthing does require some reconnaissance. Very well. But first thing when it's dark tomorrow, I want to light your policeman's lantern."

After Faedra put her pistol away, Elle fetched the notebooks. While Faedra perused them at the writing desk, Elle weighed whether she should eat of the jerked meat and biscuits she'd stashed away.

That Peasy. Declaring herself a vegetarian at age twelve—and then mocking we detractors for our inability to commit to such a sacrificial cause.

Peeved, Elle decided to eschew opening her packages for the time being. Faedra turned to her from the desk.

"Peasy gives you such clues, and I, a tennis racket?"

"Dear, you are at your most brilliant when hitting things. Balls, targets, pheasants, cruel girls—"

"Oh, how you patronise me," Faedra said with feigned hurt. She indicated Polly's fantastic paintings. "Deliriums whilst influenced by poisons, a strange exotic plant, then people becoming queer...until we'd met the dog, I'd thought the staff suffered from the lethargy of too much vegetarianism. Elle, this *telæsthesia* mentioned by our most unfriendly Miss Devereux, is that not what you do?"

"I think it means mental awareness from afar...or mental communication, Faedy, and not the moving of objects from afar."

Faedra looked at her with keen interest. "Though I've had you exercise your perturbationist skills daily, we've never tested if you could perceive my thoughts." She arched a brow at Elle's attempt to protest. "And yes, dear, I know you don't want the reputation of a common, mind-reading medium, but let's try it, just once. If we're successful, then I can purchase a crystal ball for you!"

"Mother shall spin in her grave," Elle exclaimed, but she

complied, taking a seat before Faedra. She stared deep into her wife's blue eyes.

"Naughty," Elle then said. "You are thinking about puppies again." Faedra gasped and Elle continued.

"A darling baby Labrador Retriever with the biggest paws, and the most soulful eyes one could look upon. No, Faedy, we may not have one. And I did not have to read your mind to know that thought. The art of mentalism is the art of human cunning, dear, and you should know that by now. If there's anything to this Unreal plant business and it causing true mental disturbances, I can't know until I've gone into Peasy's conservatory and met it."

"Very well." Faedra grinned while Elle gathered the notebooks and hide them again. "I hope this possible talking plant is not a mesmerist, for the last such professed hypnotist you encountered received a black eye for her trouble."

"Hm," Elle said in thought. "Mesmerism; that is an interesting observation, Faedy. I shall think on that. Peasy has been very unhelpful by not remaining to discuss these journals further."

"Perhaps she did not feel it safe to do so?" Faedra's face became serious.

"Oddly, that was not my thought. Now dear, I've a task for you."

Elle then shooed Faedra to poke about below. She instructed her wife to look within the dining room, and if Polly were there, to engage her in conversation that might reveal something. Her wife thus occupied, Elle stepped out on to their balcony to observe the great conservatory dome in moonlight. The glass was dark, though parts were lit with electrical lights. She wondered where within it Peasy flitted. Cool air filled her lungs, and she drew the curtains closed behind her to better see in the darkness.

Elle felt that Peasy was teasing her with the journals. Peasy had not seemed fearful but more in enjoyment of gifting Elle with a puzzle, and Elle did not appreciate being made part of some game. Peasy had had enough opportunities to take her or Faedra into confidence, even with dogs watching or Bascomb hovering.

But Elle did not want to share more criticism of Peasy with Faedra, who was so fond of their childhood friend.

A very different attitude from your original cry for help, Peasy.

The night was cold and crisp with a light wind, and Elle felt again that rain might come. The delicate, pleasing scent of sweet pea flowers wafted, then clung. As she looked into the dark, figures became defined in the distance, standing motionless in the grass near the rose garden.

The shapes were of maids in caps and aprons, their black silhouettes outlined by the dim lights of the conservatory. They dotted the lawn, facing this way and that, and were as silent and still as pawns awaiting movement on a chessboard. Elle retrieved her spyglass, but could only discern dark shapes and no apparent activity. Beyond them and the hedgerow stood other figures, lit by electric light in the rose garden.

She focused her glass; the garden figures became gardeners who stood close to the conservatory's lit glass, all facing its direction. Just as still as the women, they appeared to be staring within.

Elle lowered her glass, feeling she was being watched again. She looked about, then below. A matching pair of silent Gordon Setters gazed up, their eyes reflecting the dull light.

"If you could speak, I wish you'd do so," Elle said, irritated. "Since you cannot, off you go."

The dogs trotted into the darkness, their legs matching step.

Elle sighed.

"I would pack our bags and have us depart right this instant, but I know what Faedra would say: what about Peasy?" she grumbled.

She withdrew into the bedroom and shut the balcony doors.

When Faedra returned, Elle was reading Peasy's letters again, both laid side by side on the table.

"Like a highwaywoman, I've made off with the sweetmeats and nuts from the dining room sideboard," Faedra said with cheer. In her hand, she held her folded handkerchief.

"Oh, let me see. And perhaps you should refer to these delightful meats as 'crystallised fruits,' darling, considering what does not exist in this house."

Faedra opened her handkerchief parcel and Elle took a few of the treats revealed. As she ate, she went to the door and locked it.

"Polly was dining below, Elle, and she was most overbearing to Bascomb and a footman. Why, I thought them afraid, and they promptly made themselves scarce when I appeared. Polly then abandoned her meal and left as well, with barely words spoken between us. Would you say she's the shy sort, Elle?"

"One who is shy, yet overbears? You give her much, dear."

"With that mission failed, I poked below. It was cold as a tomb, Elle. They'd not bothered to keep one fire lit. On my return here, I thought to nose about Mrs Bunkley's door."

"Mm." Elle nibbled. She bent to roll up a carpet, pressed the roll against the door's bottom, and then wedged a chair beneath the handle. "And did you smell the loam and must within?"

"I did. Extraordinary. A 'natural environment' indeed. Your rug will deter insectile invaders, darling, but I doubt the little creature can push that chair." Elle could hear the smile in Faedra's voice.

"Be not alarmed by my odd cautions, dear." She walked to the balcony doors and jammed a chair beneath its handles. "After experiencing Valentin's bold interruption of our intimacies, I would rather Peasy did not surprise us with her company. It would be just like her to climb that ivy-tangled trellis outside and announce herself at our balcony, a Romeo to your Juliet, come morning. She may seem somewhat mannered now, but I'm certain she is as inconsiderate as ever."

Faedra laughed. "Oh, Elle, she has nothing but plants for company. I'd forgive her for disturbing us."

"I wouldn't."

Faedra then sighed in contentment while Elle discreetly burped behind her hand. She patted her chest as she joined her wife's side and hugged her.

"That dinner," Elle said.

"Peasy's admirable vegetarianism dissuades me from delving into your jerked meat stash…just yet."

Elle gazed tolerantly. "I wish I'd packed a ham."

"Or a bottle of your mushroom catsup," Faedra said with cheer. "Elle, I am no cook, as you know, but wasn't salt and butter entirely missing from our meal?"

"They were. Nor will we see any bread, for it requires eggs and milk. And when I make puddings and pies, well! Suet is involved. I think we've not seen even a simple bread of flour and water because unless one wants an inedible loaf it requires salt for flavour." In thought, she took Faedra's hand and led her to the bed.

"Such restrictions," Faedra said. "We can't let Peasy know of your sea salt stash, then, though that is meant for fighting spectres, not seasoning dishes. I wonder if lack of salt is why the servants are so dull?"

Elle didn't answer, uncertain about Mrs Bunkley's possible strict diet. An invalid's requirements needn't affect the meals of the whole household. She unbuttoned Faedra's bodice, then pushed it off her wife's shoulders.

"Yet Peasy remains vibrant," Faedra remarked. "And Miss Devereux seems healthy, though colourless."

Elle wrapped her arms around Faedra's waist to unfasten her skirt and kissed the bared skin above her wife's bosom.

"Oh, Elle," Faedra said.

Elle removed all of Faedra's clothing.

☠

Sometime deep into the night, Elle dreamt. She stood high above Peaseflower, like one parallel to the Earth and with the night sky behind her, and surveyed all the grounds.

Something called, deep within the maze of conservatory buildings. Verdant and lush, its limbs slowly spread but it was not a thing merely growing; it was labouring.

What was that? Elle asked, not understanding the communication.

A tiny red blight moved like one trapped in all the blue and green of the conservatory, at the place where the gardeners had gathered. Elle knew the flitting life-thing was not meant to be red.

What hurts there? she asked.

Something spoke again.

Elle woke, feeling the need to rise and attend to something urgent; a window left unlatched, a cat crying, something burning. Faedra lay still and slumbering beside her.

"What was that?" Elle muttered, then fell back to sleep again.

CHAPTER SIX

E lle woke drowsily to the sun's dawning glow and birds twit-
tering outside. Realising she was not in her own bed but
luxuriating in one larger and fluffier with a down-filled
coverlet and fat pillows, she sighed and wrapped an arm around
Faedra's middle.

The door handle jiggled. Elle stiffened. A light thud sounded
on the door's surface, as if someone had bumped into it.

"Oh!" exclaimed a voice at the other side.

That's not a maid, Elle thought.

"Elle? Elle? Good morning!" The door handle turned more.

"Peasy," Elle grated, and sat up in the room's chill, not bothering
to cover her nakedness. She put her hand out to prevent Faedra
from rising, knowing her wife liked her sleep.

"Elle, did you block this door? Are you and Faedy in a state
of dishabille? We may have last seen each other unclothed as
children, Elle, but I assure you, I don't regard your breasts as the
exception among women."

Elle groaned.

"I only want to apologise to you and Faedy for a great slight I
must visit upon you this morning—"

"As if *this* were not it?" Elle said, feeling Faedra shake silently in laughter.

"I didn't want to leave such a callous message for a servant to deliver. I've more business to attend to—Elle, can you hear me?"

"Yes, yes Peasy, oh what is it," Elle called, exasperated.

"I can't breakfast with you this morning, Elle. But do enjoy your meal with leisure and once done, meet me outside in the rose garden for your tour of my gardens! It will be such a merry time! I shall await your and Faedy's company with alacrity!"

"Very well. Is there anything else you wish to share?" Elle listened, and only silence met her.

Damn you, Peasy. "We will see you then, Peasy." When she thought Peasy had yet to move away from the door, she called again. "And Faedy wishes you 'good morning' and sends you her love."

"Oh! Oh, Faedy, good morning! I can't wait for us to be together again!"

Elle arched a brow as Peasy finally departed, her footsteps fading. She hit Faedra with a pillow. "Why didn't you say something?"

Faedra rolled over, smiling. "I was too busy laughing."

"She may not think my bosom remarkable, but she'll surely become insensate at the sight of yours."

"My darling barricade-builder." Faedra touched Elle's face and Elle eagerly laid herself atop her wife and kissed her.

"I've good reason to build such fortifications, for you are my treasure," Elle said, and kissed Faedra more. Since Peasy had assured them they might take their leisure with breakfast, Elle decided that her wife would be her first indulgence.

☠

The maid entered while Faedra was dozing more and Elle was figuring out the bath's modern plumbing fixtures. Elle poked her head out of the bath suite to observe the maid; she was not one of the round-faced girls. The maid went directly to the balcony doors, removed the chair, and then opened the curtains to let light in.

"Help me with the bath, please," Elle called. The maid obliged, her visage pleasant. When she entered the suite and bent over the tub, turning the knobs, Elle leaned over with the pretence of watching her work, and sniffed the maid's scent instead. She then understood what had been apparent when she'd been among the laundry-hanging maids.

"You smell of cucumbers," she said. "I believe you all do."

The maid turned to her as if to say something, her gaze then fixed on Elle.

"What is it?" Elle asked.

"Help us," the maid said.

"I could if you can tell me what's the matter."

"We want nothing to happen to you," the maid said.

"'We?' What do you fear?"

The maid's face scrunched, the expression seemingly forced rather than natural. Elle nearly thought the maid might cause her face harm by the action.

"We don't understand...what is happening," the maid finally said, and Elle laid a hand on her arm. The woman's body was cool.

"Answer one thing. Does something speak to you from afar? Within you head?" Elle demanded.

The twist in the maid's face shifted to the other side of her face; a seeming expression of confusion and agony.

"We...speak," she slowly said.

Elle sighed in frustration.

"Go. You are obviously not of your own mind. None of you are. And interrogating you would be like tormenting a poor child. But I also doubt it's mesmerisation, since you are capable of forming words to me—hopefully without doing harm to your brain." The maid rose and turned to leave. "And relax your face," Elle ordered.

When the bedroom door closed behind the maid, Elle spun

the bath's knobs in frustration, shutting off the running water. She wondered if a headache might set in, despite her having not used her esemplastic powers.

"They're all addled," she muttered as she rubbed her temples. "And the dogs. And Mrs Bunkley. But not Peasy, Polly, Faedra, and I. Why?"

"Elle?" Faedra said in the bath suite's doorway, and yawned. Her dressing gown lay open.

"Get in here, you beautiful woman, so that I can scrub your back," Elle said, her tone testy.

☠

Elle and Faedra attempted to visit Mrs Bunkley before breakfast, but received no answer to their polite knocking. Faedra declined Elle's offer to unlock the door with her mind. When they descended, a medley of food smells met them, the remote Bascomb standing like one invisible by the dining room's sideboard. Again, they met no Polly. Elle expected breakfast to be an unusual affair without eggs, bacon, ham, sausage, butter, or toast, and she wasn't proven wrong. The inventive cook provided potato snow and crisped potato ribbons sprinkled with cayenne pepper; stewed, button mushrooms with nuts sat on crunchy celery stalks, marrowfats *a la française*, spiced parsnip wafers, pottages of warm love-apples served in tiny cups, and pilau rice with tangy mandrang.

Faedra took to her morning meal with good-humoured curiosity and enough appetite for Elle to suspect her wife was quite ravenous after last night's exertions. She thought the mandrang dish a bit stimulating for a day's starter, since the cucumbers and diced onions contained (at least in that version of the dish) Madeira wine. But Faedra was enjoying a sizeable helping of the West Indian dish, and Elle made a mental note to return to her *Modern Cookery* book by Eliza Acton and bookmark the recipe for future meals. For herself, she enjoyed the saltless dishes well enough, but was experiencing a frightening longing for bacon.

And should I march into that kitchen and demand the reason for the lack of salt, cook would merely make painful faces, Elle silently griped.

While they ate, Faedra watched Elle with a wistful smile, and Elle wondered at the cause. She stopped eating.

"Tell me," she coaxed.

"I was thinking that you look rather like the lady of the house." Faedra grinned. "And the thought so pleased me."

Not caring that it was improper, Elle leaned to give Faedra a kiss.

"I could never manage a house this big," she remarked, as they resumed their meal. "Do you remember my home, Faedy? We speak of my lost fortune, but truly, my family was only well-to-do compared to Peasy's immensely successful father."

"I'd say the wealth from your father's antiquities hunting rather compares to my father's import business. That would have been enough inheritance to last beyond the excesses of five years."

Elle smiled. "You still suspect Valentin of hoarding some of it. I highly doubt it; he could never keep his purse closed. I more suspect he has a family or two somewhere and that they're a sizeable brood."

"Valentin, a father? Is he fond of children, Elle?"

"As ridiculously fond as you are." Elle glanced to where Bascomb would be. He had left the room, and when she looked about, no others were present. She continued in a low tone. "Though, now that we know his true nature, I hope it's not because he finds them tasty. He fancied himself quite virile, Faedy. He insisted on using a preventive."

"Really?" Faedra said in hushed astonishment.

"Oh, yes. He utilised the most expensive — and handcrafted! — of supple sheaths." Elle leaned towards Faedra with a conspiratorial air. "Handcrafted by nuns." They both giggled.

"Considering his 'vocation,' I would think he more preferred their use as preventive to disease," Faedra said, sceptical. "Elle, would you have had vampyric children? I am very confused about this 'living vampyre' business."

"It does sound like nonsense. I haven't a clue. My discussion with Miss Skycourt hadn't included his sort of vampyre. It would be simpler to accept that he has queer teeth and suffers from the delusion of being a creature."

"Except for his rising from the dead," Faedra said.

"Oh, that." Elle's good mood subsided. "For that, he deserves a well-placed kick in the condom."

☠

"Elle, what shall be my task on this excursion?" Faedra whispered when they departed through the drawing room with its flung open veranda doors. Elle glanced at the fireplace, seeing no evidence that it had been lit. "Is there anything you wish me to observe? To pummel? Perhaps interrogate?"

"Oh, what a dashing spy you would make! I think for today, darling, you must be as handsome as you can be, and charm poor Peasy to distraction."

"I will endeavour," Faedra assured. They emerged from the back of the house into sunlight. Peasy danced about down the great lawn, waving and fluttering.

"Yet another vision of white silk chiffon," Elle remarked, as they descended. "She looks like a moth. Awaiting her damselfly."

"Now Elle," Faedra said, even as she smiled at Peasy, who ran towards them. Faedra released Elle to hold out her arms, and Peasy flung herself into them, covering Faedra's face with kisses.

"Oh, Faedy! How I missed you!"

"And I, you, dear Peasy. Your company was sorely missed at dinner last night."

"Oh." Peasy clasped her hands to her breast, and Elle was again surprised to spy moisture in Peasy's happy eyes.

Heavens, girl, what happened to the practical child I knew? Love for Faedra seemed to have turned Peasy into a fount.

"Peasy, dear, the morning air is brisk," Elle said, "and your frock so light. Shouldn't a wrap be fetched for you?"

"Oh, Elle, and you in your dour black wool. I quite like that edging of earthy brown, it's so sensible. But you'll soon know why I favour light frocks in the conservatories. Faedy, how beautiful you are in that shade of blue, even more beautiful than yesterday. You are our stunning skies, streaked with Helios's gold!"

"Elle made this dress," Faedra said, demure.

"She saved her best work for you, as she should. Now, please come. Your tour of my wonders awaits!"

☠

The half-dome that Elle had spied through her glass turned out to be Peasy's laboratory. As they entered the pungent rose garden, desks, cubbyholes, shelves, and other work surfaces became evident behind the half-dome's glass. Peasy had optimum enjoyment of the surrounding exterior while she worked within. One of the lab's viewing pleasures was the singular tree of trumpet-shaped flowers.

"This is the brugmansia of South America, or as it is commonly known, the 'Angel's Trumpets.'" Peasy went to the tree and touched the large, hanging orange blossoms.

"South American, Peasy?" Faedra queried. "Sitting here amongst English roses, will it endure our spring weather?"

"That is the question, Faedy! It is meant to be behind the glass, enjoying tropical warmth, but I am testing a serum I've injected it with, one meant to enhance its natural hardiness and vitality." She held one of the flowers up for Faedra. "It smells wonderful, doesn't it?" Faedra bent and inhaled.

"It is heady. A very pungent jasmine-like scent, don't you think

Elle?" Faedra stood back so that Elle might sniff.

"But the tea of its leaves is poisonous, and a very potent deliriant," Peasy added.

Elle raised her head. "And here you are touching it, Peasy?"

"Oh, Elle, the plant is not bruised, so we needn't fear the taint of its oils. But as a hallucinogen, it is fearsome." Peasy dropped the flower. "One story tells that the brugmansia's intoxicant was given to a dead king's wives and slaves. Thus under its sway, they would enter his tomb and allow themselves to be buried alive with him."

"A narcotic to incur obedience, I know those well," Elle said under her breath, and Peasy glanced at her.

"Then...you did spend time in an asylum, just as Faedra had said. How you must have suffered, Elle."

Elle linked arms with Faedra. "It was not pleasant, but that asylum stay brought Faedra to me, and that's all that matters."

"Oh! To begin the tour on such a somber note! My friends, let's begin anew. Come see my workspace." Elle and Faedra followed Peasy into the doors of the half-dome.

Little potted plants stood on tiered shelves, while microscopes, flasks, jars, and glass dishes sat on others, and books and papers piled. Herbs hung in bunches, drying. When Faedra pointed out Peasy's refrigeration box, noting it to be of the latest technological design, Peasy unlocked it and showed her the interior, revealing vials of stored serum, plant samples, and bottled tinctures. Elle half-listened and noted a book's title as it sat atop other books on Peasy's large, cluttered desk. It read: *The Power of Movement by Plants*, by Charles Darwin.

Peasy's watercolour box lay open on a pulled out drawer beneath. A jar filled with dirty paint-water sat beside it, as well as a paint-soaked rag and brushes that needed cleaning. Elle looked about the desk but saw no paintings. One drawer had a lock, which she tested with her mind; the drawer remained firmly secure. Elle then stared at it, and it audibly clicked.

She stepped away and turned to where Peasy and Faedra knelt by the open refrigeration box.

"And the syringes are stored there," Peasy said to Faedra, pointing to a glass cabinet containing a stack of thin, black cases. "These serums are all experimental and should be locked up in an even more secure area, but since it is only I and Polly remaining, I've decided to have the research near me." Peasy then shut the refrigeration box. While she locked it, Elle caught Faedra's gaze. She indicated with eye direction that Faedra pay attention to the desk. Then she stared at it.

The unlocked drawer flew out, startling Peasy. The contents noisily rolled within, and the drawer tilted down, precariously close to falling out. Faedra leapt to her feet and moved for the drawer.

"Here Peasy, I'll—" Faedra caught the drawer and lifted it to push it back in. She looked at the contents and stilled. "Oh."

"What is it, dear?" Elle stepped by Faedra's side.

Within the drawer, a storage case lay open. The burgundy and velvet-lined bottom held a glass and metal syringe, its spare needles set in compartments. Slim vials containing tablets were stored alongside. The interior of the top case was stamped in gold: Parke, Davis & Co, London. The name alone told Elle that they were looking upon the pharmaceutical's most popular remedy.

"Either you've asthma, Peasy, or you require a 'Forced March' stimulant now and then," Elle quipped.

"Cocaine." Faedra's tone was reserved.

Peasy hurried to Faedra's side, picked up the case, and shut it. "You do not approve. And as you've a physical culturist's interests, Faedy, you certainly wouldn't. But it is my health and energy aid. It is the only way I can get the work done, and as Elle has said, the work is my own 'forced march.'" She put the case back into the drawer and Faedra helped her push it back in.

Faedra then smiled. "Might I suggest more coffee instead, Peasy?"

Peasy smiled back, self-conscious. "As heiress to a tea empire, I should not, but I will drink it by the gallon if it would please you, Faedy."

"How do the gardeners stay up the night with you, Peasy?" Elle asked. "Do they also take cocaine?"

"The...gardeners?" Peasy locked the drawer.

Oh, don't play Peasy, Elle thought, vexed. "You worked last night, did you not, Peasy? I can view your lab from our room, and I saw your gardeners gathered outside your door."

"Well, I did work, Elle, I was here all that time. I...perhaps you dreamt of my gardeners." She laughed. "Every night, I feel I've dreamt things. And I can't remember them."

"With the scent of sweet pea so pervasive, I wouldn't be surprised if one dreamt of faeries parading by," Faedra commented.

"Or of dark visions, needing painting," Elle added, and Peasy's face suddenly stilled, anguished

There, your true face. Now tell us, Peasy, tell us!

Peasy turned and flitted away. She ran out the lab through a back door.

Elle and Faedra shared a glance.

"I know I'm provoking her," Elle whispered. "But...."

"Perhaps at tour's end, she will talk," Faedra whispered back. Elle nodded. They moved for the door.

They entered a threshold where another set of glass doors met them. Faedra pushed it open for Elle to precede her, and she stepped from cool air into wet heat and a massive enclosed space. Palms stretched above to the great dome, and Elle nearly expected to see birds flying across or perhaps spy a fabled dinosaur, peeping from the soaring fronds. She breathed, and the hot, humid air was rich with the scent of wet moss and rich soil. She and Faedra shared a look of amazement, and then stepped upon the path.

The lush vegetation surrounding them was unhindered by pots, rows, or partitioned sections; the foliage, vines, and trees mingled, overlapped, and flowed. Natural balance and freeing beauty shaped the environment. As Elle and Faedra walked, a gardener—in his olive green cap and coveralls—gazed up at a banana tree and manipulated a pole ending in clippers. He carefully snipped a decayed banana leaf and it fell.

"This is not Kew, Faedy," Elle said, and an eagerness seized her, to know the unruliness of nature, just a little unfettered and unopposed. They walked down the winding path and into thickening jungle growth. The banana trees ended in a mango grove, where long, large leaves and green oval fruit hung, heavy ornaments on their long stems. Peasy stood beneath the fruit on a train track, a white fairy by a bright red locomotive engine as high as her waist. It pulled three open black carriages, each big enough to seat two.

"My dear friends!" she announced. "As you can see, Papa acquired an electric tour train for me after all."

☠

Peasy gathered her skirts and sat down in the open locomotive compartment while Elle and Faedra boarded the first carriage, hooked close enough for Peasy to turn and converse easily. As Peasy and Faedra exclaimed over her train, Elle investigated a leather folder compartment before her seat, in which eating utensils, napkins, and a folded souvenir fan was stored. Above the compartment, a small, black wooden tray was secured shut. Elle released it, brought it down, and then put it back up again. When Peasy activated the train and it began to advance, Elle stood up to see the controls Peasy worked.

Smack!

Elle sat back down, holding her forehead where a hanging mango had collided with it. Faedra burst out laughing.

"Elle! Must I remind all passengers to remain in their seats during the tour?" Peasy exclaimed, turning around.

"Must trees hang their riches over our unsuspecting heads?"

Elle said.

"Insult the trees, Elle, and they may just drop a mango on you."
Peasy laughed.

"I have nothing but praise for the mango fairies," Elle answered,
and Peasy snorted.

"Fairies," she said with disdain. "The plants themselves can
take actions perfectly well on their own."

"Can they, Peasy?" Faedra asked. "You don't sound as if you
jest." Peasy turned to touch her.

"I do not jest, dear Faedy. Plants have senses, and they will
respond. The wounded tomato emits a powerful odour to signal
distress; the *mimosa pudica*—the Touch-Me-Not—shrinks from
the merest contact to protect itself, and the Venus Flytrap knows to
close its formidable leaf blades around prey. The subject of plant
sensitivity, Faedy, is the introduction to the tour. There." Peasy
slowed the train and brought it to a stop. Clusters of creeping
plants with tiny fanning leaves grew on the slope of black earth
before them, surrounded by the roots of a spreading mango tree.

"Note the beautiful compound leaves of the Touch-Me-Not,
also known as the sleepy plant. Now Faedy, touch one with a
finger."

Faedra did so, reaching around Elle and touching the tip of
one tiny branch of leaflets. The fanning leaves withdrew upon
themselves, row after row, until the branch's leaflets were tightly
folded.

"What a singular plant," Faedra said in hushed astonishment.

"Plant movement," Elle murmured, recalling Peasy's book by
Darwin. She reached out and touched another, and they watched
the folding cascade again. "Perhaps not so singular, Faedy. The
sweet pea and the cucumber do coil their tendrils around objects,
pulling themselves up as they grow."

"Exactly, Elle," Peasy said, delighted. "All plants move; they
merely travel at a pace unperceived by human attention."

"But...Peasy," Faedra said, perplexed. "Such tiny plants, the pea and this Touch-Me-Not. Where would they house their thoughts?"

"Their thoughts, Faedy?" Elle questioned.

"What I mean to say, Elle, is, does not such movement require commands from a brain?"

"Oh, Faedy, it most certainly does! And perhaps a plant's 'brain' does not resemble our accepted understanding of a centrally controlled system. A plant after all, is unlike the animal, and the animal, unlike it." Peasy started the train again.

"And if such plants should want to talk to us?" Elle suddenly pressed. *As in the manner of* telæsthesia?

Peasy let out a noise of surprise. "Oh, Elle. Plants haven't mouths," she chastised.

They passed beneath the last of the mango grove and entered the conservatory proper, surrounded by leathery and fleshy trunks, black earth and swollen roots, branches heavy with ovoid, pear-shaped, and odd-shaped fruit, and flowering shrubs also bearing fruit. The humid air was pungent with the scent of tropical flowers, and Elle wondered if such an environment resembled the fabled Malay Archipelago Peasy's cousin Cherish adventured in. Peasy pointed out fruit and named them: guava, yellow and red dragon fruit, scaly skinned snake fruit, the Malay gooseberry, sapodilla, tamarillo, prickly pawpaw, monkey-apple, and several kinds of passion fruit with their striking white and purple passiflora flowers. She picked two melon pears from their bush and handed one each to Elle and Faedra. Elle retrieved the fruit knife and napkins from the front pocket, unfastened and laid down the hanging tray, and served Faedra slices. Peasy declined when Elle offered her a slice and continued to drive the train.

Cocaine has certainly affected your appetite, Peasy, Elle thought as she ate. The melon pear's flesh was sweet and juicy, and Faedra dabbed juices from her mouth. Peasy then reached up and picked two succulent star fruit from a branch and handed them to Elle.

"These are very ripe now, and can be eaten in its entirety,"

Peasy said.

"This abundance, with edibles everywhere," Faedra exclaimed. "What an Eden you've built, Peasy." She ate of the star fruit Elle handed her.

"The gentry would fight for the privilege to debut such exotic fare at their dinner tables," Elle added. "You would be the most sought after grower in England, Peasy."

"My interest *had* been in exotic foodstuffs," Peasy said with an indifferent air. "But I no longer desire to feed people." Elle glanced at Faedra, who seemed to share her surprise, and raised a brow.

"Very well, you keep your exotic bounty to yourself." Elle put away the tray and disposed of the melon pear rinds. "No longer desire to develop Peaseflower Court for the public—" Peasy turned and gave her a sharp look. "And choose to leave your hamlets to care for themselves. Then what is your interest now, Peasy?"

"Why, conservation, of course." Peasy tone was cool. "I wish to save and preserve as much as I can."

"And with this tropical clime, I believe you can. Such perfect humidity and heat," Elle observed. "Kew could never accomplish this."

"My conservatory harbours a subterranean world of furnaces, Elle. An army of fire-breathing boilers labour beneath us."

"Yet with your greatly reduced staff, how do you maintain the feeding of those furnaces?" Faedra asked, curious.

"That, dear Faedy, Papa had the foresight to take care of, for he favoured the use of modern advancement. The conservatory furnaces are fully mechanised, and you will also notice the same with our watering systems." Peasy then produced a parasol, opened it, and handed it to Elle. Intrigued, Elle accepted and held the parasol over Faedra and herself.

Water sprayed above from seemingly nowhere, a light misty rain nourishing the plants surrounding the advancing train. Rainbows appeared within the mists. Peasy waved off Elle's attempt to place the parasol over her as well. Their hostess surveyed her plants while glistening drops beaded in her black hair and ran down her white skin.

"A conservatory like this requires more than modern solutions," Peasy said. "There must be a vision for the future, and preparations to ensure such future. Like Kew, I've begun a germplasm bank. That is a 'seed bank,' Elle."

"Of course, Peasy." Peasy gestured to the dome they slowly passed beneath.

"It is a daunting vision, conservation, and I find myself in the minority with such dedication. This giant, sprawling house that Papa started, and is now mine. It is precious beyond words, and requires so much work. I try not to wonder how I will go on alone, with mother ill, but surely if Elle can have someone by her side, there's hope for me yet."

"Peasy, your passion and intellect are certain to captivate any you woo. You will find that someone for you," Faedra assured, and Peasy beamed at her, breathing in happiness.

The misting rain ceased, and Elle shut the parasol, thinking how very silent Peasy's paradise was, with no birdsong, animal cries, or the buzzing of insects. She would welcome the sight of a darting damselfly to activate the stillness. Picking out the complimentary fan in the compartment pocket, she flicked it open and fanned herself. The logo of Bunkley Teas decorated the paper.

Peasy still gazed at Faedra with adoration, and Elle idly wondered who the heiress of Bunkley Teas hoped to marry someday, for any man she ended up with would own everything of Peasy's, forcing the loss of her autonomy.

Unfortunate that Faedy hasn't a sister, Elle thought drily. Peasy's neck and face seemed to maintain its coolness, unperturbed by the heat. Faedra, pinker next to Peasy's whiteness, was slightly flushed.

"In such humidity, Peasy," Elle said, fanning more. "One is

tempted to disrobe and roam as God made Eve, entirely naked."

Faedra laughed, but Peasy scowled, and Elle wondered at her sudden distemper.

"The plants do not care about nakedness," Peasy said. "Such a foolish myth."

☠

When Peasy returned her attention to her locomotive, Faedra touched Elle's hand. She indicated the surrounding jungle with a subtle indication of her finger. Gardeners in their olive green caps and coveralls stood in haphazard fashion behind foliage and tree trunks, as still as the plants they blended into. In their sentinel-like state, they seemed bleached of living colour.

If not for her wife's huntress's eye, Elle would have continued dismissing their shapes for more plant mass, making up the body of the richly organic scenery. Faedra looked from left to right as the train trundled on, her gaze alert though unperturbed. Her wife was perhaps gaining the same impression Elle felt in studying the strangely quiet men they passed. In their odd respite—some standing with closed eyes—they seemed, like the maids, utterly benign.

Elle returned her scrutiny to Peasy, who simply focused on the tracks before them. If she was aware of her staff's presence, she paid them no heed.

Faedra shared a glance with her and shrugged.

"I've noticed, Peasy, your maids standing about on the lawn on occasion," Elle remarked, and she felt her voice broke the hush like a plate dropping. "While engaged in no activity nor chatter. Do you instruct them to partake in such pastime?"

"Why yes, Elle, it is Eastern meditation practice." Peasy glanced back and smiled. "Far more beneficial for inspiring proper, disciplined work than theological values. What a funny look on your face. What did you think they were doing?"

Meditating, Peasy? In the damp and darkness of the night?

"Praying," Elle answered under her breath.

Their jungle surroundings parted. The tracks swung near the conservatory glass and by doors leading outside. On the lawn, a lone conservatory house stood, and behind it, the shining edge of a huge concave mirror emerged, its mounted surface facing the eastward sky.

"That is my House of Succulents," Peasy said, pointing. "Which requires a more dry heat than green plants can bear; thus their isolation. It's only fitting that I store my dehydration dish there."

"Why, your vegetable and fruit chips are optimally positioned to receive the morning sun," Faedra remarked. Elle chewed on a pinkie finger. She had a strong desire to jump off the train and run back to the men and question them about their meditation practice rather than discuss dehydration cooking.

"They are, dear Faedy!" Peasy turned to beam at Faedra, much to Elle's annoyance. "In that way, they receive the full benefits of all-day exposure."

"Does your Rare House also enjoy a placement outside the main conservatory, Peasy?" Elle asked.

Peasy switched her gaze to her, lips curled, and Elle was uncertain if the smile was simply mischievous—or touched with portent.

"It enjoys a most especial placement, Elle. One, as I explained to Faedra, that must remain quite inviolate."

☠

Elle was of the mind to forego the rest of the tour and with brazen impoliteness, demand a visit to the Rare House, regardless of its mantraps. She needed to sleuth, something impossible while trapped on a train with the droning Peasy. She could not say she wasn't enjoying their tour, however. Their train left the glass and its view of the Succulents House for the interior proper.

In that open space, gardeners far more industrious than the ones "meditating" in the jungle laboured among Peasy's floral exotics. Ghost orchids, allium gladiators, bright borage, and the swirling leaves of the escargot begonia; Elle and Faedra could not help but exclaim over such rare botanical sights that even the most privileged of Englishwomen could ever hope to view.

"Peasy, your conservatory is the pride of England—of the world! Her Majesty would delight in all the rare treasures you've collected here," Faedra praised.

Peasy spun around with such energy Elle nearly fell back.

"It is what I hope," she said, hushed, and her dark eyes gleamed.

Their train then passed into a darkened entrance framed by curtains, leaving the great domed area behind. The interior of a sizeable house came into view, the glass blackened and revealing light only from above. Trees and fallen logs stood in grass and moss. Mushrooms, toadstools, and cascades of umbrella-topped fungi sprouted from trunks and clustered on the earth.

"My fungi forest," Peasy announced, breaking the silence. "There are many edible fruiting bodies here, as well as poisonous ones. Fungi compete for nutrients and space. Therefore, I've not been very successful with raising truffles. But that may change."

"Your fungi forest possesses a fairy circle. Look there, darling." Elle pointed out the ring of mushrooms to Faedra.

"You are a fount of quaint myths, Elle!" Peasy teased. "I've yet to see any little creatures dancing around it."

"That is because they don't want to be seen, Peasy," Elle said.

"Well, that particular circle is made of edibles, so their dancing ring shall disappear soon enough."

The train exited through more curtains for a half-moon tunnel, faced with frosted glass. Pale light shone through great, green squash leaves sprouting from tangled vines woven into the arched framework overhead. From the weave hung smooth and bumpy-skinned squashes and green, yellow, and orange gourds, their heavy bodies swaying.

"Peasy!" Elle said in alarm, and covered her head with her fan. Faedra laughed.

"But Elle, you could...," Faedra whispered and pointed to her own temple.

"Only if I'm aware that it comes for my head!" Elle hissed.

"But Elle, aren't they beautiful?" Peasy exclaimed. "My Tunnel of Gourds, filled with wonderful butternuts, acorns, patty pans, muscats, hubbards—and see there, such lovely, long zucchinis. So thick and well-formed," she added, beaming at Elle.

"And pumpkins!" Faedra said, before Elle could retort. "Oh, I love how you cook pumpkin, Elle."

"I am fond of squash flowers. They are wonderful when fried in butter and oil," Elle said, nervous.

"Faedy, beware, a very large pumpkin above you just bounced on its tether. Now Peasy, if we reach the end of this perilous tunnel unscathed, what will we find there?"

"Why Elle, that would be my poison garden," Peasy said with delight, and her face shown white in the pale light.

CHAPTER SEVEN

O f all of Peasy's gardens (which Elle thought might benefit from an illustrated touring map) only her poison garden bore a great, carved sign. Erected overhead, a grinning white skull decorated the black placard and its white letters. It read:

POISON GARDEN
Poison is in everything, and no thing is without poison.

When their train entered the garden proper, Elle surveyed their white glassed surroundings, filled with boxed and container plants, and unconsciously stiffened. Were she in a field or wood, open space would have granted her safe retreat from an encounter with a deadly specimen. Instead, danger flanked, innocuously and intimately close. The stick-mounted signs informed: mandrake, wolf's bane, mourning bride, belladonna, hemlock, henbane, foxglove, thornapple, and yew.

"And there, hellebore," Elle said, hushed. "Touch nothing, Faedy, for a baneful herb's toxins can be absorbed by mere contact with its leaves."

Peasy brought the slowing train to a stop.

They sat in the red train, encased in a white house and surrounded by a garden of death.

"Now we're in the midst of danger!" Peasy whispered excitedly. "Is it not a thrill? Elle is correct, Faedy, unlike my brugmansia, you must assume that these specimens bear their potent oils on their leaves. And should any dry part of a foxglove break near you, do not inhale! That is why, when my gardeners are present, they are well-garbed and don respiration masks. A simple brush against deadly nightshade's leaves can aversely affect you, though its beautiful, dark berries entice."

"The deadly nightshade?" Faedra repeated.

"That beauty there, Faedy," Elle said, "with its bell-shaped, purple flowers. It is also the belladonna, whose fruit may be called 'sorcerer's berries'."

"Their berries are like dark jewels," Faedra exclaimed, "and so beautiful."

"Hence their sobriquet, Faedy." Peasy gazed at Faedra with admiration. "For they are as darkly becoming as you are as fetching in your illumination."

Heavens, I may retch, Elle thought.

Faedra smiled with less her usual warmth, her tolerance for their friend's fawning perhaps finally giving her discomfort. Faedra glanced at Elle as if to see if she were well.

Elle smiled in assurance. Peasy's uncouth behaviour never surprised her, but her poor wife needed respite.

"Peasy, is there a difference between wolf's bane and mourning bride?" she asked to distract their hostess. "I had thought them the same."

"Why yes, Elle. They are different species of aconitum, or as you would know them, as different kinds of nightshades. My garden hosts many kinds of aconitum, as it is England's most poisonous plant. Which Polly had somehow forgotten." Peasy sniffed.

"Polly? Are you saying your remaining scientist *accidentally* tainted herself with toxins of the aconitum whilst in here, Peasy?" Elle asked.

"Well, accidents are that, aren't they? Her present pallor is indicative of her most recent self-poisoning. I placed my poor cannabis plant among the deadly nightshades for good reason. She was harvesting it to its death."

Elle spied the well-picked cannabis stalk, surrounded by belladonna. *What a careless mistake for a botanist. It's too careless.*

"Were it not for these signs, I would not know what dangers were in store, myself," Faedra remarked.

"Indeed, Faedy! It is fortunate that my former toxicologist delighted in labelling the specimens by their antique and picturesque names. One like yourself, Elle, could then easily identify such dangerous plants and stay away."

"Your warning is heeded, Peasy," Elle said. "I would not want to mistaken the unassuming hemlock for parsley. But I am surprised to see the common henbane nurtured here." She pointed out one specimen gone to seed for Faedra, who was not familiar with the saw-toothed leafed plant and its jawbone-shaped rows of seedpods, arranged like human teeth.

"What a strange and sinister...," Faedra said.

"*Weed*, Faedy?" Peasy said. "It is a coarse, hairy plant of dreadful stench, found in many a graveyard. But Elle, we must give its wretched attributes the same scrutiny as my exotic deliriants, among which number the spiritual kava-kava and the sacred peyote cacti. For all within this garden has medicinal potential. Paracelsus did say it is the dosage that makes the plant either a poison or a remedy. Consider then, that my deadly garden is a true *pharmakon*, for its contents can both kill and heal."

Peasy turned back to the train's controls and activated it, advancing the train down the track.

"Which then leads us to what may be the secondary purpose of conservatorial work, though no less important," she said. "The research laboratory compound of Peaseflower. The labs are currently in the embarrassing state of seeming abandoned, but I assure you, my experiments continue."

"Experiments for improving plant health and endurance," Faedra clarified.

"Oh yes, Faedy! Among many such augmentations, like for longevity." They had exited the poison garden and were then approaching a curved tunnel with a landing platform bearing glass doors. Peasy brought the train to a stop.

"Yes, longevity matters to me, very much," she said.

☠

When they disembarked, Peasy sent the train rolling ahead, informing that it would stop on the western side of the building and in her orangery, where they would board it once more. Elle gazed back where they'd come, attempting to gauge the distance they'd travelled. If they were at the other end of the conservatory, then the Rare House lay near. They entered a one-storey, glass-roofed laboratory building, which formed a box formation around a large courtyard. Though the walls facing outward were conventionally solid, the walls facing into the courtyard were still of glass, and Elle could see to the other side, where the laboratories continued. An isolated conservatory house sat within the courtyard, long in body and with two short wings at the head. Gravel and creeping green plants surrounded it. Elle thought the house stood forty feet from the lab walls, yet it seemed as distant as a solitary castle.

Is that you, Rare House?

She wanted to ask Peasy, but their hostess moved swiftly through the empty laboratories with their many lab tables, jars, sinks, counters, and glass cabinets, filled with withering specimens, and talked all the while.

"I have allowed experiments that may be considered heterodox," Peasy was explaining to Faedra as Elle trotted to keep up. "But what gentlemen of science fail to realise is, what is unknown to them has been *known* to our Earth for millions of years. Who is to say I cannot answer a question by supposedly unconventional means that my fellow scientists did not know could be asked? What makes up our Earth is already here with us within these glass walls, and it needs only to be recognised and given language."

"If these plants could speak," Faedra said.

"They would not gibber about being breathed into being by a god," Peasy scoffed. "Paradise created *itself*. Oh, my dear friends, never mind my mood. I also have my battles with the natural philosophers and their god. Outside these two aspects of supposed understanding—bungling science and foolish mythology—lies our truth."

"And what is that, Peasy?" Elle asked. She found Peasy's atheism intriguing. Peasy smiled.

"Why, Elle, it's simple: the botanical world has nothing to do with humans." Peasy walked ahead, then spun for Elle, her gaze sharp.

"Nor do plants care," she added.

They made their way towards the western side of the laboratory compound, the isolated conservatory house still in view, and Elle searched its grounds, attempting to discern a path or door that led to it. Its glass was mostly frosted, but where clear panes were present, fronds pressed from crowded ferns. The courtyard remained austere; no plants, sculptures, or benches decorated the gravel crawling with green creepers. She thought the plants familiar.

Touch-me-nots, she realised.

Elle returned her attention to Peasy, who was explaining to Faedra the contents of the orchidology lab they presently stood in. Rows of large capped jars nurturing green orchid roots sat on shelves and tables, labelled and neatly spaced. But Elle became aware of a scent that disturbed the ordered, neat appearance, drifting from the laboratory ahead. It was the dense, sharp odour of cannabis.

"Well," Peasy said, her smile stiff, as if she were aware of the scent too. "Let us proceed into the seed lab. There, we may find my remaining botanist, Miss Polly Devereux."

"A seed lab, Peasy?" Faedra said as Elle followed, and they stepped into the lab.

"Oh yes, Faedy, it's where we propagate cuttings, seedlings, and graft certain specimens."

Beyond the shelves and tables of many tiny plants, Elle spotted Polly's back. The botanist quickly hid within an office. Peasy sighed.

"Miss Devereux, we'll be leaving for our afternoon dinner soon. It's expected that you'll join us." Peasy's tone seemed to broach no dissent.

"Yes, of course, Miss Bunkley," Polly called. Peasy touched one of the small plants.

"She neglected to water these cuttings," she muttered, and proceeded to fill a cup at the sink. Elle noticed another seed experiment. A tray of small pots contained the long stems of wheat, along with—

"Rye," Elle said, looking at the heads.

"Ah yes, the pretender grain," Peasy said, turning. "By mimicking wheat, it has become quite the successful progenitor, hasn't it?"

"It mimics?" Faedra said.

"Yes Faedy, it does; there are many plants that do. And here is nature's mundane miracle, the power to duplicate another. In truth, the solution is mimicry." She turned one pot to better view the plant. "Rye is but a common weed, one that infested wheat fields. But over a period of time, it began imitating wheat's qualities, ensuring it too would be cultivated for its grain and become a successful species. And it has." Peasy gave the specimen a cool glance. "But it's still a weed."

"Moving plants; mimetic ones," Faedra said in thought. "These are actions requiring thought, awareness! The plant world is truly unknown to us."

"That is exactly what I've been saying, Faedy," Peasy said, her face alight. "No one yet fully understands—and will they ever?— the lives of plants, and the possibilities already inherent in them. Have you read Charles Darwin's works, Faedy?"

While Faedra and Peasy discussed Darwin and moved for the next room, Elle became aware of another odour; the disagreeable scent of old fish.

She peered at the rye heads. Black spurs grew among the grain: the fungus disease, ergot.

Faedra, while following the pontificating Peasy, glanced back at her spouse. Elle motioned that her wife move ahead. Elle then stepped quickly to where Polly had hidden herself and peeked into the tiny office.

Within sat a cluttered desk that smelled even more strongly of cannabis. Another of Polly's personal journals lay open, to the page spread of a precise painting of the holly, Golden King. Polly seemed to have been perusing her own book at leisure, for no watercolour paints were present. A tincture bottle sat beside a countertop's metal sink and Elle was tempted to reach over and inspect the label—or give the bottle a sniff. But Polly presently knelt under the counter, shoving something paper-wrapped into a refrigeration box containing more tincture bottles. Hairy, sharp-toothed leaves showed within the paper before it disappeared into the box: henbane. A fat, tightly rolled cigarette sat snuffed out in a laboratory glass dish.

Ugh, she's a ganjha smoker.

"Ah, cannabis," Elle said, smiling. "I find its tea an effective soporific for my female complaints." Polly glanced back, startled.

"Yes," Polly said hastily. "Well, I find it keeps my mind sharp." She locked the refrigeration box, and grabbing the tincture bottle, put it in her pocket.

"You work with poisonous plants, don't you, Miss Devereux? Peasy has told me—"

"What? What have you heard, Mrs Black?" Polly demanded.

"For it's probably all wrong." Elle raised a brow in surprise.

"Miss Devereux, I'm merely referring to—"

"Miss Bunkley can be mistaken about many things," Polly interrupted. "She is a foreigner."

"Miss Devereux, what a thing to say." Elle hadn't heard Peasy insulted thus since their school days.

"Sorry, sorry," Polly said, but she didn't seem so; instead, she appeared agitated, as if things distressed her still.

Elle was tempted to tell the woman to calm down before she became soppy, but a cautioning might only excite Polly's paranoia more.

She harbours too much mistrust. She's not the sort meant to enjoy cannabis.

"Miss Devereux, I only remark because we'd emerged from the poison garden, and—"

"Did you touch anything there? You should wipe your hands, Mrs Black." Polly brought out something from her pocket and turned her back. Water ran in the sink. She then turned around and handed Elle a dampened handkerchief. "Here." She pressed it into Elle's hand.

Surprised by the gesture, Elle moved automatically to wipe her fingers. She smelled the brief, sharp scent of unripe tomatoes.

What?

Elle swallowed, thinking of nightshades. She returned the handkerchief to Polly. "I'll use your sink instead to wash my hands, thank you."

While quickly lathering her hands, she watched Polly in the little mirror hung above. Polly smirked, as smug as a child who had stepped in secret on another's toy and broken it.

☠

Polly then declared that she should join her employer, and Elle had no choice but to follow. When she sniffed her hands, she smelled only soap. In the laboratory ahead, Peasy and Faedra stood over a table upon which sliced apples lay.

"Peasy is explaining an advancement she is working on; the rapid growth of fruits and vegetables," Faedra said to Elle when Elle joined them, and Faedra offered an apple slice, feeding it to her. "This apple was grown in the conventional manner, with its natural time on the tree. Sweet and textured, isn't it Elle? But here is another slice, grown with acceleration." Faedra fed that slice to Elle as well. "It is not so impressive a specimen, I'm afraid."

"Its body is weak, and the flavour hardly present," Elle said.

"I've not been happy with the results of this particular growth serum and may end its research," Peasy said. "There is a significant problem with hastening the process of maturation; quality is amiss. The aspects of sturdier development, refined flavour, and mere vigour of the body, all of which result from the proper maturity achieved from natural living, I speak of pure, good health. These are all missing."

"Yet the subjects serve well enough as they are," Polly remarked.

"No they do not!" Peasy said with a savagery that took Elle aback. Peasy turned to glare at Polly and then returned her attention to the slices of apple on the counter. Faedra glanced at Elle, concerned.

"It's all wrong. The growth is flawed! They should have been allowed their deserved time on the vine," Peasy said.

Vine? Elle thought, wondering if Peasy was still speaking of apples. She stared at Peasy's white neck and rigid shoulders, and heard nothing more from Polly.

She can't even flush in anger.

"Come," Peasy then said, turning to regard them with a smile. The effort was brittle. "Sampling apples must have stimulated the appetite. After all this boring scientific discussion, I'm certain you look forward to the repast prepared."

☠

The next lab was a main juncture, facing the courtyard and the front of the conservatory house they'd been circling. The two wings of the house were then evident, filled with palms and ferns, some stretching into its vestibule's dome. Elle looked through the lab's bolted doors and down the path to the house.

"Peasy, that conservatory house there—"

"Yes, Elle, it is my Rare House. There reside my most precious and rarest of rescued species," Peasy answered.

"Like the one from Unreal Atoll?" Elle asked.

Polly stiffened, and Peasy turned to gaze at Elle, keen and penetrating.

Why do you look pleased?

"Yes, Elle, exactly so." Peasy's tone was touched with glee.

"This house is what you protect with mantraps, Peasy?" Faedra said. "I'd hope you were speaking in jest."

"No, Faedy, I did not jest. I've something more valuable than cannabis to protect in there."

Peasy glanced in Polly's direction, and the botanist stepped farther away. Peasy then picked up a warty ornamental gourd from a lab table and handed it to Faedra. She walked over to the lab's courtyard doors, unlocked and unbolted them, and carefully pulled them open. Elle wondered at her caution, for all was still and silent out in the vast courtyard.

"Now Faedy, do not—I repeat—do not step beyond the door, but toss that gourd out into the yard as far as you can."

Faedra did so, taking a step forwards within the lab and tossing the gourd, underhanded. It sailed out into the yard for the Rare House's shut entrance. The Touch-Me-Nots' leaves shrank from its airy passage.

Shuk-shuk-shuk-shuk—

Elle's breath stopped as wooden shafts flew from either side, one piercing the gourd in midair. It abruptly landed, pinned to the ground. More leaves of the Touch-Me-Nots shrank beneath it, and projectiles flew. Peasy shut the doors and bolted them before the last sharpened stick struck the gravel.

"It is interesting what one learns from the Malay Archipelago." Peasy gazed out at the yard, littered with embedded shafts. "One needs only to mechanise the technique for deadly effect."

Elle looked to either side of the courtyard, knowing the glass walls belonged to the very labs she and Faedra had walked. She could not tell where the projectiles had originated from, nor the mechanisms Peasy spoke of. Her heart pounded, and her breath quickened.

Faedra, obviously disturbed by what they'd witnessed, said nothing. She silently urged Elle to walk away with her, Polly already making haste for the laboratory's exit at room. Elle gave a brief shake of her head and motioned for her wife to follow Polly. She would speak to Peasy.

"Why did you ask us here, Peasy," Elle quietly demanded when Faedra had walked ahead. "Why give me those notebooks? Are we not here to help a friend?" Peasy hesitated in step, her gaze stark.

"I know you're here to help," she answered. "I did ask it. And I had thought if I told you…but I've changed my mind, Elle. Your arrival—Faedra—so many thoughts I've had.

"Yes. I've changed my mind." Peasy looked away and spoke no more.

"Peasy," Elle said with force. Her heart did not stop its rapid beating, and she wondered at her own agitation.

Peasy met her gaze.

"I've made my decision. I'm so sorry Elle. For all the trouble I will cause you."

As Elle took in Peasy's gaze, one that had settled into a seeming resolve, the retort, "what are you talking about", died on her lips. Peasy hurried away to rejoin Faedra, and Elle could only wonder what Peasy was really apologising for.

The laboratory facing the Rare House exited into Peasy's great orangery, filled with many ladened citrus trees. Faedra linked arms with her spouse and they listened while Peasy pointed out the various fruits, but Elle was too distracted to appreciate the sight. Though the orangery was warm, Elle did not think her own sudden warmth was due to its influence. Her heart and breath remained fast and agitated, and when she swallowed, her mouth was dry. She looked to where Peasy and Polly walked ahead.

The sunlight was too bright. Polly's body began to shimmer, and when the botanist glanced back, she seemed to smirk.

That bitch.

Elle swallowed again with difficulty, her tongue become thick.

"Your pupils are so large, Elle," Faedra said in a low voice.

"I am unwell," Elle whispered.

"I will excuse us," Faedra said but Elle held her arm. She then brought Faedra's head down for a kiss.

"This disorientation will pass," she whispered when their lips parted. "Like any narcotic I'd been made to take. The asylum addled me with worse, Faedy. I know what to do. Let us proceed to dinner, and I will drink much water."

"Narcotic? Elle, what has made you ill?"

"I suspect a handkerchief, dampened with tincture of belladonna."

"What?"

"It's not enough to overwhelm." Elle looked to Peasy and Polly, who continued to shimmer. "A mean trick's been played on me, Faedra. But I'll not be sent back to the manor." *And forced to leave you alone with them.* She held Faedra's arm closer, steadied by her wife's strength. "Has Polly touched you at all, or have you accepted anything from her hands?"

"No!"

"Beware. And watch her during dinner."

Faedra then moved for Peasy and Polly, bringing Elle along

with her.

"Faedy, Faedra—" Elle said. Polly, seeing the look on Faedra's face, scurried away. Faedra released Elle and pursued Polly around a grapefruit tree, her fists up.

"*What* did you do to my—" Faedra demanded.

"It was a jest! A *jest!*" Polly protested, and ran more. Peasy burst into surprised laughter.

"Oh, just like when we were in school!" she cried. "What has happened? Though I'm not surprised Polly has done something stupid." Elle swallowed, watching Faedra and Polly move in different colours.

"Why haven't you rid yourself of Polly?" Elle demanded.

"I didn't know she'd be this much trouble," Peasy muttered. "Now she won't leave. I'm not prepared to end the matter by killing someone...yet."

"Faedra can make her leave," Elle said. "And she needn't a sharpened stick to do it." Sorrow seemed to cross Peasy's face, too swift for Elle to be certain.

"It is too late for that," Peasy said.

"I'm sorry! Sorry," Polly cried, but Elle could not tell from Polly's scrunched face if she were becoming soppier due to remorse, or from having been found out.

"Faedy," Elle called. "I think Miss Devereux has learned her lesson. Let's continue to dinner."

"Elle?" Faedra gave Polly a last threatening glare and returned to Elle's side. Just as she was about to protest, Elle whispered to her.

"Faedy, if I withdraw, I feel Polly will win."

Faedra exhaled, exasperated. Peasy then declared that, though ignorant of what had gone on, she hoped all amends had been made, and that she too hoped to be forgiven for wishing the tour to continue. Obviously unwilling to complain when Peasy was seeking peace, Faedra said nothing, and Polly did her best to fade into the background. They boarded the train waiting for them at the orangery's exit. Faedra seated herself and Elle in the third and last carriage. Polly boarded the first carriage, and Peasy set the junction for the western track.

During the journey back to the main dome, Peasy said little, though they passed new gardens not seen from the eastern track, containing variations of the more commonly known fruits or flowers. One house, its signs and tabletop furnishings unfinished, Elle thought might be a workshop or education centre, though Peasy made no remark upon it. They then returned to the dome proper, once again riding within the domain of exotic edibles. As the train moved through the growth, the too-bright world undulated and all of nature's colours bloomed and bled, more vivid than Elle knew them to be.

I'd forgotten what it was like, under the sway. Star fruit hung from a branch, bouncing and spinning. She made them drop into her hands with her mind and gave one to Faedra. She swiftly ate the juicy fruit, wanting to still their wiggling star-bodies. Peasy stopped the train by glass doors leading outside.

They disembarked, exiting the building into a path lined by tall hedges. The change from heat and humidity to the sudden coolness of English countryside made Elle giddy, and the world danced a little. They then emerged from the hedges into more of Peasy's ordered outdoor gardens.

Oh, that is pretty, Elle thought upon viewing an eight foot high herb wall. It expanded and contracted to her addled gaze, a living wall breathing. Peasy led them to it and pointed out the sage, thyme, dill, basil, fennel, rosemary, sorrel, and parsley that rose and fell. The wall snored. Elle glanced at Faedra, who, being still out of sorts by her confrontation with Polly, had a dab of red within her golden self, and her body was rimmed with blue.

An aura? I can see auras now?

Elle scrutinised Peasy.

Peasy was all of green, bright and brilliant as an emerald, but she was cracked with red; riddled. Elle cocked her head.

Peasy glanced at her. "Elle, are you—" Elle suddenly leaned into Peasy and inhaled; Peasy smelled of cucumber.

"Elle?" Peasy said in surprise.

I should be alarmed. I should tell Faedra; but tell Faedra what? Elle raised Faedra's hand and sniffed it. Her wife still smelled of the lotion she favoured. Elle then turned to Peasy.

"How very poised you look, Peasy, as you've been all day. A splendid slice of cool cucumber."

Peasy laughed, the sound both delighted and incredulous.

"Oh, Elle," she simply said, and then turned to lead them down to another hedged garden, in which a marble fountain flowed. A table was set with a grotesque majolica fish at its centre, its wide, fat-lipped mouth spouting flowers. Peaseflower manor stood above in the distance. Elle judged by the house's direction that Peasy's lab and rose garden might be only a hedge over, thus bringing them full circle in their tour.

"Elle," Faedra said as they approached the table. "I will excuse us."

Elle squeezed her hand. "Faedy, it is a minor delirium, truly. I can recover just as well here at the table as at the house. Let's not give Polly the satisfaction." Faedra breathed deeply and pursed her lips. She seated Elle, then herself, and moved aside the majolica fish so that she might glare at Polly, who took a seat on the opposite side of the table.

Have to keep an eye on Polly. Have to figure out the cucumber. But the fat lips of the grotesque fish moved, distracting her. Bascomb filled her water glass, and Elle stared at him. Like Peasy he was all of green, but peridot-pale, with no red in him. Elle drank all of her water.

To start, Bascomb served each of them a peck of young, tiny peas, then young carrots, steamed asparagus, sieved spinach, roasted butternut, boiled French beans, stewed tomatoes, Globe artichoke bottoms sprinkled with parsley, roasted new potatoes, a spring fruit soup, crisp cauliflower, sapodilla fruit, passionfruit, red and white dragons, guava, macadamia nuts, and peaches boiled in sugar with a light dash of bitters. Luscious, red strawberries sat in green majolica serving bowls, rolled in sugar crystals, and when Elle happened to look away, they whispered vulgarities at her. She needed to think—and watch Polly—and therefore ate the rude strawberries to quiet them.

All the while, the fountain splashed and flowed; Bascomb appeared, then disappeared; Polly munched and kept her hands to herself; Peasy talked; and Elle thought that even with her affected perceptions, Peasy's discourse sounded more strident, and Faedra's patience a little frayed.

"It is necessary to preserve even the most endemic of species because when their places are gone—and they *will* be gone—so will the plants," Peasy said. "And I don't believe a god desires such destruction so that humans might have purview over an outraged Earth. It is a cruel fact that nothing may last before humanity's appetites." She sipped her water, and Elle saw that Peasy's plate was barely touched. Peasy set her glass down. "Perhaps it is futile, what we do, for Peaseflower and I are a vanished world, a paradise that ought not be true. Humanity's gift is incursion, with synergistic precision. They bring extinction to everything."

"Such a dire statement, Peasy," Faedra said, her tone solemn. "And don't you mean that 'we' bring extinction to everything?"

"Yes, 'we.'"

Elle silenced more of the obscene strawberries by eating them and drank much water. Being addled did not affect her opinion of cook's handling of the dinner. She thought the meal the most raw that they'd had so far, and a disappointing show of cook's skill.

I shall need a second stomach.

"Our lower extremities will be working very hard and a great amount of air produced between us after this meal," Elle murmured into Faedra's ear.

"You are feeling better?" Faedra asked.

"The strawberries have learned their lesson and ceased speaking, which means the intoxication is lessening; in time for the wine, it seems." They watched Peasy rise and present two wine bottles on the silver tray Bascomb carried.

"A vineyard is no easy task to nurture." Peasy held up one of the labeled bottles. "Our first Peaseflower wine." Faedra and Elle politely applauded while Bascomb uncorked the bottles and then began pouring. After filling Polly's glasses, Bascomb came around to fill Elle's and Faedra's.

Polly reached for her glass of red, knocked it over, and splashed the table with ruby liquid. The stream ran towards Faedra. Faedra stood as the flow approached her dress while Bascomb poured for Elle, unperturbed.

"Oh, sorry!" Polly stood up as well and reached over the tabletop to dab at the flow with her napkin.

Faedra, watch Polly's hands, Elle thought at her wife, even as she did the same.

"Miss Devereux, please!" Peasy snapped. "I would like to toast now." She waved off Bascomb when he came around to pour for her. "Bascomb, you know I abstain from spirits." She raised her water crystal and Faedra, Elle, and Polly reached for their glasses and did the same.

"To dear childhood friends," Peasy said, "and to our steadfast devotion to each other, and to our love." She looked at Faedra.

They drank. Elle thought her sip of red wine tasted woody. She set the glass down, but then Peasy toasted again.

"And to a future, my good friends, of growth, prosperity, happiness...and longevity." Elle raised her glass again and took the obligatory sip.

Faedra is sipping white, Elle then realised, and she surveyed their glasses on the table. Her own white wine glass was missing, and Faedra's red wine glass had never been filled.

Then, to Elle's surprise, Faedra suddenly excused herself and Elle from the table, giving only a vague complaint as explanation. Peasy expressed concern, but Faedra was already dragging Elle through the garden's hedges. They burst on to Peaseflower's rolling lawn, and Faedra climbed it, pulling Elle along. The round-faced maid with the blonde fringe stood outside the drawing room's open veranda doors. As they passed her, Elle thought the maid's bland gaze held curiosity.

"Faedy, are you—?"

"I am well, Elle, I just had enough of our ongoing charade. You put on a valiant front, but I felt more and more that I'd failed you—either by not punching Polly, or making you return to the manor."

"It was my pride that wanted Polly to not see me succumb, Faedy. Truly, it was a minor dosing. Please do not blame yourself." The maid's twin stood at the foot of the stairs, folded linen piled in her arms. She also watched as Elle and Faedra ascended the stairs.

"But it's more than that, Elle. I'm—I'm very disappointed with Peasy. With the opinions she has expressed at dinner, and her strange paranoia! And with how she treats her mother. And how she has treated us, after sending us such an urgent letter. I will speak to her a final time to make clear my mind, but I blame myself for having us come. We should leave."

"Then we will." Elle said in surprise, and allowed Faedra to hurry her into their room. Her wife let go of her hand and went to their suitcases. "Faedy, please be assured, I spoke to Peasy and she made it clear she no longer wants help with whatever is going on here. Feel no guilt about leaving. Now if you'll excuse me, darling, I must go expel my insides." She ran for the bath suite and promptly vomited into the lavatory bowl.

Faedra entered the suite and comforted her while she knelt over the bowl, then left when Elle felt the need to vacate from her other extremity. She finally emerged from the bath suite, clammy and shaky, to see the two round-faced maids helping Faedra pack. Faedra left the chore to pour Elle a glass of water.

Elle sat down on the bed. "Those wicked strawberries. I need to sit down."

Faedra laid the back of her hand against Elle's forehead. "You are sitting, darling, and you are not recovering from whatever Polly did to you. You feel of fever." She tried to put the glass in Elle's hands. "And you're shivering, like ague."

"Faedy, I think I'm—"

Her lower organs seized, the contraction curling her body. The glass spilled, and she clutched at the coverlet. When she could relax, her body seized again.

"Elle?" Faedra said in alarm. The maids backed away, their eyes wide.

"I am—having bearing-down pains," Elle gasped. She reached for Faedra and clenched her wife's arm. The next contraction forced her eyes shut.

"Breathe, darling, I'll have hot wa—" Then Elle's body seized in Faedra's arms, her limbs convulsing. Pain shot to her fingers and toes.

The wine!

"Elle," Faedra said in fear.

"Poisoned," Elle uttered.

Faedra lifted her and set her down in the middle of the bed. Elle heard her wife turn about, as if searching.

"The maids fled," Faedra said. "I will make certain a doctor is summoned." Elle tried to pry her eyes open, hearing Faedra run out the door.

"No, Faedy. You must—" Her body seized again.

"*Run,*" Elle ejected.

CHAPTER EIGHT

*I*n the asylum, Faedy, there were three ways to survive, and
all these ways may be applied when needed. One was to
obey, another was to collaborate, and the third was to
become angry. Anger arms one well when emerging from the
stupor administered against one's will.

Elle burned on the bed and held conversations with Faedra,
though none of the four identical faces of four round-faced maids
who hovered above her were of her wife. If Faedra could hear,
she needed her to know; she needed Faedra to know what to do
if poisoned.

*When you succumb, for the body and mind must, you will
lose both, and you will know and not know yourself, at the
same time, for a very long time. In that place of 'not,' yet also
'thus,' you may remain, but you can come back; you will come
back. A thought most precious, most dear, will be the thread to
bring you back.*

Until that vision to lead me back became you, Faedra, that thought had been of my vengeance.

Elle descended.

She sank into the bed, the floor, the concrete of Peaseflower, and then into the depths of the planet itself. She was a flaring comet, burning until she was a pure conflagration, pulsing and echoing. The Earth echoed back, a repetition that reverberated through her inferno, and she knew it was the sound of her heart, beating too fast.

Slow, slow, she told it, even as her brain burned. *Slower.*

Something called from the surface of the planet.

Faedra?

She rose, a snapped rubber band.

Elle was a flame in the night sky. She gazed down on Peaseflower as firmament, the blazing stars her eyes. She detached from flaming head, fingers, and toes to exist, a mere ghost, and saw below the one that called, hidden in the Rare House. It was thick and green, flourishing and dying, and when it breathed, she expanded with it. Elle felt its veins, blood, vines, and roots, and in its breath, she heard the multitudinous thumps of many, slow hearts.

Faedra, Elle demanded.

The plant repeated her word.

Elle felt weighed down. Was it her roots? Too much water? She was heavy with many children who slept and suckled from the vine.

You're pregnant, she said. *With Faedra.*

Elle was both breathing plant and sky, and a veil dropped away where the back of her skull might have been. She saw the red spot, from her dream, in the conservatory again; dancing, crying. One of her children had broken off, run away; gone mad.

I will fix it, Elle said. Then she saw a black spot of death in the house.

She fell to Earth, or the Earth rose and met her. Her body swallowed her ghost; merged. She then sat up in bed, her ghost animating her body in a room that fluxed and pulsated. Fingers, toes, and limbs burned anew, but she did not need them to move. Four round-faced maids watched as she elevated above the bed. She turned her body with a thought and flung the bedroom door open with another. Elle flew into the hallway. She sent a thought at Mrs Bunkley's doors and they burst apart, spilling dead fronds and skittering beetles. Amid dust motes and darting damselflies, Mrs Bunkley sat, a decayed husk, her wizened face collapsed.

Elle rushed back into her room and commanded the balcony doors to open. Raindrops sprayed. She flung herself out into the night and white lightning sky, dragging the maids behind her.

Down the wet, rolling lawn she alighted, and then glided in the rain, approaching more maids standing still and silent in the grass. Massive, slow waves moved from one side of her perceptions to the other, and Elle's body flared and then subsided with each undulation. The dark sky hung, pregnant with water, a smear of frozen lightning fused to the ground. She gathered wet maids, potted plants, and watching dogs in her wake, all tumbling after as she glided down to Peasy's laboratory.

Just over the hedge, the rain-soaked gardeners stood outside the streaked glass, looking within. Blurry Peasy was ranting, red pulsing in her blue-green. Peasy carried sharpened sticks, and then flung them aside. Another figure stood inside the lab behind her, tense, and with a cloth pressed to her eye: Polly.

Elle leapt the hedge, the maids, pots, and dogs following. The gardeners turned their heads in unison. They watched as she stared at the glass doors and sailed by.

Oh no, I passed — stop-stop —

Elle collided with the brugmansia and fell to the ground. Maids, pots, and dogs dropped.

Poisonous trumpets rained down around her, and the state of her true body became known. She could barely sit upright, with her burning hands curled close and her legs like charred sticks. The crowd of gardeners split slowly into two, giving her full view of the lab and Peasy scattering papers and books. She was retrieving the box with the syringe.

The cocaine.

Peasy prepared her dose. Behind her, Polly watched and slowly lowered the cloth held to her face. She revealed a bruised eye.

Faedra hit you! Elle crowed. *A fresh mark too!* She was not too late; she would find Faedra. Elle stared hard at the lab's doors.

Open, she commanded.

The glass doors flew apart with a gunshot's bang. Rain blew in and Peasy looked up, her needle poised at her bared arm. Polly lunged for her and sank a second needle into Peasy's head.

Thunder cracked and papers, equipment, and specimens flew, a tornado within the lab as Elle tried to order her panic and take hold of Peasy. She could see nothing in the chaos she created except Polly's hand, compressing the syringe.

Stop!

The papers ceased whirling. Peasy stood lax and blank of gaze, the syringe still in her head. Polly spied Elle, her good eye wide. She turned around slowly as one in liquid, and picked up a chair.

I'll get you first, Elle threatened, as Polly advanced with the chair held up, her footfall leaden in the gelatinous air gone green, blue, and red. The raining world bent around Elle, and she tried to mentally fling the chair from Polly's grasp. But her body chose that moment to melt into the wet earth, her being flaring and echoing.

No! Not now!

Her heart echoed-echoed. Polly stood above with the chair. Elle felt her melting self scooped up by firm hands and then she was borne away. Four maids ran Elle through the hedge and back up to Peaseflower. Lightning flashed, and Elle's vision bobbed, her head lolling back. The world shook upside down as gardeners fled the rose garden before Peasy's sudden emergence, her slight body a flaming, red matchstick.

"We must help her," Elle cried, but she knew her shut mouth did not make a sound.

"Come back!" Peasy screamed in the rain, little fire-fists beating the air. The needle sat embedded in her head. "*Come back here!*"

Elle was cheese on the stove; curds and whey dripping through the maids' fingers. Bascomb stood by the veranda doors as the maids ran passed. Then Bascomb stood there again, in the hallway the maids ran down, fleeing for the stairs.

"She will poison us all," Bascomb said in Faedra's voice.

Stop, stop. Put me in a Charvolant. The pantry. The sugar bowl.

The maids ran her back into her bedroom and laid her on the bed. She sank into it, a puddle dripping through the house, and then on and on, long and far into the planet. Then she thought no more.

☠

"Elle. Can you hear me?"

Elle swam up from darkness, and forced her lids to open.

"Elle."

She saw gaslight. She was propped up on the bed of her Peaseflower suite; Faedra's side had not been slept in. Peasy sat before her on the bed, and Elle was still dressed; the same black dress from the tour.

Am I dreaming? Her organs and muscles ached too painfully to be a mere dream.

Peasy stared at her, a red-red thing.

Elle blinked. Peasy remained red. Elle was still in delirium, the room slowly bending and swaying, and her limbs were still charred sticks, but she would use them. She flexed the pained fingers of her hands, lying palms up on the bedspread, while red Peasy stared into her eyes.

Peasy's hair was in disarray, and her dress, stained. The blacks of her eyes nearly obscured the whites. She was a pulsing devil-red with edges of fading, weakening green.

Cucumber disappearing.

"Elle, it has been a few days...do you know me?" Peasy reached for a pitcher on a silver tray atop the bed as she watched Elle. She poured a glass of water and offered it.

Stop poisoning me, Elle thought, but she accepted the glass with clawed hands and drank. The water did not taste tainted.

"You had taken ill, Elle, right after our tour. You entered such a long state of delirium."

What happened?

Woody wine; convulsions, Faedra.

She dropped the empty glass on to the bed and Peasy did not bother to pick it up. Near the open bedroom doors, a maid lay still and silent on her side on the floor, her front up against the wall. Her hair was blonde like the round-faced maids.

What happened?

A needle in Peasy's head.

Peasy only stared at Elle, though she seemed to know where Elle looked.

"You had attacked the maid," she whispered.

Elle returned her gaze to Peasy, her distant heart echo-echoing.

"Elle, how it hurts to tell you this again. I only hope your madness does not repeat. But to not tell you would be wrong. Faedra is gone, Elle."

Elle thought the silent room lacked something. The ticking of a clock.

"It was the water velocipede. We'd gone out, she and I. I—I had persuaded her to take time away from your bedside. How I wish now that I hadn't. The boat capsized, and Faedra was trapped beneath.

"We are still searching the river. Oh, Elle! When we told you, you fell into hysteria! You were not yourself! You were not like anything we knew. For days you were nothing but mad."

Elle saw the writing desk. The red carnation from the tennis court sat atop it, as red and fresh as when she'd removed it before descending to her and Faedra's first dinner at Peaseflower.

"Elle," Peasy said, her voice slow. "You do understand me, don't you?"

"Faedra is an excellent swimmer," Elle said, her voice raspy. "And she always brings her pole to the water." She looked over at Faedra's fishing pole, still wrapped and leaning against the bedroom wall. It shimmered. "Remember that swimming hole, pole? The one we swam nude in when we picnicked off the Thames?" She turned back to Peasy. "Have you ever had a loved one go mad-mad-mad, Peasy?" She rose from the bed, unsteady, and Peasy stood as well and stepped back. "Do you understand, at all, what it's like to watch over a mad little wife?" Peasy continued to step away, and Elle turned her back to the doorway in order to follow Peasy with her gaze.

"Well, the fishing pole knows," Elle said.

She flung Peasy up against the wall with her mind. Peasy shrieked, three feet above the floor.

"What?" Peasy cried. "Elle, what is happening?"

"Peasy, I was not given the same deliriant as you. I was given much worse. But unlike you, I've no memory loss of my nights, and especially of last night. I can remember."

"What mammalian power is this?" Peasy's waving arms scraped wallpaper. "There's a name for it. Yes! A perturbationist's power. An anomalous perturb—"

"What do you babble on about, Peasy? You must be hallucinating." Elle leaned towards Peasy and sniffed. "You no longer smell of cucumbers."

"What?" Peasy said.

"That rotting scent is henbane," Elle said. "You reek of it."

"Nonsense, I am not addled," Peasy retorted.

"You know as well as any countryside witch what it can do to you. Every night, you don't remember, is that not what you said, Peasy? That is because every night, Polly injected you with henbane, and under its influence, you were susceptible to her will. She *turned* your mind, Peasy. In the morning, you recalled nothing, for that is henbane's gift: it brings *oblivion*."

"Elle!" Peasy snapped. "*Elle!*" She began to breathe, her chest rising and falling.

"Now that you know, help me retrieve Faedra," Elle urged.

"Ha-ha-ha!" Peasy laughed.

Elle drew back, startled by the hilarity and grief she saw in Peasy's face.

"I need her, Elle," Peasy said. "I need someone by my side."

Elle dropped Peasy and turned for the door.

"*Faedra!*" Elle cried. She saw Polly instead. Polly swung one of Faedra's golf clubs for the side of Elle's head.

Stop, she thought at it, but the slowed stick still connected with a loud smack. Polly grunted as if she were swinging through water. Elle saw the floor meet her face and tried to cushion the impact with her hands. She hit the floor and hot blood ran into her shut eyes.

"Don't!" Peasy cried above her. "Don't hit her again! We need her to take the blame, don't you see? She went mad once more, did the deed—killed her wife. We can have that." Elle felt a hand touch her and suppressed a flinch. She hoped to feign unconsciousness.

"I'm trying—oh, I'm trying so hard to keep you alive, Elle," Peasy said. "Do you think they'll believe your mad ravings in the asylum?"

Someone kicked Elle in the abdomen and she let out a groan.

"*Polly!*" Peasy screeched.

That soppy—takes more than—been kicked by better—

Her head rang again and Elle blacked out.

☠

Elle woke to the rapid sounds of wheels moving on a wet dirt road. She was in the Charvolant, the back of the silent, sandy-haired driver before her. Her head throbbed and dried blood caked the side of her face.

She raised herself with effort, and then let her head fall back on the seat. Above, the cloud-filled sky was night. Was it the same night as the wine and dinner? Was the needle in Peasy's head the same night? She stared, watching it all vibrate. The moon breathed.

"To the local asylum, is it?" she said. The driver did not answer.

"Be a good man and—hello, Unreal plant? Unreal plant, are you in there? Tell this man under your sway to turn the vehicle around. You still haven't given me back Faedra." Elle sat up more. Far ahead in the moonlit horizon, she saw a smokestack belching smoke. The smoke danced, turning colours, and Elle was not surprised that she was still under chemical influence.

Is that the colliery? That means we're nearly twenty miles away from Peaseflower.

"Driver...I am asking you," Elle grated, "to *stop*."

She held fast to the side rails and seized the handbrake with her mind. She brought it back with a grinding of gears, and the Charvolant lurched to a hard stop, swerved to the side, and jerked her forwards. The driver flew over the front of the buggy and landed with a wet thud on the road. He flopped and tumbled over the side.

Elle scrambled out of the Charvolant, tripped, fell, and then scurried for the roadside. The man sat propped up against a pen's fence below, where the dark and silent cottages of a humble hamlet stood. His limbs were askew, and his head lolled, as if the neck were broken.

"Oh dear, oh dear," Elle ejected, and then shushed herself, not wanting to wake the cottage's occupants. Two goats and a kid woke and walked over to where the man leaned. They nibbled on his head.

"Are you dead, are you?" Elle hissed. She slid down the wet slope. "Or am I hallucinating that I killed you? Because that was too easily done!"

A goat ripped the man's scalp off. Elle fell on her behind and suppressed a scream.

While the goat chewed on the scalp, another tore away the man's ear. Blood, clear and pale as tree sap, oozed down his impassive face.

What?

Elle dropped the hand at her mouth. She curled up, feet tucked close and her arms wrapped around her knees, and stared as the goats munched on the man's white, cauliflower brain.

CHAPTER NINE

V alentin sat in the back of a milk wagon, resting against the ten-gallon milk cans that clinked as the flat bed rolled. A brown flat cap was pulled low over his eyes as if to avoid the evening sun's glare, and his worn coat's collar was lifted, hiding his face. He wore a neckerchief and wool waistcoat, his shabby trousers having seen better days, and he dangled feet shod in a pair of worker men's boots. In his coat's breast pocket was a punched train ticket from London to Durham.

A telegram was also folded in his pocket, one he'd received earlier that day. He had boarded the train as soon as he could. The telegram held a simple message and an address:

Valentin. Come to me. Faedra is missing. Be discreet.

Valentin hunched in his coat and looked as unassuming as possible.

The milkmaid driving the wagon called to him. "Here's the cottage you be wantin'. The Punwick's." She pointed down the side of the road, where a humble abode sat by a small goat pen. Children played among the houses and women hung wash.

"Thank you!" Valentin jumped off, and the milk wagon rode on. He walked down the slope for the cottage and removed his cap. The goats in the pen chewed and watched him as he passed. His black hair still bore the glisten of pomade, and he'd run dust through his locks to lessen the effect. Valentin knocked on the door and a little girl answered.

She said nothing as she held the door open, her brown eyes wide, perhaps at the sight of his height and dark looks. Valentin smiled to reassure her. Inside, an old woman sat at the table and pounded her small mortar with a pestle. Valentin smelled mashed comfrey leaves and wrinkled his nose. A younger woman worked at the stove, and she turned to see what was the matter, her boy clinging to her skirts. She opened her mouth to say something, but it was Elle on the floor who caught his eye.

She sat by a babe, fat and healthy enough to sit up in its basket, the child holding Elle's attention. The kohl Elle favoured had become smudged, and her black skirts bore streaks of mud. She had a gash at her temple that had gone pudgy and purple, but by its darkness, Valentin thought it already healing. She dangled the brass tools of her chatelaine before the grabbing baby and made it laugh.

The old woman looked at Valentin with suspicion but rose, mortar in hand, and dipped fingers into it. She went to Elle and painted the head wound with a wet, brown poultice that made Elle wince. Then Elle glanced his way.

"Ah-ha-ha-ha-ha!" She burst into laughter and pointed. Her hazel eyes twinkled gaily.

He entered and knelt before her, staring into her eyes. Her pupils were as large and dark as a newborn's gaze.

"What has happened to you?" he softly exclaimed.

☠

After Elle contained her amusement, she properly introduced Valentin to the cottage's occupants, identifying him as her once-husband. She was relieved that the telegram message carried to Durham had been successful in reaching Valentin's Huguenot chapel. Mrs Punwick shooed her children out to play, then picked up her laundry basket. She left her cabbage soup to simmer and went outside to hang the washing. The old woman lit a short pipe and smokeed it while she watched Elle and Valentin. Valentin returned her gaze with wariness.

"Don't mind nana. She's a witch," Elle assured him.

"Elle." Valentin helped her to her feet, and then at the baby's protest of Elle's absence, fished in his waistcoat's pocket. He brought out his pocket watch on its chain and dangled it for the child.

"You look a proper ruffian, I suppose," Elle said with humour. "Though if you intended to pass as a labourer, you forgot to roughen your manicure's work. Your fingernails are prettier than mine, Valentin."

"You are under the influence of chemicals." His tone was both curious and accusatory. He knelt to give the baby his watch.

"I suffer now only from residue effects. Much like the aftermath of having drunk too much wine. In my case, just two sips of *vinum ergotae*."

"*Vinum*—? Wine of ergot?" His gaze was incredulous. "Ergotism is a peasant's disease, and the wine is a physician's remedy." He took hold of her shoulders and bent to inhale at her neck. "It's true, it is in your sweat. That foul fish odour is from the black spur that infests rye: ergot!"

"Did I not already say that? Regardless of how sick I am—"

"Has a midwife examined you?" He sniffed lower and placed a hand at her belly. She firmly removed it.

"I'd forgotten your fondness for using your nose. You need only ask if I were bleeding, Valentin. Though the ergot wine excited uterine contractions, I fortunately had no placenta to eject, and thus no other damage was done; I am certain of that. As I was saying, we must rescue Faedra!"

"Then Faedra is not merely missing, but held captive." Elle was surprised to see the intensity that entered his gaze. "You will explain it all to me, and then we will plan. Drink more."

He fetched the cup and pitcher from the table and poured water for her. "Ergot! What a vile affliction. I have witnessed villages possessed by the infected rye's madness. If your poisoner meant for you to hallucinate, opiates would have been kinder. You must cleanse your body of the chemicals."

"I think the intention was not to merely addle me." Elle drank the water. "I suffered more from the convulsions and the excruciating burning of my extremities." Valentin's mouth turned grim. "Yes, you know of what I speak: the horror of St Anthony's Fire. That was how I knew it was ergot. But once I survived the Holy Fire, then the phantasms began." She stared hard at him.

He flew up until he hovered a foot above the floor. The baby cooed and pointed, and nana looked on, impassive. Despite the surprise on his face, Valentin remained still, his legs and arms spread. He suddenly grinned.

"I would applaud your show of strength, Elle, if I were not preparing myself for possible flight around this cottage."

"Don't worry, I won't launch you. This proves that the augmentation of my abilities was not a hallucination." She set Valentin gently down on his feet again. No pounding megrim ensued, nor did a great exhaustion seize her. But a sorrowful anger did take hold, for she felt that the expansion of her esemplastic abilities had cost her dearly.

I failed to protect Faedy.

"I had been foolish, and underestimated their need to keep their secret," she said with angered misery.

"You've yet to tell me who these captors are." He took hold of her chin, raising it, and studied her neck. She shrugged out of his touch.

"Now why are you looking there?" she demanded. The baby began to protest again, and Elle picked her and the pocket watch up. She gave the child to Valentin. "I do not smell pleasant to her, thanks to the ergot." The babe immediately quieted in Valentin's arms. "The first poisoning to fell me was done through my fingers.

A kerchief dampened with tincture of belladonna. I should have known by the scent, for the kerchief smelled like the plant; of unripe tomatoes." Elle's fists balled. "That ganjha smoking, sopface. I'll blacken her other eye. Tainting my hands was merely the first assault upon my perceptions. Thus confused, I became lax and drank what was truly intended for me."

"An Indian ganjha smoker has taken Faedra?" Valentin said in confusion. He jiggled the baby to soothe it.

"Not an Indian, Valentin, I speak of Soppy Miss Polly. Who hasn't the decency to ingest her cannabis as a tea, but rolls it and lights it. With any other woman I might have found that bold and daring, but with her, it was simply crude."

Valentin sat with the baby, his face bearing patience. "Come, sit. And try your best to explain why and what happened to you, if you can."

☠

Having slept the day until Valentin's arrival, Elle finally felt the worst effects of her poisoning recede, though her head and body still felt as if she had been tossed down a cliff. The ergot's sway was still strong; she doubted she'd be free of hallucinations for a few days more. Right then, Valentin shimmered, but he did not distort, change shape, or become something else entirely. They left the babe in nana's care and retreated to the room upstairs so that Mrs Punwick could return and continue her work. Valentin took the cup and pitcher with him. In low whispers, Elle explained everything, from the summoning, to the strangeness of Peaseflower's servants, then Faedra's disappearance and Peasy's betrayal, and on to the circumstances of her near commitment to another asylum.

"Peasy and that Polly didn't know that I'd been through this sort of experience before: 'lost time'. That's what we called it in the asylum, for the injections were meant to make us docile...and turn our minds. One moment I'm pulling someone by the hair for pissing on me and then next, I'm somehow in the garden, my face feeling sunshine. Then another wretched needle is stuck in me, probably for sending dirt and worms flying with my mind, and I'm suddenly wailing in a tub full of hot water." Elle poured another cup of water and drank more. When it was empty she set it down. "I'm very glad Faedra rescued me. It took a while to come to some common sense, one not intoxicated. Poor Faedy, sharing her room with a mad, little animal."

Elle looked away, solemn. "Now, I must rescue her."

"Do you know where she may be held?" Valentin asked.

"I know, as surely as I heard her heartbeat. She is in the Rare House of Peasy's conservatory."

☠

When Mr Punwick returned home from the colliery, covered in coal grime, a meal with meat, potatoes, and gravy as well as cabbage soup awaited him, prepared by both Mrs Punwick and Elle. Despite Elle's desire to return to Peaseflower, she could not deny that she still needed to eat. She also wished to express her appreciation to the Punwick family for their care and hospitality. Poor folk had their pride, so she could not offer coins (sewn into the lining of her dresses for such emergencies), but she could send Valentin out to purchase foodstuffs for a satisfying meal. At the table, she noticed Valentin ate with his usual reserve: as a man with no great appetite.

Knowing the pleasure she took in satisfying Faedra with her cooking and brews, Elle doubted she would have ever been happy with Valentin, her pride always challenged by what would appear to be his finicky eating when in reality he was merely being a vampyre.

At dinner's end, nana wiped away Elle's poultice and by Valentin's look of approval, Elle assumed her head wound no longer appeared ghastly.

"I was also cut there during the Sundark affair," she complained. "I shall sport an imposing scar soon, to frighten women and children."

"All the more to frighten your enemies with," Valentin said. "Since you insist on being this psychic detective, Elle, you must intimidate with more than your darkened stares and blood-red hair." Elle huffed.

She then gave her good byes to the Punwick family. While Valentin retrieved his watch from the children, she stepped out with a bundle of men's clothes under her arm. He joined her in the dark and she walked to the spot by the goat pen where the driver had been eaten. She unrolled the clothes and showed Valentin a man's shoe. It still contained a foot.

Valentin picked the shoe up and poked in the chewed part where flesh and bone would have been. He withdrew a finger covered in congealed sap.

"Your vegetable man," he said slowly, staring at his finger.

"I kept this foot for you to see," Elle said. "Else you'd think I dreamt that part. Goats ate him, Valentin! Though I had to aid the feeding by undressing the poor man and giving the goats his body parts. Like a wicked murderer, I had rid my crime scene of the evidence." She sighed. "I'm sorry he died, and that I had been too confused to understand what I'd done. I thought myself in the midst of another manifestation. The goats came during my indecision and ate of his head."

"He was a living man." Valentin looked at her for affirmation. "He walked about...and such."

"He was, Valentin. I speak not of animated gourds dressed up in men's clothes, but a person alive, cognisant, functioning, yet with a vegetable brain! It looked like a giant cauliflower. Now I'm glad Faedra dislikes cauliflower." Valentin pulled the pale foot out of the shoe with a squelching sound. He sniffed it.

"However, I enjoy cauliflower," Elle added, "and ate quite a few florets during that vigorous dinner, despite the air it gives me."

Valentin fed the foot to the goats. Elle took hold of his arm at a sudden realisation.

"Valentin, they fed us their brains!"

He patted her hand, lost in thought. The goats gulped down all of the foot and looked for more.

"I've never seen the like," he finally said.

☠

The first thing she and Valentin argued about was the Charvolant, which she'd driven into a hollow, a quarter mile from the Punwick cottage. She had activated the spools, calling back the kites until they rested on the driver's seat. He looked upon the buggy, scoffing that he'd not seen such an archaic vehicle in years, and thought the high-flying kites might give away their approach to Peaseflower.

"Would someone truly be watching the night sky for them, my military man?" she asked, incredulous.

Valentin put a finger in his mouth, wet it, and then raised it in the air. "I feel no wind to help propel them now that they are spooled, do you?" he said with an arched brow.

"I didn't want attention drawn to the thing," Elle sniffed.

Since they were among poor folk, a horse and cart was a precious item to borrow, and Elle was reluctant to involve others in an affair that was dangerous. Valentin did not want her to hike either, in which time they would lose the cover of night, and she did not want him to carry her on his back and run to the estate, which he assured her he could do.

"And if Faedy is in no condition to walk out on her own—shall you carry us both?" she said.

When he pushed the Charvolant back on the road, she then knew that there were limits to his vampyric endurance.

But she did admire, while seated in the driver's seat of the buggy and watching him leap nearly two storeys high to fling the kites, the supernatural grace of his form.

So...once I was married to that, she thought, as she watched him land like a cat for the third time.

And she was a bemused mix of pride, hurt, and deep resentment at the thought, knowing that during their marriage, he would have never let her become aware of that side of him.

When Valentin had flung one kite high enough to catch the upper winds and she'd activated the spool—sending the device spinning and paying out more line—she decided to help him with the second kite. He was twelve feet above again, throwing his arm forwards when she mentally snatched the kite out of his hand and sent it soaring above. She was surprised at the height the kite attained and quickly released its spool. Valentin let out a startled shout and landed in the roadside grass, rolling. When he regained his feet, he looked at Elle.

"I am not yet accustomed to the new extension of my mental powers," she said.

Valentin hopped to sit beside her and attached the steering bars. "I will remind you." After he released the brake, the Charvolant rolled swiftly forwards. They rode in darkness, the gas lamps unlit. "Though such brain application should be reserved for more pressing actions, Elle. You may fatigue, so beware."

"That had already happened," Elle muttered, recalling her ability's desertion right when Polly meant to batter her with a chair.

"Despite how you came by the unleashing of your brain's power, I am gladdened by your new strength. I want you to survive any foe you may face."

"And why should you care? I am not your fighting cock. When I lost you, it placed me on the hell road to an incommutable vow. I will not lose another love like that again."

Valentin's smile was dark and sharp. His fangs glinted in the moonlight.

"Do not fancy yourself so precious," she said.

"I think only of how fortunate Faedra is," he said, his tone smooth. "Very well, my pocket warrioress, slayer of mechanical houses, pinching phantoms, and defeater of the Holy Fire. Rest and gather your fortitude. Once we reach this fabled Peaseflower, we will retrieve your beautiful wife."

CHAPTER TEN

E lle dozed against Valentin as he drove, his coat tucked around her. She was trying to steal his body's warmth. But she was also using his familiar scent to ground her.

I've not gone mad again, nor am I hallucinating this moment. We are *advancing to the rescue.*

The world, at times, did pulse and breathe, changing colours, and the lingering effects of ergot were manifesting a new sensation: her head encased in wobbly gelatine. She became weary of viewing the night through jiggling jelly and closed her eyes, thinking of Faedra.

We are coming.

She sent the mental projection out should the Unreal plant hear, and by it hearing, might Faedra know the thought too.

Take care of my wife, Unreal plant, or I shall set fire to you myself, Elle warned, and then turned her attention to Faedra. *And I've brought he-who-was-once-dead, Faedy, for he is a vampyre, and that's as good as bringing a hound to sniff you out and fetch you, isn't it?*

Elle nearly laughed aloud, knowing Faedra would laugh too, and then sobered again. She tried to tamp down the fears rising.

"That betrayer," Elle said, straightening in her seat. Her head casing of gelatine was lessening.

"Elle?" Valentin said.

"Berating myself for believing in a false friend," she said.

"Ah, this Peasy. During our marriage, you referred to her at times. I thought you two not very fond of the other."

"We weren't, but not to such extent that she would be so dishonourable as to take Faedy away from me." Elle sighed. "However, Peasy is under the influence of henbane. Just as gin may destroy the character of a person, hers may be altered because of it. This crazed woman is really not Peasy."

"Under an influence, she may be, Elle, but you have not seen your friend since childhood. In that time she could have changed into something else, entirely."

"Peasy is not a vampyre," she said.

"No? And why do you even mention that?"

"Because at the cottage you inspected my neck, Valentin, and I have to assume you did so for bite marks. Now why would you think vampyres would be out here, in the boring countryside?"

He did not answer, paying mind only to the road.

"How are we to maintain civility if you continue to keep secrets," she exclaimed. "It's just like you, to never talk when it doesn't suit you."

"Never mind this Peasy and the possibility of vampyres." His aspect was solemn as he watched the road. "We've a few miles, yet. Tell me of your life. Your dear, simple housewife life, when you are not seeking to defeat spectres and false friends. I want to hear of that, rather than dwell on the habits of dark creatures."

"Very well, lieutenant." Elle gave him a mock salute.

"Captain," he said, terse, then balked. He looked at her, the night's darkness hiding what his eyes held.

She smiled, knowing he could see it, and wondered if she had the mental speed to stop him with her mind should he try beguiling her.

"Did you not want to hear of my womanly habits?" she then said, and when he returned his attention to the road, she proceeded to do so, telling him of her cooking, cleaning, washing, and gardening; of the canning she was in the midst of, of her brewing, of the foundling blankets she was knitting and the socks she was darning—

"Do you indulge in *any* frivolities, Elle?" Valentin said in astonishment. "Especially with such an amiable wife to share amusements with. I knew you to be too practical for fêtes, but Faedra does not deserve to spend her evenings watching you darn."

"I assure you, I know how to please my wife! And we do conduct ourselves on a budget, Valentin, unlike yourself, who frittered my fortune away." He did not rise to the bait, and she continued. "Sometimes we enjoy a show, or a concert, and dance on occasion at the women's club, and oh! A lovely swim on 'women only' days at the bathhouse. But we would like to visit the more exclusive Vesta for—"

"The Vesta! How did you learn of such a club? No, Elle, you mustn't go there. It is the lair of bored, aristo deviants, amused only by their own lascivious appetites."

Elle burst out laughing. "You make it sound like a penny dread."

"Elle, it is so! Such private clubs are unfit for you. If you bring your wife, the toms will surely steal your woman."

"Valentin! How can you know?"

"Because those who love their own sex are bees with very few flowers. They will rush to Faedra like she were the rarest blossom."

Elle sighed and looked at the moon above. "And take her. You are correct, Valentin. It has already happened."

☠

Elle was idly aware of the scent of blackthorn blossoms when Valentin spotted the high blackthorn hedgerow in the darkness. He affirmed that it ran a long length, delineating the border of an estate. They had arrived at Peaseflower.

"Your vampyric vision is extraordinary; I see nothing. Will you leap the hedge?"

"At that height, not with you on my back, lest we both end up stuck on the thorns."

"There is a gatehouse, Valentin."

"I see it." He pulled on the brake, slowing the buggy to a stop. "Wait here. I will return after I've subdued the gatekeeper."

"But he may be a plant-person. I now believe they all are. Please don't harm him, for he is under the sway of the Unreal plant, and therefore no threat to us."

Valentin sat back down again. "Elle. Do you truly trust this queer, sentient plant?"

Elle sighed, recalling her fevered psychic visions while poisoned. Her mental communion with the Unreal plant had been profound; naked. She was certain she came to "know" it, just as it peered into her heart and simultaneously "knew" her. The plant had no "bad" intent, of that she was certain. Yet it was also a plant that most likely did not know what "bad" meant.

"I will tell you, captain, I trust it for now, for I must," she finally said. "It has Faedra. And I certainly trust the plant more than I do Peasy."

"Perhaps the plant is some trapped dryad," Valentin muttered, and released the brake. He drove the buggy forwards. "And I hope it hasn't beguiled you."

"A dryad! What an extraordinary thought! What do you intend to do, Valentin? Drive through the gate?"

"Yes, Elle," he said, curt. "And if the gatekeeper causes us trouble, I will feed him to goats."

The gatekeeper caused them no trouble; he was standing still and barefoot on the lawn when they stopped before the gate, and he opened it for them as if they had been expected. Once Valentin drove through, the gatekeeper moved to the side of the Charvolant where Elle sat, and she felt a sudden stab of guilt, looking up the twin of the driver.

"Help us," he simply said.

"Yes, that is why we're here," Elle replied. The man then went to shut the gate. He returned to the lawn. Valentin stared as the gatekeeper stood again in the grass, still and silent.

"He is a plant," Elle said to Valentin, apologetic. He harrumphed.

"He smells just like that foot." Valentin drove the Charvolant on.

Halfway to the manor, Valentin brought the buggy around and put on its brake, leaving the kites flying.

"For our escape," he said. When he disembarked and came to Elle's side, he did not help her down but presented his back. "You still have the look of one making merry with fairies, Elle. Hop on."

"What a fine steed you are," Elle said in humour, and climbed on to his back. She wrapped her arms around his neck, and he held her legs securely around his waist.

"And you are but a feather, my inebriated witch. Where shall we find this Rare House?" Elle gave him a rough outlay of Peaseflower's grounds, and then explained the mantraps.

"I think entry must be done from above, or below," Elle said. "But I never saw how to access the underground and its furnaces."

"We can't spend the night looking for an underground entry," he said. "We'll go directly to this Rare House then, and see how fortified it is."

"I don't know if—"

Valentin set off into the surrounding forest, cutting off Elle's protest. He headed west of the conservatory to avoid the manor, and ducked and weaved through the trees, moving quickly.

"Beware my head," Elle exclaimed, hoping he wouldn't run her into a branch. "Valentin, you should know; Peaseflower hasn't any livestock, and all walking here are of vegetable, not blood. Unless we find you a rabbit or pheasant in the woods, there's nothing to slack your thirst should you need it."

"Not one chicken on the grounds, Elle?"

"Not even an egg. And the dogs may also be plants. Don't you dare bite Faedra or me," Elle warned.

"It is tempting." His voice sounded like he was grinning. He laughed when Elle growled at him, her arms tightening around his neck.

He ran swiftly along the forest outskirts. Once past the brace of tall windbreakers that stood before the estate, ivy-infested Peaseflower came into view, serene and silent in the moonlight. Anxiety hit the pit of Elle's stomach at the sight.

The reaction was not unexpected, considering what she'd suffered the last time she'd been within its walls. Valentin paused, raised his head, and sniffed.

"What is it?" she whispered, but he ignored her and proceeded. She raised her nose to sniff the air too.

There it was, borne on a night zephyr. The scent of sweet pea flowers.

"The sweet peas are reminding you of another time, aren't they?" she accused. Irate, she smacked him on the head.

"Elle," he ground out. "Be silent."

"They were planted outside our hotel," she whispered in anger. "And laid on the pillows of our bed."

"I remember."

"Really? Well, Valentin, I've replaced that so-called honeymoon with better memories. Memories so ecstatic in their heights, I still swoon at their recall." He marched on, not speaking, and Elle snorted.

"Don't tell me you placed value on that night."

"Of course I do. You were exquisite."

Elle raised a hand to hit him again when he stilled.

Elle quickly peered around his head, and saw one of the estate's black and tans before them, watching. Its eyes reflected in the dim moonlight, and behind it, across the vast lawn, the conservatory stood, surrounded by garden hedgerows. The manor lay in the far distance.

"Is this one of your vegetable dogs?" Valentin whispered. "It smells like the others; like cucumbers."

"Yes, it is under sway to the Unreal plant. At least, I hope that's still the case. Since it hasn't the capability to answer questions, let us continue."

Valentin hefted her and hastened his pace, the silent dog trotting after.

They skirted the conservatory length while hidden by the forest, nearly fifty feet of lawn separating them from the glass walls. The manor remained unseen on the eastern side. Elle gazed at the soaring palm trees and cascading foliage within the great dome area and thought of the warmth harboured there. All was dark but for a few spots of electrical light. Nothing stirred.

The dog trotted away, leaving them to join more dogs like itself that dotted the lawn, standing about like rooted statues. It took its place among them and fell into stillness as well.

"These plants," Valentin exclaimed. "What help are they?"

"I don't think they know to concern themselves." Elle recalled Peasy's words: *the botanical world has nothing to do with humans. Nor do plants care.*

Well, care enough until I get Faedra back, Elle thought darkly.

"Where is your friend?" Valentine whispered. "Did you not say she worked into the night?"

"I did, and doubt she'd change her habits now. I could not spy into her laboratory, which was back where the manor lay, and is surrounded by hedges. But there, Valentin: the orangery. Beyond it would be a compound of laboratories, surrounding the Rare

House."

Once passed the orangery, Valentin let Elle down. "This long row; these are the laboratories?" When Elle confirmed, he picked up something in the dark from the forest floor, then threw it. It bounced across the fifty feet of grass to land close to the lab's wall: a rock. The lawn remained unperturbed.

"A stick," Valentin suggested, "swept before us like the blind do, will encounter a concealed jaw trap before we step in it."

"What of the flying projectiles?"

"Where would they come from?" Valentin said, and motioned to the forest and then to the building.

"Very well, captain, you first," Elle said. A door opened and she and Valentin spun to see what made the sound. One of the round-faced maids emerged from the orangery. She shut the door behind her and walked across the grass to meet them. One side of her face bore a long gash, crusted with old sap. The eye was obliterated. Despite the damage, the maid regarded them with a calm pleasantness.

"Did Polly do that to you?" Elle exclaimed as the maid came before them. "When you and your sisters carried me away, you could have fled into the forest. Or hidden me *somewhere*. Even tossed me into the Charvolant with a driver so that I might flee, and not get clubbed by that sop, Polly. Oh, you are a plant not used to thinking in this manner, are you?"

The maid only stared with her one good eye, and Elle sighed.

"I'm sorry," she said.

"Mother is tired," the maid said. "Please help us."

"Yes, I understand. She is over laden with children, and Faedra is one of them. Lead us to her, quickly."

The maid turned and walked back to the orangery.

"Are there more of her, within?" Valentin whispered as they stepped on to the grass.

"I don't know. It is not their usual place. Perhaps she's acting on her own, since she is damaged." Elle thought of the maids who might be gathered right then on the manor's lawn. A sharp stick suddenly pierced the maid's body and ran out her back. She bent like a willow.

Valentin picked Elle up as she suppressed her scream. He ran back to the forest as more projectiles whistled past them. The maid stumbled, struck by more, and then a giant jawed trap flipped open beneath the ground, tossing turf. The maid fell into it, the jaws snapping shut, leaving half her body beneath the ground and her legs sticking up in the air.

Valentin put Elle down behind the cover of trees and Elle beat the air with her fists.

"No, not again!" she ejected as Valentin held her back, but Elle knew there was nothing she could do. The maid's legs were still.

"Did you see?" Elle hissed. "How was it done? Because I couldn't, everything's become jelly again!"

"You activate the ergot in your blood when excited," he said, distracted. He let her go and his fists opened and closed at his sides. "This is far more sophisticated than I expected. I did not see, but I heard…taut strings, perhaps strung all through the grass. One merely has to step on them. If there is a pattern, I do not know it. And there's too much grass." He turned to the woods and searched, finding and discarding sticks and small rocks.

Elle put her fists to her temples. Valentin was correct, she needed to calm, as the remaining intoxication was causing the world to spin. Could she have saved the maid with her power instead of watching what happened in shock? But then was not the time to dwell on it.

"Mechanised, Peasy had said," Elle vented. "But I can't do anything about a mechanism until I've seen how it works first." Valentin looked at her in curiosity as she turned away, ignoring the maid's still body. She gazed down the conservatory towards the dome area.

"Valentin, if we move down there, to where it may be only thirty feet's distance from the glass; can you leap to that roof?"

She pointed to a lower rooftop.

"Thirty feet is too far. I cannot leap it," he said. She nodded and closed her eyes, lifting her hands.

"What are you doing?"

"I'm attempting to fly." She took a deep breath. "I will carry us both." After a moment, she heard Valentin fidget.

"Are you hallucinating again, Elle? For you are not truly flying."

"I know I'm not, Valentin," she snapped, and dropped her hands to look at him. "I did lift you at the cottage. I feel—I feel I've lost the knowledge of it. Why does my ability desert me when I most need it?"

"The death of the maid has frightened you, and now you are in fear for Faedra." His tone was gentle. "It is an emotion that can make impotent the most formidable of hands."

Elle swallowed. "As I recover more from the ergot, I also fear I'll lose the enhancement entirely, right when I need it to save her. No! I must not think that. I must regain calm. But now everything is dancing in mockery of me—trees, moon, and shadows—and my heart beats too fast. You are a magic lantern devil to me, at this moment, and I know you haven't a goatee."

"It is the anxiety caused by chemicals." Valentin pressed her head to his chest, and she took comfort in the embrace. "Let us retreat to a safer distance and find another way inside. Once you regain your equilibrium, no one may stop you."

☠

"No, I believe the dogs stood over here," Valentin whispered. They had retraced their steps to a possible safe point; the area where they'd last seen the setters standing, all of which had disappeared.

"And I know it was more over here," Elle said, "for I recall the tall trio of palms within the glass when we passed the dogs. And see! There is a door you may force open—while I watch and let you open it."

"I see the palms, but how do we know you did not hallucinate the palms with the dogs?"

"Oh, we are wasting time!" She picked up her skirts and proceeded across the grass.

"Elle!" Valentin hissed, and ran before her. He advanced with his arms out, at the ready for attack, until they reached the door. It was a simple matter for him to force the lock until it broke, and Elle allowed him that achievement rather than mentally unlocking it herself. He glared at Elle as she passed him and entered.

The first thing Elle did once inside was to urinate beneath the palm trees. After she relieved herself, she felt better. She rejoined Valentin, who stood on the eastern train track leading through the mango grove. He glared at her once more, his arms folded.

"Pah! Your piss still smells of ergot. How long ago did you drink that foul wine? Now you must sweat; sweat all the chemicals away."

"That can be easily done in humidity like this. The underground furnaces are efficient, aren't they?" She studied her once-husband. "Do you sweat, Valentin? You never smelled of it."

"If I drink much water, I do." He walked the tracks and she followed.

"And do you urinate, Valentin? I've known your penis to do only one thing."

"Does Faedra endure such chatter? I now reconsider if we should reunite her with you," he said, irritated.

"Are you not presently henpecked yourself?" Elle asked, incredulous. "For your woman has given you the look of it."

"She—" Valentin said in protest, then stopped himself, shutting his eyes in frustration. When he finally met her gaze, his was dark with anger.

"Often, I had to beguile you, Elle. For unlike any woman I'd kept company with, my tongue loosened around you. And I *dislike* that in your presence, I find that ease."

"Have you children now?" she queried.

"Why do you ask *that*?" Elle was surprised to hear the anguish in his voice.

"Because recently in my presence, you fell into great ease with the Punwicks' babe. You've the touch of a father, Valentin."

He turned away and made distance between them, and Elle saw that right then, she had pressed him too far. She looked at his straight, military bearing and the hanging of his head, and chastised the unfledged wife she'd been for not spying the true man in her husband.

I did not see the years you bear on your shoulders.

He gestured in her direction, the motion curt.

"Come." He marched away.

They made quick time through the forest of exotic edibles, Elle picking a juicy star fruit to eat and slack her thirst. But perhaps the conservatory's heat and humidity was causing her blood to remain agitated. When they entered the garden of fantastic flora, fuzzy orchids made monkey-faces at her, and the lilac spoon flowers spun. Elle stared as the flowers of the eucalyptus macrocarpa popped their buds and lolled their many red stamens like wagging tongues. As she and Valentin walked the pitch-black fungi forest, mushrooms blazed with eerie foxfire and glowed, a brilliant blue-green.

"Their phosphorescence is bright enough to read a book by," Valentin murmured.

"Oh? Do you see them too? I don't like the peeping little men beneath." Elle held tighter to Valentin's coat when they progressed through the tunnel of hanging gourds into the poison garden. As they passed the deadly plants, she felt unsteady, and the idea of a fall into plants that could sicken her more nearly made her laugh aloud.

"Be careful in here, Valentin," she said. "Death is everywhere."

He reached behind to hold one of her hands, and she stared at his back rather than at the plants. If the henbane really did chatter its seed teeth at her, she did not want to be tempted into kicking it.

At garden's end, Valentin veered to the left and passed the platform leading to the eastern labs. Peasy's train sat by it. Elle didn't need to tell him where to go, for the scent of citrus floated down the dark tunnel. Elle saw little lights fly by as if made by tiny fairies in flight, their glowing paths spiralling through the air. When Valentin did not remark upon them, she decided not to point them out. They entered the great orangery.

She noticed then that she was hot; too hot, with quickening breath and a heart beating faster. Either fatigue was catching up to her or she had become even more agitated, so close to Faedra's captivity. The world's colours began to pulsate with the echoes thrumming in her chest.

"Bugger," she ejected.

Valentin turned in surprise and then took hold of her chin. "Your eyes, Elle."

"Valentin, I am having...a delirious reoccurrence." She sat heavily on the ground beneath the lemon trees, and her tongue felt thick. *I will* not *swoon. I will calm.* "I must close my eyes, and I may doze. You are to wake me in ten minutes if I do not rouse myself, do you understand?"

"Elle, I can go—" Elle grabbed his arm and looked into six spinning pairs of his eyes.

"*Stay*, and rouse me. Understood, captain?"

"I will be at your side," he reassured, and Elle shut her eyes, her heart echoing.

☠

She fell asleep, or at least she thought she did, for she stood in the Rare House, a place she hadn't known before, with a dream's immediacy rather than by the trials of hallucinogenic journey. A plant taller than her stood centred in foliage leaves and snaking vines. At the head of the thick stalk, wrapped in a giant spathe, an immense flower of undulating folds bloomed. Green pods of the same height also grew on the vine, some lying on their sides or hanging from above, wrapped in velvety sheathes Elle knew she could squeeze between, to rest at last in their snug bedding. She was tempted, but each pod already had an occupant.

Mrs Bunkley stood before Elle, in front of the flowering Unreal plant. She wore a hat, necklace of pearls, and an elegant red dress, exactly as Elle had seen her when a child.

Hello, Mrs Bunkley said, smiling.

What is this? Elle said, recalling the woman's husk.

I have found a voice, Mrs Bunkley said.

Very good. Though with you, language has its limits. Is Faedra with you?

Yes, Mrs Bunkley said.

Keep her safe. I am coming.

Yes, Mrs Bunkley said.

And how are the other children in your wombs?

Mrs Bunkley's face grew sad.

☠

Elle sat up.

Valentin turned to her. He was crouched and had been watching the rest of the orangery. She gripped his arms, reassured by their physicality; she was no longer in a dream-state—she hoped. The world's shimmering had receded.

"Was I gone long?" she whispered.

"Perhaps for ten minutes." He examined her eyes. "Do you still feel in the midst of trance?"

"I believe the strength of it has passed." He helped her to her feet. "Now pinch me. *Ouch!* Yes, it has passed. The plant in the Rare House has the power of the mind, Valentin, to send thoughts to people and animals from afar. Have you felt it?"

"I know of what you speak," he said in surprise. "The plant has this ability? But I have sensed nothing of the kind while here." He closed his eyes and raised his head, as if listening for something, and Elle wondered when he'd had occasion to experience mental communication. He then opened his eyes. "I hear nor feel nothing of the psychic nature. I am of a race excluded from the living realm, so perhaps it's not possible for me to hear a plant speak, for what are these plants and trees, but of the living?" He glanced about in emphasis of his point. "I don't think they would want to talk to me."

"The plant's gift must be a defence attribute, for all the servants are in its sway. And now we know those servants are its offspring as well."

"And the true people and animals they imitate? Are they dead? Ingested by this plant?"

"No, they are alive, but I do not know for how long." She gripped his hand. "I am well. Let us go."

☠

Valentin took that opportunity to win one argument: he persuaded Elle to wait in the orangery while he investigated the laboratories ahead, making certain Peasy, Polly, or other dangers did not await them within. His once-wife was still ill, if not also greatly fatiguing, for her head wound still looked ghastly. He had not known when he'd married her—his precious pocket wife— that she'd such infrangible tenacity. Despite her current delirious state, Elle was perfectly capable of marching into the Rare House and claiming her captive spouse, but any respite he could coax her to take would prepare her better. He left her hidden beneath the orange trees, his coat to cloak her, and entered the dark of the laboratory rooms. There, he allowed his true nature to manifest.

His fangs emerged, his senses heightened, and his muscles swelled. The faintest human sound or scent would be known to him. He moved, quick and silent through the circumference of labs surrounding the courtyard and cruciform layout that was the Rare House, and encountered no one. But the quick tour gave him the opportunity to take in the place he was meant to breach. The isolated house was one long nave with very short transepts, the vestibule portion topped by a small dome. The only entry to the house was the vestibule side, which faced the lab leading to the orangery. Creeping plants covered the entirety of the courtyard's gravel floor: the Touch-Me-Nots that Elle had spoken of.

When he returned to the orangery, he found Elle stuffing her cheeks beneath the orange trees, citrus peels littering the ground. At sight of him, she swallowed, and then munched more. Her kohl-smudged gaze seemed to pin him, unwavering, and Valentin was drawn to the familiarity her stare inspired. Memories of other women with kohl-lined eyes and secrets in their gazes came to the fore, staring at him from within caravan wagons, tents, and smoke-filled rooms. Elle cocked her head, as she usually did when staring, and looked directly into his soul.

"My, what a beast you are," she said.

☠

Elle looked at her once-husband's supernatural demeanour, the enhancement of his teeth, eyes, and musculature, and thought the energy he exuded was interesting. She finished her orange.

"We are still alone?" she said.

"We are; I will create an entryway into the Rare House, then return and fetch you," he said. "Come." He walked for the orangery's exit, and Elle followed. As they traversed the lab attached to the orangery, Elle saw plants quiver in their pots and was uncertain if she imagined it or was herself the cause. She told herself to calm. The glass walls and doors at lab's end revealed the unassuming courtyard that led to the Rare House.

All was dark. The lab doors were locked and bolted from

within, and Elle wondered if the sophisticated-looking locking mechanism might be too complex for her abilities, or Valentin's strength.

"This lab has many objects I can use to activate the traps," Elle said. "Why don't I toss everything into that courtyard until no projectiles are left?"

"That would be quite disruptive, Elle, and may call this Peasy's attention to us. Was our rescue of Faedra not meant to be in stealth?" Valentin pointed to the Rare House's rooftop at wing's end. The edge of the wing stood less than twenty feet from the lab walls. "I'll break into the house from above. We will enter from there."

He jumped for the lab's ceiling and gripped the rafters' framework. He swung both feet up for the skylight. *Thump.*

"Peasy must enter that house by going underground," Elle muttered, turning to stare at the Rare House. Valentin paused and hung from the rafters.

"Searching the orangery's floor will be—" he began.

"I know, I know. It will take too long to find an access to below. And there may not even be one in the orangery." She turned to look at him. "Well, get on with it, captain."

Valentin gave her an exasperated look, and then swung both legs up again. *Thump.*

So...he is capable of exertion beyond the bedroom.

Elle watched him swing two more times, carefully forcing the lock so that the glass did not break. She decided not to inform him that she could have unlocked the skylight at any time.

"I love watching Faedra in the gymnasium," she remarked.

"I believe I would too," Valentin said as he pushed the skylight open. He squeezed through before Elle could retort.

Valentin made his silent way across the rooftop for the Rare House. Elle stood at the glass doors to watch his progression.

Hunched and his hands low, he ran to the left and followed the circumference of the labs' rooftops until he reached the Rare

House's left wing. He leapt over the courtyard, and his landing on the wing made no sound. Elle dropped the hand she hadn't realised she'd put to her throat. He advanced, searching for a skylight to break into. Elle watched him step until he stood at the dome above the entryway. He unlatched a glass panel and opened it. Then he doubled over, arrow shafts protruding from his chest and out his back.

He slid down the glass, smearing it with blood, and fell into the courtyard. When he hit the ground, more shafts whistled across the yard.

Elle ripped up two lab tables with her mind, their metal fixtures screaming. She sent them spinning into the doors, shattering them, and out into the courtyard. Projectiles struck as she ran between the spinning tables and trampled shrinking plants. The whole world seemed to shoot at her until the rain of projectiles ceased. She reached Valentin, dropped the tables, and fell to her knees beside him.

He was snapping the shafts sticking out from his chest, his hands shaking and his fangs and vampyric gaze gone. His shirt was soaked in blood.

"The rest," he gasped, "push them out."

"You will bleed more."

Valentin clenched her arm and Elle gazed upon him, grim. "They are poisoned, aren't they?" she said. "I will be quick."

She pulled him forwards to sit, wincing at his shuddering groan. She stared at the shaft heads poking from his back and mentally pulled them out of his body. More blood poured from the holes. Valentin's face contained an agony Elle had known and seen replayed in her nightmares. She looked into his stricken eyes and knew what would come next.

"My Valiant." She held him and kissed his forehead. "Know that I don't hate you."

"You're...still angry with me."

"Since you look so poorly, not very much right now," she

whispered.

"Go," he gasped. "No need to watch. I will be...asleep."

"I'm no longer that girl who could not face your leaving," she said softly. "Let me comfort you now, as I could not back then."

"Elle...I'll return," he whispered.

"Come find me," she urged.

She held him close as his eyes shut. The iron-scent of his spilt blood, one that she'd never escaped, filled her, and she relived the smell of gun powder; of morning air, crisp and wet, and the ringing of gunshots in her head. His warm body lifted and lightened in her embrace as he exhaled his last, just as it had before.

"My boy," she said. But the stark utterance was not the screaming lament of that long ago time. He belonged to another, and she had someone to rescue. She laid Valentin down, covered him with his coat, and stumbled away. The bolted glass doors of the Rare House mixed her moonlit reflection with the sight of giant, still ferns lit by tiny lights, within.

She looked at one of the fallen tables, studded with sharpened sticks. It trembled and rose in the air. She turned for the doors and sent the table crashing through her reflection.

CHAPTER ELEVEN

I t there were more hidden arrows within, Elle was ill prepared to receive them. Fatigue made her tremble and drop the lab table, unable to lift it again. She tried to calm and not berate herself for wasting her ability's strength on breaching the doors. As a dangling pane of glass fell and shattered to the floor, Elle knelt and picked up one of the fallen, sharpened sticks. She saw Valentin's coat.

"Oh, forgive me," she sighed, and dropped the stick. She took the coat from his body and went to the shattered doors. She flung the garment through.

Her mind sent it flying before her, and she lifted her skirts and ran in. No projectiles whistled while she and the coat pushed through ferns until they'd traversed the entryway. Elle dropped the coat, and then had to kneel, once more trembling from fatigue.

"Come now. Arctic sled dogs fare better. I have only...to dangle Faedra before me," Elle muttered, and pulled herself up to stand again. She stepped into the house proper.

In the dark and stillness, water softly fell, somewhere ahead. Small palms and towering ferns, their feathered fronds forming massive umbrellas overhead, stuffed the humid place, and Elle couldn't tell in the dark what might be considered precious specimens or not. It seemed such greenery was present to rarefy the air with freshness and the scent of rich soil. She glanced up and spotted a skylight, and saw then why Valentin could not find a way in before trying the dome's compromised door. The skylight bore a heavy bolt. Elle returned her attention to the only path she could discern in the foliage. As she advanced, the sound of cascading water grew louder. Soft light glowed ahead and Elle held her chatelaine still. She crept through a break in the ferns and peered into a common area, dully lit with scattered electric light.

Peasy sat in ragged chiffon, asleep in a great, carved chair. Thorns grew from her arms and face, and on her head was a wreath of red roses. A long staff rested in her arms, sharpened at one end like a spear. Beside her, Faedra's blue and gold dress neatly draped a table with her shoes and folded undergarments, as if awaiting their mistress to don them.

"What? Flying tables...ridiculous," Peasy mumbled. "Ridic'...."

Elle blinked and stared; Peasy remained thorny. Then she regarded the garden Peasy sat vigil before, flanked by paving stone and with one corner harbouring a mounted waterfall shower, the soft cascade draining into the stone.

The Unreal plant stood, like in her dream, upon a tall stalk with its spread spathe and blooming flower. Its vines tangled on the earth, twined up poles, and hung down from wooden beams. A grove of giant, long pods surrounded the Unreal plant, sprouting from the hanging vines and gently glowing from within, revealing dim shapes. More vines ran from each pod, and nestled in their foliage leaves, white fruit sprouted. The lesser ones formed pumpkin-sized eggplants, while the greater ones shaped into human heads with bodies, limbs, and fingers, all growing into definite form and features, and devoid of flesh colour. Faedra stood among the leaves next to one pod, a vine's stem atop her head. Nude, her eyes closed, and her body far paler than Elle knew her to be, only her arms and legs were pink, like a berry just gaining its ripening colour.

Elle stepped on to the stone paving and made her careful way to Faedra. Peasy snorted in fitful rest, and Elle ignored her. She gazed upon her sleeping wife and touched her arm.

The skin was smooth, cool, hairless, and soft like an infant's. Elle raised Faedra's arm to her nose and inhaled: cucumbers.

"You are a simulacrum," Elle whispered.

"Elle," Peasy exclaimed, and Elle whirled. Peasy blinked on her throne, rousing.

"How is your cauliflower brain?" Elle said. Just as she was about to focus her powers on Peasy, she tugged on Faedra-plant's cool hand. A snap sounded and Elle turned back in surprise.

She'd pulled Faedra-plant from her stem. The detached simulacrum stepped towards her, a somnambulist following the tug. Faedra's pale lips parted and she inhaled, long and slow.

"Faedy," Peasy said in a hushed voice. Faedra-plant's eyelids fluttered. When they rose, Faedra stared down at Elle, the vague, enchanted gaze of a newborn. Her pupils filled her blue irises. She smiled.

Child, Elle thought.

"Elle, that's my Faedy," Peasy said, rising.

"Peasy—oh, get rid of your horrid stick! You are not a dead king and Faedra is neither your wife nor your slave."

"Elle, why should you care? As I've said, that's my Faedy and yours is in the pod!" Peasy pointed at the standing pod. "But now you've ruined everything, you've picked Faedy too early!"

"This is not how you simulacra awaken?" Elle turned back to Faedra-plant and grasped both her cool hands. "She has the manner of a babe."

"I did not ripen with as dull a consciousness as Faedy is presently showing." Peasy looked at Faedra-plant with dismay. "I knew that Polly had poisoned her. I knew it!"

"Polly poisoned Faedy—my Faedy?" Elle demanded. She searched their surroundings, wondering if Polly lurked, a henbane-loaded syringe at the ready. She'd yet to free her own Faedra and may need to contend with two madwomen.

"No Elle, I mean the fruit itself, my Faedra!" Peasy turned to regard the dark as well, stick clenched in both hands. "If I hadn't needed Polly to help me put true-Faedy in a pod...Polly had been injecting the fruit, Elle, with *my* growth serum. She accelerated their maturation so that they could be picked and infiltrate the staff faster." Before Elle could act, Peasy spun to regard Faedra-plant again. "I'm certain she tainted the Faedra-fruit with more than that."

"Peasy." Elle moved to block Faedra-plant from Peasy's view. "Peasy-*plant*. You were that, weren't you? Since our arrival?"

Peasy's face darkened to humour. "I was." She found her chair and resumed her seat, her chin raised. "Once Polly was rid of the true Peasy, Elle, she thought Peaseflower hers for the taking. She did not bother returning to the Rare House to taint me as I grew. Unmolested, I ripened. Then I stepped off the vine. I walked back to Peaseflower to take back what was mine."

"You saw Faedra's answering letter," Elle said. Peasy waved a hand as if in dismissal and laughed.

"Had I been stronger I would not have had you come, at all. To that end, I've been strengthening myself; augmenting my attributes. Do you know what that means, Elle? I've awakened my potential. I'm referring to that which had lain dormant in my biological structure. I added a little something to stimulate it. Even when that something comes from other plant species."

"Have you been injecting more cocaine, Peasy?"

Peasy struck the armrests. "It's not cocaine, Elle! I've been injecting my life's extension. Such as more durability. More... hardiness. These are the gifts of my fellow plants. The result of such grafting is a little odd growth here or there, but I can prune those off." She brushed her thorns in emphasis.

"I think you've grafted a little too much, Peasy."

Peasy laughed. "All the more to resist Polly's influence over me. Yes, I did listen to you, Elle. Sometimes I do. After I sent you off to the asylum, I'm afraid my tête-à-tête with Polly devolved into a little war. I could not risk her coming into the Rare House again and killing Faedra." She gestured to herself. "Thus, my augmentation."

"Peasy, had you kept a *friend* by your side, you would not have had to do that to yourself."

"Elle. Please don't be offended, but how would you have helped me against Polly? By baring our souls with your dark gaze and pointing: *j'accuse?*"

"Why yes," Elle said, and pointed at Peasy.

Peasy screamed as she flew straight up into the air and stuck to the glass ceiling, her stick falling from her hands. Elle kept one hand pointed at her and then stared at the skylight's lock.

Unbolt, Elle thought at it.

The skylight burst open with a bang. Elle mentally shoved Peasy through it and slammed the skylight closed.

Lock, Elle thought, pointing. The bolt shut fast. Peasy screamed down at her, the sound muted, and struck the skylight with her fists. She then stiffened as a sharpened stick appeared in her body, piercing her through. Peasy, tumbled, a dark spinning shadow, from the rooftop glass.

Elle turned quickly for Faedra-plant. "I'm sorry. I'm sorry, because you are so very fond of her."

Faedra-plant smiled. She shook her head, a blonde lock falling before her face. The motion was slow, as if the simulacrum were still waking. Elle touched Faedy-plant's face in concern and smoothed back the loosened hair.

"Come with me," she said gently. She led Faedra-plant back to her vine and the standing pod attached to it. The pod's skin was veined and translucent, the matter within aglow. Elle could not know if her addled perceptions made it appear so. She retrieved her novelty pocketknife on her chatelaine, the one shaped like a woman's heeled leg. Popping the blade open, she pierced the pod's skin at the top and carefully cut. Viscous matter, pale, gelatinous, and faintly glowing, oozed. Elle clenched her teeth and cut more. Within the thick folds, she saw Faedra's nose, then her chin.

She pulled back the pod's skins, tearing them, and Faedra-plant took hold of the folds as well. Elle reached into the oozing matter and pulled out an arm. Faedra's wedding band glistened on the finger. Elle reached up and pushed back the pod's skin and Faedra's head emerged, her eyes and mouth closed. Then her wife convulsed. Faedra retched and viscous matter left her mouth and nose.

"Oh Faedy!" Elle whispered as Faedra fell to her knees, tangled in the pod's skin. She heaved and coughed, and raised feeble hands to wipe at the matter covering her eyes.

"Help," Elle said to Faedra-plant, and the plant came aside, taking hold of Faedra. The plant then pointed beyond the grove of pods to the softly cascading waterfall shower. They lifted Faedra to her feet and walked her to it.

Once Faedra was beneath the water, Elle hugged her, unable to let go. She pressed against Faedra's warm chest and water streamed down her head and cheeks, mingling with her tears. Faedra coughed more and then sneezed.

"Elle," she said, her voice roughened. "I knew you'd come."

☠

Elle finally released Faedra, especially as she was getting soaked and her wife needed to wash. Faedra seemed to quickly regain both strength and assurance of her limbs. Her eyes opened and she worked to get rid of the matter sticking to her body. Elle combed through Faedra's tangled locks while her wife's twin came to stand beneath the water too, smiling in enjoyment of the spray. Then she proceeded to help Faedra with wiping down her body.

"Extraordinary," Faedra said, taking hold of her twin and staring into her eyes. Elle wrung the viscous matter out of Faedra's hair and then felt something nag at her perceptions. Frowning, she stared into the dark.

She could not tell if the Unreal plant had spoken; the disturbance seemed more than a plant's attempt at communication. She let go of Faedra's hair and stepped away, trying to read into the darkness beyond the dim electric light.

"What was that?" Elle said. If the mother-plant spoke still, she hadn't proper attention to give it. Her mind was preoccupied with thoughts of retrieving garments, clothing the two Faedras—and the persistent belief that something was disturbing the edges of her addled awareness...something that might be Valentin, risen again.

And he won't be pleasant. She was about to look for Peasy's sharpened stick when she heard Faedra fussing. Elle turned and saw Faedra scuffling with her languid, yet intrusive twin beneath the shower. They were a tangle of wet limbs and pressing, slick breasts.

Oh my goodness. Elle put palms to her cheeks.

Her Faedra said something to her.

"Shhh," Elle hushed, still staring.

"Elle," Faedra said with worry. "I'm asking how you wounded your poor head."

"Horrible, horrible narcotics and their adverse effects on the libido," Elle said. "I shall tuck this glorious vision away, and it shall inspire me whenever the day is too disagreeable, or when Faedy's not home to ease such need." Elle then took in Faedra's gaze. "Did I just say that aloud?"

"Elle you need to—" Faedra emerged from beneath the shower, her twin still attempting to clean her. "Leave be," Faedra snapped to her plant-self. "There is much that needs to be done here, but you must rest." She took hold of Elle and walked her quickly to Peasy's knocked over chair and set it right. She urged Elle into it, and Elle sat with a plop.

"I'll sit for a moment." She felt ready to swoon again. She swallowed against the feeling and tried to look about. She spied nothing in the dark foliage surrounding them. "But please hurry and dress."

"I will." Faedra took up her chemise and bade her doppelgänger don a petticoat.

"And Faedy, Valentin is here—"

"What?" Faedra's gaze was sharp as she tried to pull her chemise down her wet body. Her plant-twin patted her on wet skin with the petticoat, dropped it, and proceeded to slowly put on skirts and bodice.

"He died, trying to get into this house. He." Elle's voice suddenly hitched.

Oh no, not now! Her eyes stung. She'd had one death too many from him, it seemed. "And he will rise again," she continued, steeling her voice. "We must go."

Faedra glanced back at the faintly glowing pods. "I understand, but more need freeing, Elle. I must see to them."

The foliage rustled. Elle sprang to her feet and stood before Faedra and Faedra-plant. Peasy pushed through the plants, enraged. Broken shafts riddled her chest. She reached for the sharpened stick stuck through her middle and slowly pulled it out. Gelatinous, white blood poured from the wound, then stopped once the wood popped out.

"That *hurt*, Elle," Peasy reproached.

CHAPTER TWELVE

E lle was about to retort when Faedra stepped to shield her and glare at Peasy.

"Faedy," Peasy squeaked. "True-Faedy." Her hands went to her thorny face, self-conscious.

"That was the bodily improvement you spoke of, Peasy?" Faedra's tone was wrathful. "Before you trapped me in a pod? Rather than let me throw Polly out for you, you chose a *serum* to be your aid. You cannot imagine my disappointment in you!"

"Oh Faedy, please understand," Peasy cried, and clasped her hands.

"Faedy, you do know she's a plant," Elle said.

"I do, Elle, and one that has been errant, contrary, and all together wicked!"

"I—I had reasons, Faedy—"

"Peasy," Faedra interrupted, "we haven't time for it. The first poor creature to become trapped by the mother-plant has slept long enough. Elle, I need your help." Faedra beckoned for her spouse to follow and turned for the grove of hanging vines and pods. As she walked by the Unreal-plant, Faedra touched it briefly and with seeming reverence.

Aren't we a party, Elle thought to it when she passed by, and hurried to where Faedra waited near grove's end. At her wife's direction, Elle made an incision in a pod half her own size, lying on its side. Faedra then ripped open the rest of the casing, revealing a Gordon Setter. As she pulled the great dog out, slick with fluid, it started out of sleep and began to retch.

"Much like exiting the womb—blind, weak, and utterly disorientated!" Faedra exclaimed, and picked the heaving dog up. She ran with it in her arms for the shower and laid it down beneath the spray while Peasy followed her.

"Faedy," she began.

"Peasy, I've had enough from you," Faedra snapped as water fell on her and the sneezing animal. "Instead of playing tennis with me, you had all the time in the world to help release everyone! What does this tell me?"

"I—I was under the influence of henbane, dear Faedy! Polly did it to me. Ask Elle!" Peasy pointed in Elle's direction. Elle sat down by the emptied pod, Faedra-plant joining her.

"Don't point at me," Elle said. "You sent me to an asylum."

"You did *what*?" Faedra exclaimed as she tended to the dog.

"Oh Faedy, I was only trying to save Elle from Polly!" Peasy pleaded.

"Was it the plan to also save me, Peasy, when you had me shanghaied into the Rare House?" Faedra demanded. Peasy burst into tears.

I cannot believe this, Elle thought.

"Peasy, sobbing is not going to work," Faedra said. "You will think on what you have done. Am I your friend or no?" Peasy opened her arms to hug Faedra and then wailed, for her hands and limbs were covered in thorns.

Elle glanced at Faedra-plant beside her and smiled. "That is what I love in you," Elle said softly. "That you can still see some redemption in someone, whether it's a thorny little madwoman or myself raving in an asylum...but I doubt either of us is worthy of such faith and love." Elle regarded the two and the recovering dog, panting beneath the spray. "I meant to kill Peasy when I flung her to the rooftop. Instead of my trying to kill her again, she stands there, arguing with Faedra. Just like when we were schoolgirls." The humour faded from her lips, and she looked at Faedra-plant. "Tell me I'm wrong in my conviction, and that you are right," she whispered.

Faedra-plant's face stilled to solemnity. She turned her head, as if listening to something invisible, and Elle saw the Unreal plant behind her, framing Faedra-plant's profile. At that moment, they seemed one. Faedra-plant's lips parted, and she spoke, slow and soft.

"Peasy is disea —"

Elle heard foliage rustle beyond the mother-plant and she grabbed Faedra-plant's hand to silence her. A woman furtively cursed.

Elle let go and leapt to her feet. She ran around the pods. A can's contents sloshed somewhere in the common area and Elle smelled kerosene. When she rounded the pods and fruit, she saw black-eyed Polly splashing the moss and vines with a kerosene can. Elle's detecting suitcase stood beside the botanist and Elle's policeman's lantern, unpacked and glass door unhinged, sat on the moss. Polly jumped at the sight of her, and then shook the can at Elle.

"Get back! Get back, you!" Polly threatened, and though Elle saw Polly holding nothing but the can, she raised her own hands. Faedra-plant, Faedra, and Peasy ran through the pods and joined her. Peasy then screeched at the sight of Polly and raised her thorny fists.

"You!" Peasy shouted.

Polly stumbled back, wide-eyed. Elle's suitcase tipped and fell open with a heavy thud. She looked down and dug out a white package.

My sea salt! Elle thought. With a bloodcurdling yell, Polly heaved it at Peasy.

The bag burst on Peasy's face and salt poured down. Peasy screamed, her face and neck cracking and blistering wherever the salt touched. Her flesh sizzled. Then Peasy's fists clenched; with shaking effort, she seemed to will the damage away. Blisters, cracks, and oozing eruptions healed. When she stood upright again, only a few white scars crisscrossed her face and flesh. Peasy laughed and looked at Elle.

"Do you see, Elle?" she crowed. "Augmentation." She turned back to Polly, contemptuous. "You are a fool, trying that again."

Polly's face scrunched. She lit a match and tossed it at the kerosene-soaked moss beneath the Unreal plant. Fire erupted.

Peasy screamed as Elle framed the fire with cupping hands.

Bell jar. Her mental jar capped the flames tight, strangling them of air. She squeezed her jar down until the fire snuffed out into a tight, black cloud. Then her jar fragmented, the cloud releasing and billowing. Elle grew lightheaded.

Her eyes rolled back and her knees gave way. Thorns pierced her backside.

"*Ouch, Peasy,*" Elle yelled. She clutched the wounded area and straightened, wide-eyed. Peasy stepped back.

"You fell at me, Elle!" she said. Then both Faedras took hold of Elle on either side, steadying her.

"But the fire," Peasy ejected, pointing to the blackened area. "What just happened? Or did that just hap—"

"Peasy, what fire?" Elle said. "You henbane-addled cucumber." She looked at Polly, whose face was as white as a spectre. Sudden wrath overtook Elle. "And what are you doing, *looting* my suitcase?"

"I think she meant to blame you for the arson, Elle," Faedra said. "And so poorly."

"My policeman's lantern uses *candles*, not kerosene, you imbecile," Elle shouted.

"Y-you're a witch!" Polly accused, pointing at Elle.

"Yes, of course I am. And you're a toad. Did you torch your last place of employment too, Miss Devereux? What sort of madwoman are you? You're so careless I wonder if you really meant to ruin Peaseflower by getting rid of everyone in it!"

"Those dismissals weren't my fault! The plant—I—I just wanted the Mrs Bunkley-plant to dismiss the one—that nosy toxicologist—" Polly sputtered. "And then she got rid of all of them!"

"You," Elle snapped, "are *nothing* but excuses! Perhaps to cover for a lifetime of mistakes. First you dose those you dislike, and then you poison to kill. First you give one injection to *turn* people's minds, and then you drive them insane! Look at Peasy. She's a fright! Did you have to overcompensate by poisoning me with Holy Fire, you unimaginative girl?"

"With holy, what?" Polly said.

"Or was that not your fault, too? I saw the black spurs on your rye samples."

"That wasn't—" Polly protested.

"Ergot," Peasy said and laughed. "How—"

"Malicious," Elle said. "You could have used hashish, or mescaline. But you wouldn't know how, would you, Polly, even with your chemical knowledge? Learned in *university*?"

Polly's eyes widened like one wanting to flee.

"Can you name your school, Polly? No, don't answer that question. Here you are, surrounded by exotica, but you still rely on a rubbish heap weed like henbane, or common belladonna, found anywhere in England. You know no better for that is what you truly are: a simple, countryside *murderess*. What did you do to the true Polly Devereux?" Elle accused. "Were you her housekeeper? Her *maid*?"

"I was her assistant!" Polly screeched, stamping her foot. "Her *assistant*. I *helped* her. I dried her specimens, washed her jars! Her stupid, *stupid* jars! She said she couldn't bring me to Peaseflower with her! That there was no place for me here." Her reddened face twisted. "So I took her place. I *took* it."

She reached behind her and drew out Faedra's silver Smith & Wesson. She pointed it at Elle, then at Faedra.

"And I'll take *more* from you after I'm done," she said.

Valentin burst through the foliage and grabbed Polly from behind. He sank his teeth into her throat.

The pistol fired as Faedra pulled Elle away. Polly's screams deafened, and Valentin flung her gun-arm down, skating the weapon across the floor. Faedra-plant picked it up. She calmly aimed the weapon at Valentin and fired.

Valentin jerked as if hit, his head rising to display his blood-smeared face. Snarling, he snatched Polly and plunged back through the plants. Faedra-plant fired after him again.

Faedra firmly took the pistol away. "Enough of that." She looked at Elle.

"Go. And don't let him bite you," Elle said.

Faedra ran after Valentin.

"This is absurd. A man with—? No," Peasy said in confusion, then laughed. Elle snatched the red package called *Especial Surprises* from her opened suitcase and held out her hand for Faedra-plant, who joined her. Peasy muttered to herself, holding her thorny head.

"I've made my decision," Elle whispered to Faedra-plant. "Help me run, as I'm still not quite myself after that fire trick." She took Faedra-plant's hand, and the plant smiled. They plunged into the foliage for the Rare House's exit.

"What are you—*Elle*?" Peasy shrieked. Elle fled with Faedra-plant. They ran out of the Rare House's shattered doors, past the strewn courtyard, and into the laboratory compound.

☠

Faedra moved quickly through the foliage, her pistol at the

ready, and followed the trail of blood to a transept wing of the Rare House. The world outside was only just then lightening. Dawn was coming. By that dim light and the stickiness beneath her bare feet, Faedra knew there was much blood on the floor. She heard running steps and turned with her pistol. Someone was fleeing the house. If it were Valentin, he might have left Polly behind. Faedra turned back to the trail and continued until she neared the end of the transept.

A hatch in the floor sat open. Faedra approached with caution, and felt heat radiate. Furnaces far below roared as they worked. When she peered into the opening, she saw a metal ladder, leading into darkness. The trail of blood ended there.

Faedra kept her Smith & Wesson aimed at the open hatch and allowed a silent sigh. Elle had let her run after Polly, even though the chances of saving the woman were slim. The thought of not having tried would have plagued Faedra for her lifetime. But Elle had not given her permission to do something as foolish as pursue a starving vampyre into a trap and then forfeit her own life. Especially after Valentin had died in front of Elle a second time.

Faedra made her decision. She flipped the hatch closed, and for good measure, latched it. Elle might remind her that Polly had meant to shoot if Valentin had not stopped her, but more likely, Elle would not. The fact remained that Valentin, despite his hunger, had the choice to not kill Polly, and even the Faedra-plant had understood that. Faedra backed away from the hatch, and then ran back to where she'd left Elle.

Her spouse and the others were nowhere to be seen in the common area. The wet black and tan sat in repose where they had stood, still weak but wagging its tail.

"It was Elle who fled the house, wasn't it?" Faedra said to the dog. "And Peasy must be in pursuit." She turned to leave when the mother-plant spoke. The communication felt like assurance; Elle was well, the plant seemed to say.

"What was that?" Faedra said. Again, the mother-plant sent reassurance.

It was a vague communication, like listening for a whisper only to feel breath on the skin instead. Faedra missed the immediate and clear connection felt while in the pod. She shook her head, wanting to depart.

I am certain, the mother-plant seemed to emanate.

"If...if you say so," Faedra said. "My plant-self is with her, after all, and you watch them in that way, don't you? Through my plant-self's eyes. But...no. I must—" Then she smelled smoke; a wisp like the curling from a lit cigarette.

When she looked at the blackened moss beneath the mother-plant, it was smouldering. She ran up and scattered the plant matter that had begun to burn and stomped on them. Then she rushed to find a container to carry water.

After dousing all that Polly had tried to burn, Faedra set her bucket down and received yet another concern from the Unreal plant, the thought resonating to the fore.

"I know, and I understand," Faedra said. "Some haven't time left."

She searched within Elle's suitcase, finding the hunting knife with the mother-of-pearl handle she'd hidden in the lining. She'd placed it there for Elle in case her spouse needed to clean a fish or skin a rabbit while on a case.

"I will release everyone now," Faedra said, approaching the Unreal plant, "and lighten you at last." She went to a large, decaying pod beside the mother-plant and carefully slit it open, revealing the still, grey face of Mrs Bunkley.

☠

Elle and Faedra-plant sat in the locomotive of the train, positioned at the laboratory platform to depart backwards down the eastern track. She placed the red package marked *Especial*

Surprises in Faedra-plant's lap and pulled the red string. They unfolded the wrapping together.

"You know what these are, don't you?" Elle smileed. "For you had purchased them for me."

Faedra-plant smiled as well, one corner of her mouth slow to lift. Her right eyelid lagged as she blinked. Elle saw that the plant's bodice's fastenings were uneven. Elle unhooked them, refastening them properly. She looked into Faedra-plant's eyes again, the pupils large and sleepy.

You are like a baby-farm infant, given too much opium.

"Would you do me the honour of sharing your first kiss?" Elle asked, and the Faedra-plant smiled broadly. She pressed cool lips to Elle, and Elle was overwhelmed by the scent of cucumbers. When their kiss ended, she embraced Faedra-plant to her and blinked rapidly.

You haven't much time, and I must not think about that, now.

Peasy burst from the laboratory compound doors. "Elle!"

"Time to depart." Elle pushed the *start* button. The train rapidly retreated and Peasy ran up the tracks in pursuit.

"Elle, you rude little mentalist *mammal!*"

"Wife-stealer," Elle retorted, and pushed down on the accelerator pedal as the train entered the poison garden. Rolling past the deadly plants, Elle picked out a match from within the red package on Faedra's lap, ignited it, and then removed a string of red Chinese firecrackers.

"But Elle, you have your own Faedra back now, why take mine?" Peasy wailed. She lunged for the locomotive. Elle flung the lit firecrackers at her.

Pop-pop-pop-pop!

Peasy shrieked as they exploded in her face, bursting red paper bits and clouds of smoke. Elle accelerated more for the tunnel of gourds.

"Once I've my hands on a grater I will make a cake out of you," Elle called, and flung another string of firecrackers at Peasy. A pumpkin detached from above and landed behind Peasy with a wet crack.

"Then I'll slice you up for the perfect tea sandwiches." Elle lit another string and tossed it. Peasy screamed as it exploded, blackening the front of her silk chiffon with scattered gunpowder.

"The rest I'll make into soup. Won't you like to fling one at your supposed suitor, darling?" Elle then asked Faedra-plant, who laughed, husky and low.

"Yes Elle! *Yes*! I have greatly wronged you. I shouldn't have done it!" Peasy leapt and landed against the long nose of the locomotive. She clambered on and Elle threw another string of firecrackers at her. More exploding powder turned Peasy's dress front black.

"Elle, *will you stop*," Peasy roared. She clung to the engine. Elle did not answer as they passed the dim world of fungi; the phosphorescent mushrooms fading as light strengthened in the dawning sky. Elle dangled a lit match between her fingertips, and then flicked it at Peasy, who flinched. The train rolled in silence.

"What—" Peasy said in confusion as Elle rose, Faedra-plant with her, and lifted her skirts. She climbed into the first carriage and Faedra-plant followed.

"Peasy, it was not false-Polly who poisoned me with ergot," Elle said, and stepped into the second carriage, Faedra-plant following.

Peasy laughed. "Elle, what do you—"

"Only the mistress of the dinner table could serve me that wine, not Polly. Only you could instruct Bascomb to fill my glass with red and serve Faedra only white." She looked back at Peasy, whose stricken face was dotted with blistering burns and thorns.

"It's true," Peasy said, her voice stark. "But wouldn't you have done the same, Elle, to have your own Faedra?"

"Peasy, you don't deserve your own Faedra." The train entered the exotic flower garden. The morning sun gained in brightness, bringing warmth to the world as if nothing had gone wrong. Elle climbed into the last carriage and bade Faedra-plant sit with her.

She took the red package from Faedra and pulled out the last string of firecrackers.

Peasy struck the locomotive with her fists. "Elle, how dare you judge me! What gives you that right? I am a botanical being with a finite life. Don't I deserve my happiness? I will live! I will, and if I can't have my Faedy, then the original Faedra will be returned to our mother so another might sprout and grow. Our seeding would be complete. Except for you, Elle, I'd never include you in our family. What a distasteful thought, having fruit walk about, sprung from you."

"I would be rather bitter fruit," Elle said. "But if I allowed it— let you have your Faedy—would you be content with just that, Peasy? Faedy-plant, you, and your little paradise of Peaseflower? Perhaps with my murdered mammalian remains fertilising the apple orchards?"

"I did *send* you to an asylum, Elle, I didn't want you *dead*." Peasy drew herself up. "I've plans, Elle, you know I always do. I will... experiment more, achieve more! I'll ensure plant life's longevity, strength, and durability! No more will humans threaten us with extinction. Botanical life will regain the world."

"Regain the world?" Elle repeated with a raised brow. Faedra-plant laid her head on Elle's shoulder, apparently bored.

"We are botanical beings, Elle, with legs, hearts, brains, mobility, speech, and the ability to think! Just as you do. Now we are your equals, the perfect biological response to humankind's wanton destruction. I will have airships." Peasy motioned with grandeur. "And we will seed the skies."

"Such ambition. And might that include an invitation to our queen to view your accomplishments...and the Unreal plant?"

Peasy stared, though she said nothing, her lips twisted into a secretive smile.

"Dear Faedy-plant. Who knew our tiny Peaseblossom would dare so much?" Elle petted Faedra-plant on the head.

"Faedy—Elle, why are we riding about in this train?" Peasy

cried, striking the locomotive again.

"Because we needed to converse, so that I might know your cauliflower mind. And to also give me time. If once you were sorry for all the trouble you would cause me and have caused me, Peasy, now I am sorry for what I will do to you."

Peasy leapt from the locomotive and into the first carriage. She lunged for Elle, the thorns on her reaching arm growing with a cracking sound. "No! You are a destroyer, Elle! Like all of humanity, you destroy!"

"It is true; I would be judge and executioner," Elle said.

"Faedy," Peasy pleaded to the Faedra-plant. "Oh Faedy, how can you stay there with that meat-person?"

Faedra-plant did not answer but only took hold of Elle's arm. They were approaching the glass wall, within sight of the House of Succulents. Elle lit her last string of firecrackers.

"I—I must be strong!" Peasy said. "And be committed, for the sake of my kind. For our future! I will not let something like *you* harm me, Elle."

"Peasy," Elle said, her tone gentle. "Once noble, well-intentioned Peasy. That harm you speak of. Polly has already done it to you."

"No!" Peasy screamed.

Elle threw the firecrackers into Peasy's carriage.

Peasy scrambled out of the car as the firecrackers exploded, her dress catching fire. She slapped out the flickering flames, and Elle took Faedra-plant's hand and fled the moving train. They ran out the doors of the conservatory and into the crisp, morning air. Elle urged Faedra-plant for the House of Succulents. The giant concave mirror, sitting behind the house, dazzled from the morning light. Elle entered with Faedra-plant, walked down the centre lined with cacti and tables containing pots of succulents, and glanced up. She unlatched the skylight with her mind and popped it open.

Faedra-plant leaned on her, the dry heat of the house affecting the plant. Faedra's eyelids drooped.

"It won't be long now," Elle encouraged. "And then you may stand on the lawn, like the others, and receive plenty of air and water." The plant smiled in response.

Peasy ran up to the house's entrance and stopped, her chiffon dress smoking.

"*What* am I to do with you?" Peasy rasped.

Elle simply regarded her. The prickly cacti began to shake, some hopping in their pots, and Peasy regarded one side and then the other, alarmed by the rattling. She ran in, hands out. The doors slammed shut, and Peasy glanced back at them, startled.

"Elle, these plants have done nothing to you," she said in fear. The plants stilled. "Elle." Peasy's tone turned conciliatory. She advanced, a thorny hand out. "Let us make amends. Let us talk. Elle, please."

"Faedra once punched girls for you, Peasy, because you were little, and you were alone. Like you are now."

Peasy clasped her hands before her. "Yes, Elle. Yes. I am that girl now."

"No, you are not." Elle stared at Faedra-plant, and she began to rise. She floated to the skylight opening. The plant laughed.

"What? Elle, stop that, stop it *now*!" Peasy stamped her foot. Faedra-plant alighted on the rooftop and looked down.

"You are not that Peasy whom Faedra loved, Peasy-plant," Elle said quietly. "And I'll do to you what she should not." She held up the match safe on her chatelaine. Thumbing it open, the safe's compartment was empty.

Elle gazed wide-eyed at the empty safe and then at Peasy.

Peasy roared and reached for Elle, her thorns stretching. Elle put out her own hand and formed a mental wall between herself and Peasy, impeding Peasy's advance. But the thorns continued to stretch, and Elle glanced to the house's end and outside where the concave mirror stood. She felt her own hand shake as Peasy pushed against her mental wall.

Elle stared at the concave mirror. It fell with a bang, the mirror rolling towards them. Bright light shone into the house and Peasy raised her arms to block the brilliance. Elle retrieved the magnifying lorgnette on her chatelaine and held it up. She focused a small, hard dot of sunlight on Peasy.

"Elle? Ouch!" Peasy exclaimed. A little hole in her chest began to smoke, and black saltpeter covered her bodice front. She looked up and stared at Elle.

"Oh, Elle," she whispered.

Peasy's chest exploded.

Charred chiffon tatters fluttered and fell, afire. More flames burst to life on Peasy's chest and she sucked them in, as if trying to contain and smother the fire within her own body.

"Not my plants!" she shrieked.

"No, not your plants," Elle agreed. She dropped her lorgnette.

"*Faedra—*" Peasy screamed, fire erupting from her mouth. Her hands and face shrivelled as all her body's water went to the flames. She crumpled, knees collapsing. Her falling body curled into a smoking heap. Plumes rose from her blackened eye sockets.

Elle looked up to where Faedra-plant watched. "Faedy, come down." She held out her arms. She caught Faedra-plant with her mind as the plant leapt.

"Does this upset you?" Elle asked, when the Faedra-plant stood once more by her side. Elle trembled from fatigue, unable to meet Faedra-plant's gaze. The plant looked down at Peasy's smouldering remains.

"She was diseased," Faedra-plant said.

"Let us go." Elle took an unsteady step.

And landed her foot on Peasy's shrivelled head, crunching it. Elle closed her eyes.

Now I'm truly sorry.

☠

The train came around again while Elle leaned against Faedra-plant, the conservatory dome's glass becoming brighter and brighter. Faedra-plant helped Elle into the moving carriage. Elle collapsed, her head in Faedra's lap. Light framed Faedra's golden head as she watched over Elle, and Elle saw it then: the weariness. The waning of the ill.

"No more death," Elle said, but her mouth did not move. She tried to raise her hand for Faedra-plant's face, and somehow the plant knew and grasped her hand. She smiled down at Elle, the expression weak.

What did Polly do to you?

"Stay, please," Elle whispered.

"I love you," Faedra-plant said.

"I love you, too," Elle said, her heart breaking. Faedra-plant became still.

Elle saw the light leave her eyes, and felt her cool hand lighten, the soul departing.

"*No*," she cried.

CHAPTER THIRTEEN

Though the day was bright, rain fell.

Elle no longer knew what was happening when, or why. Faedra—her Faedra—carried her back to the manor, raindrops striking her wife's calm face. She heard Peasy talking somewhere beside them, sounding small and confused. A dog snuffed at her dangling feet. She knew things again when Faedra was laying her in bed.

"Your plant," Elle uttered.

"She rests in the Rare House," Faedra soothed. "The mother-plant wants you to know. What happened was best for her...and for Peasy-plant."

"I'm sorry," Elle said. Faedra held her, and Elle buried her face in her chest.

"My brave woman," Faedra said softly. "You are the bravest."

"I am murderous," Elle sobbed.

"No. No." Faedra kissed her eyelids, her tears. "You are my heroine."

Elle wept until she finally slept, welcoming oblivion.

When she woke again, it was to the steady pitter-patter of rainfall. One of the round-faced maids sat in the room with her, silent and still, and she looked towards the water-streaked balcony doors. The bed, the quiet, the woman playing both minder and nurse; they were reminders of other rooms with doctors, patients, and illnesses.

I'll accept your morphine dose now, doctor, if it will take this pain away.

Elle closed her eyes and slept more, saddened.

Narcotics had their dark side. Instead of lightening their victims by their absence, they carved out a void within, needing filling. Melancholy became magnified. Elle knew the mother-plant was right. Faedy-plant was meant to pass away, a malformed babe too injured to live. Elle had enough of tears, even if her body wanted more. When she woke again, she stayed awake.

Faedra entered their bedroom after Elle had emerged from a hot bath, the round-faced maid brushing Elle's hair. Faedra ran up and embraced her spouse.

"Tell me what you've been up to," Elle softly demanded, and once she was back in bed at her wife's insistence, Faedra did.

Valentin remained missing. Faedra had investigated the subterranean furnaces and concluded from the blood evidence that false-Polly's body had been fed into one of them. Seven of the people placed in pods did not survive, which included Mrs Bunkley, Bascomb, and cook, all of whom were older or aged. Nine still lived, including six staff members, Peasy, Faedra, and the gamekeeper's black and tan. After recovering, they had returned to the Rare House while Elle had slept, to rid the place of traps and to put the rest of the conservatory in order.

"You glow with health," Elle then said, and she didn't think it was the last residue effects of ergot that made her wife seem so.

"The others confess to feeling years younger, though they remain dazed," Faedra said. "It appears that all the survivors had no family or friends outside of Peaseflower. I think Polly deliberately chose them."

"With Mrs Bunkley-plant's help, since she would have known her staff's history. A very clever person might have succeeded with the scheme of replacing staff with false people." She held Faedra's hand and sighed. "Even with Valentin's help, it was a trial, breaching Peaseflower. How fortunate that you emerged less dazed but ready to lend aid."

"Well, I had competition for your attention," Faedra said with a grin, but it faded — perhaps from recall of Faedra-plant's fate — and Elle squeezed her hand in reassurance.

"Elle, the false-Polly. How did you know she killed people — yet somehow didn't intend to?"

"I think at some point she did intend to. She had a way of botching things. Like an inexperienced farmhand who mishandles slaughtering a pig, and causes it to scream and scream until someone helps him kill it. False-Polly, angered at the true Miss Devereux, poisoned her employer, making her suffer, and then she must have killed her. Arson was a means of destroying what she'd done, and the effects of self-poisoning that Peasy witnessed at false-Polly's arrival? That was her mishandling her murder weapon: belladonna."

"But the ergot, Elle," Faedra said. "If it was the wine...."

"My swift Fae'," Elle said, her tone soft. "You already suspect the truth. But do you accept it?"

Faedra held Elle's hand and kissed it. "Yes." Then she kissed Elle's forehead.

"I know you have to see to more," Elle said. "Please eat something, even if from the orangery...before attending to the dead."

"The hunt for food will not be necessary, as I've prepared edibles for all," Peasy announced, and she entered the bedroom carrying a tray ladened with cut fruit, nuts, a glass of juice, and a cup of coffee. Elle nearly jumped out of the bed in alarm, but Faedra held her steady. Peasy wore a work smock over her dress, her gardening gloves tucked into a pocket and a pair of clippers hanging from her chatelaine. Elle suspected that under her skirts, Peasy was shod in galoshes. Peasy's countenance was so full of vigour—hair bright and complexion glowing—that Elle thought her a second Peasy-plant, and was tempted to mentally pin her against the wall again.

"And you needn't worry, Elle, Faedy's been fed." Peasy placed the tray on Elle's lap. Faedra then pulled biscuits from her pocket and laid them on the tray, and Elle recognised them as the ones she'd packed. Her detecting suitcase had been retrieved and lay open nearby. Faedra clasped Elle's hand.

"Are you well?" she asked, adding in a lowered voice. "She insisted on visiting."

"Of course she did." Elle patted their clasped hands. "We forgot to barricade the door."

"Elle?" Peasy said.

"Quiet, Peasy," Elle said.

Faedra grinned. "I would remain, but—"

"Go," Elle bade, smiling. "And if you spy Valentin at all, perhaps napping...." *Beneath the earth.* "Send that scoundrel to me."

When Faedra left, Elle proceeded to devour her food, eyeing Peasy all the while. Peasy sat gingerly on the side of the bed, her hands clasped.

"Now Elle, it is me," Peasy said.

"Why shouldn't it be you?" Elle said.

"Well, it can be confusing *in vivo*. I believe another of myself was also growing on my personal vine when—when things happened. I even stuck myself with a pin to see if I bled red, and I did." She brightened. "I can't say I was tired upon emerging, though I was quite disorientated. I've been busy taking care of the pod remains in the Rare House—clipping the vines and such so that our mother-plant might conserve her nutrients and recover. Then I prepared foods for all."

"Are you injecting yourself with cocaine again?"

"Why—how did? Oh, don't be silly." Peasy fidgeted. "The mother-plant told me that stimulant would be to my health's detriment. Being in the pod, Elle, is quite rejuvenating, especially when the nutrients are plentiful. I've been cleansed of my addiction, and will taint my body no more."

"I told Faedra to fling your doses and syringe into the river."

"Oh."

Elle drank all her juice—a sensual blend of orange juice and mango—and decided to forego the coffee. More sleep would be what she needed. With Peaseflower in Faedra's hands, all would be well. Peasy moved closer on the bed, hesitant.

"Mother's dead," Peasy said, her voice small. "My own mother, I mean. I knew when she was gone...while we were in our pods. But we're all just matter and dust, only to come again, aren't we?"

"Peasy, I can't philosophise right now." *And unlike you, I may scream and cry once again.*

"Yes, yes Elle, of course."

Elle sighed. She could be so harsh. "Peasy, forgive me my thoughtlessness. I am sorry she's gone...she loved you very much."

"Thank you, Elle." Peasy's gaze fell to her lap. "I know she did. I know this now, more than I'd ever felt since understanding that I was adopted. I was loved. The communal connection of the vine is an extraordinary gift. I don't feel abandoned. And therefore, strangely, have no need to scream and cry."

Elle paused in eating her cantaloupe slice.

"But now, I feel my aloneness." Peasy cleared her throat. "And therein, perhaps, lies some grief. I slept whilst *in vivo*, but I knew fear, confusion...and death. I know there was another like me, in the world and—and she did things. Oh, Elle. Can you tell me of the horror that's been done?"

"Yes, of course," Elle said through a mouthful of melon. "But first, fetch me my stash of jerked meat from my suitcase."

☠

Elle did not feel she had much to relate. It was a simple tale, only made complex with the constant obfuscation by the Peasy-plant and false-Polly—who both somehow worked in tandem to thwart Elle's investigation as much as against each other. However, Peasy-plant's actions had consequences enough to occupy Peasy's mind, concerning friendship, betrayal...and unspoken desires. Such information, for the time being, could distract her from the practicalities of her true mother's death and those of the other six, whose bodies Faedra was presently taking care of.

The old cemetery on former Fairditch land shall see new occupants.

When Elle related the circumstances of her poisoning, Peasy interrupted. "Such madness you endured, Elle. You were plainly given a narcotic with a strength beyond the dream delirium of the opiate."

"I know that Peasy, It was St Anthony's Fire, because it burned."

"Ergot? How utterly medieval. Why would the false Polly dose you with that to induce phantoms and frenzy when my conservatory possesses the sacred mushroom, *teonanacatl*, and the peyotl cacti...and that darling little toadstool, the Fly Aga—"

"Do any of those torment the body?" Elle interrupted.

"I...speak from experience, they do not make the body suffer like ergotism can." Peasy's head dropped. "Oh, Elle."

"I will be blunt." Elle's tone was tired. "It could only be given to me with the complicity of the dinner table's mistress. Peasy-plant was the one who poisoned me."

Peasy looked up in fright and shock.

"And perhaps I will give Peasy-plant this little doubt," Elle said. "Polly was driving her mad with henbane. Polly might have prepared the ergot, and Peasy, recognising an opportunity, might have agreed to administer it."

"An opportunity," Peasy said stiffly.

"Yes, Peasy."

"Elle—" In anguish, Peasy covered her face with her hands.

"I'm still weighing whether living out my life trapped in an asylum without Faedra was kinder than plant-Peasy allowing Polly to kill me." Elle's tone was matter-of-fact.

"Can you ever forgive me?" Peasy wailed. "How did I let this happen? False-Polly had not seem such a—not as bright as her brilliant work had made her to be! But many gifted individuals lack in social skills. And then to learn now that she really was a stupid girl? How can someone like that be such a danger? *How?*"

"Peasy." Elle sighed. "Like in school, you failed to notice a simple truth: the devastation cruel girls can wreak."

☠

Elle rose later, needing to prove her body's recovery, and took a walk, avoiding the conservatory proper and Faedra and Peasy's work there. Since Faedra-plant's death, Elle had not had a delirious relapse. No longer did the world bend or her mind feel as if all its doors were flung open. She was an ordinary woman again in an ordinary world, with the mundane need to breathe rain-freshened air, listen to birdsong, and feel the breeze on her face. If the ergot left her with anything, perhaps it was with an ocular sense that made things a little sharper and brighter, but she was certain that effect would fade.

She did not test if her ability's enhancement remained. On her arm she carried a large market basket retrieved from the kitchen, and crossed Peasy's hedged vegetable gardens for the fruit tree orchard. She had a great desire to touch apples, smell them, eat a few, and then find fuzzy peaches to fondle.

While she was standing on a ladder picking rosy Annurca apples, the plant-maids approached. They looked up, two of their group with round faces and blonde fringes. Elle looked down and realised that, during all her time asleep, she could not recall dreaming of the Unreal plant. She descended and put her basket down.

"Speak your mind," Elle said.

"Polly was disease," a maid said.

Elle paused at the thought. The mother-plant, previously isolated on its atoll, knew no other comparison for malevolent intent.

"And you came to my aid when she attacked in the rose garden," Elle said. "Thank you. But did you help me because I was being threatened...or because you needed me to help you?"

"Harm is bad," the maid said. "Are we safe now?"

"Peasy-plant had plans that would harm humans. Have you entertained the same thoughts?"

The maids stared blankly.

"That is, if you can entertain thoughts. I speak not to the mother-plant, but to you, vegetable-people. What are your intentions whilst co-existing with humankind?" Elle asked with patience.

"We are fruit. We mature, and then we die," one maid answered.

"That is your function? Your only intention?"

They stood in silence, seemingly pondering her question.

"We will seed, and that is all," the maid answered. "Are we safe now?"

"It would appear so." Elle sighed. She returned her attention to the ladder, only to pause, her scrutiny of the maids sharp. "Why was Peasy-plant so complex of thought and action, if you maids and gardeners are not?"

"She had time to grow," three maids said in unison, startling Elle. She nearly thought she could see the mother-plant in their eyes. "She was left longer on the vine."

"And we," another maid added, her gaze placid, "were injected."

Elle's throat caught, thinking of the Faedra-plant.

They helped carry her basket, and she made them pick fruit, melons, and harvest vegetables to fill three more baskets.

☠

After Elle had packed a great hay box (used to ship the garden's bounty to the Bunkleys' London home) with a letter of instruction to Mrs Haggins of how to gift their neighbours, church, and the soup kitchen, she had more food baskets prepared for delivery to the Punwick cottage. Good deeds done, she sought out Faedra and Peasy, who were in Mrs Bunkley's study, surrounded by papers and accounting books.

"I do not know how to manage this home," Peasy cried when Elle entered.

"Peasy, you have overseen all manner of conservatory houses and teams of gardeners, groundskeepers, and scientists. Perhaps you just don't want the responsibility," Elle snapped.

"Elle," Faedra said.

"Even when ill, Mother insisted on running all of Peaseflower," Peasy retorted. "We kept no land or house steward. And it isn't only the manor I must oversee. This was Fairditch land. There are the farms to consider, the hamlets, the forests—"

Elle sat down. "Peasy, hush. We've another matter to discuss." She then related her interaction with the maids.

"But Elle," Faedra said when she finished. "I thought you had... well, considered destroying them." Peasy gave a high-pitched squeak.

"I did," Elle admitted. "Only because Peasy-plant revealed intentions that the other plant-folk might have shared. Peasy, Faedra and I discussed this, for we engaged with your plant self and understood the depths of her schemes. What would happen should Her Majesty visit your conservatory—and become duplicated?"

Peasy shut her mouth, her eyes wide.

Elle nodded. "Now you understand. I don't believe your plant-self intended to merely take over airships."

"Elle," Peasy whispered.

"Yet the plant people, innocent of her plottings, approached me in good faith," Elle continued, "and I'll return their goodwill in kind—for now. Peasy, they'll end up seed, but when will that occur?"

Peasy composed herself. "I have asked that question. The mother-plant is young, and this is her first flowering, therefore the fruit-people do not know. These fruit—it is extraordinary mimicry. The process beginning with the luring of 'prey,' if you will, into pod-traps, and then producing fruit duplicating them. In this manner the Unreal plant ensures propagation, for legs can travel far, like spores on the wind. However," she said, as Elle and Faedra shared a look of alarm. "The fruit-people seem content to remain on the estate or return to it, and therefore will decay and die right here. They'll need much tending, my poor creatures."

"Peasy," Faedra said. "When you reopen your estate—"

"And calling them plants or vegetables is truly a misnomer," Peasy continued. "They bear seeds, and though now detached, I believe they still grow, maturing as they draw sustenance from the—"

"Peasy," Elle said with some severity.

"Elle, I understand about empire matters. I do! But you've said yourself, they've no evil intent. For the mother-plant's sake, they must be kept safe," Peasy pleaded. "Faedy, you spent enough time within the pod to know. They are all she has left, as the Unreal Atoll is gone."

Elle sighed. "Peasy, they are duplicates of true people. They cannot remain on staff or where returning staff can see them. They do resemble people's colleagues and *friends*."

Peasy hunched in the desk chair, hands to her face in despair. Faedra touched Peasy's shoulders.

"Six dead by my ignorance," Peasy said in a stark voice. "Bascomb and Cook served the Fairditches. They were old and alone, and the manor was their only home. They and the four will be mourned only by Faedra and me." She dropped her head.

"That's seven, Peasy, including your mother," Elle said quietly. Peasy raised her wet-eyed gaze to her.

"Elle...what of the ones still on the vine?" she asked in a small voice.

Elle looked at Faedra in exasperation. "Faedy?" She had not expected Faedra to leave undeveloped simulacra to still grow.

"Let us consider how to explain this situation to the world outside, first," Faedra said.

☠

Elle insisted on a simple story: a threat incomprehensible had overtaken the estate, brought on by Polly's mysterious experiments with ergot and the mishandling of its effects. The circumstance needed containment, and Mrs Bunkley had dismissed nearly all the staff to avoid scandal and their becoming tainted. Those who remained had succumbed, resulting in memory loss. Perhaps due to such effects, Mrs Bunkley could not explain her actions or seek help, until Peasy, bewildered by what was happening and somehow ignorant of Polly's actions, did seek aid.

"Elle, I'll look like such a fool," Peasy exclaimed.

"But Peasy, you were a fool. You were entirely unaware of what was happening and wrote us, did you not? Then you *succumbed*," Elle added pointedly, "just as your journals attest, when we arrived. False-Polly fled, her true identity and actions uncovered—more or less—and thus, here we are."

Peasy sighed. "Very well. I do want the true Miss Devereux vindicated, if any good can come of this. She was—she was an exceptional mind, and would have made a valued contribution to science. We will have a staff meeting to collaborate this story, and then I will record the entire incident, recalled to my point of 'memory loss,' or in truth, my placement *in vivo*. But now, what to do with my fruit-people?"

Elle threw up her hands.

"May we have tea first before discussing that?" she asked. "And can someone find us some ham?"

By tea's end, Elle decided to wash her hands of the matter of the duplicates. It was Peasy's fault by refusing to not send them away, even to London, which Peasy had called an impure environment and unsuitable for her maturing fruit. Faedra then informed them she herself had to return to London; her week's reprieve was done. Yet Elle, thanks to Peasy's entreaties, still needed to stay on. It annoyed her that Peasy seemed just as distraught as she felt inside at the thought of her wife's departure in the morning. But Elle also rationalised that at least her Faedra would be away from the dreadful place.

Later, when Elle was supervising dinner preparation and had stepped out of the scullery door, she spied Faedra and Peasy near the laundry line, deep in discussion. Peasy suddenly sobbed and wept, and Elle knew by her wife's expression and comforting embrace, that something breaking Peasy's heart had been said. Elle withdrew into the kitchen, sober.

She left the two alone until dinner was to be served, though she knew even bonding as friends again would not ease the pain of unrequited love. After dinner, Peasy bade her and Faedra an early *good night*.

In their suite, Elle brushed her hair and watched Faedra move about clad only in her chemise.

"Though I share your attentions with Peasy, she must find her own Amazon, and soon," Elle remarked. Faedra laughed.

"She should fall in love with anyone who inspires her heart to do so," Faedra said. "And that can be any sort of person."

"Yes, but she did see you nearly naked, Faedy, and that impression may last a long time."

"When?" Faedra said, appalled. "If you speak of when I was only in a chemise—" Elle eyed Faedra in the mirror and smiled.

"When you are soaked, dearest, your nipples are a delight to behold."

Faedra folded her arms over her breasts. "Why didn't you tell me."

"And the fabric that clung to your wet buttocks. Had I been capable and the others not present, I would have—no, I truly would have. *Tipped* you there, for all to see."

"Elle," Faedra said, breathing deeply. "My bedraggled, wild-eyed little witch."

With a mental command, Elle flung Faedra on to the bed, making her bounce, and rose from the dressing table. She eagerly laid her body against her wife's and pulled Faedra's chemise up. She ran her fingers along Faedra's inner thigh.

"I've yet to affirm that you're entirely my Fae'," Elle mused. "Why, *this* certainly feels like my Fae', though the living vegetables are cunningly deceptive. Answer me this, you possible, plant impostor: what is my very favourite intimacy I like to perform on you?"

"No, I won't answer—I shan't," Faedra gasped.

"Ah, I see. So my prisoner will be difficult? I will interrogate you all night if I have to," Elle said, and proceeded to do so.

☠

That night, Elle dreamt, and it was Faedra in the Rare House, dressed in blue and gold and wearing her black cavalier hat, standing by the mother-plant.

Good night, she said to Elle.

Faedra? Elle said. She tried to touch her, but Faedra in the Rare House was already shutting her eyes, so Elle let her sleep.

I'll be here when you wake, she assured, and then closed her own eyes as well.

☠

Elle woke to the sound of curtains being drawn by one of the round-faced maids. The second one hovered over the bed, as if studying her.

"You know maids ought not to do that," Elle muttered low, hoping her voice did not wake Faedra. To her sleepy surprise, the maid smiled, then picked up Faedra's packed cases and left the room with her twin.

Elle remained in bed and decided to investigate the maid's surprising show of emotion some other time.

After breakfast, Peasy sobbed by Elle's side as they watched Faedra's Charvolant race away.

"If that missing Valentin should approach you in London," Elle had murmured to her wife when hugging her.

"I shall pull his ear for you," Faedra had promised.

With Faedra gone, Elle set her jaw and turned her attention to the manor.

She did her best, but she felt her wife had the better head for supervision. Elle ran her own home well enough, but only because she preferred to do everything. Her mother had been that way, therefore Elle did not suffer the presence of servants much. And there were hardly any servants' presence to suffer. Peasy saw her precious plants as needing help first, and thus enlisted everyone's aid towards their care, even Bascomb-plant's.

"Elle," Peasy said when Elle confronted her with the manor's needs. "We needn't a kitchen staff presently, for everything we can eat is right here, in the garden. We've zucchinis, lemons, cabbages—"

"Peasy, you may gnaw on a raw cabbage if you like, but the rest of what's harvested does not wash and chop itself up!"

Somehow, after she's made certain all the humans were fed, including the vegetarian, Elle had to puzzle out the hiring back of the human staff.

"Elle," Peasy said to her at breakfast, while Elle, grumpy, was pondering how to tackle Mrs Bunkley's staff records. "Have you noticed how articulate the fruit-people have become? With the Unreal specimen entering dormancy, its *telæsthesian* effects may be lessening, and the fruit-people are gaining autonomy at last."

Elle only stared at her, the toast she held to her mouth dripping yolk on to her shirred eggs.

"Heavens, Elle, must you flaunt your mockery of my vegetarianism?" Peasy said, aggrieved.

Peasy had determined—based on Cherish's Unreal Atoll letter—that because her cousin had found evidence of human inhabitance dating as much as four to six years old, the Unreal plant's dormancy after flowering might last the same length of time. Elle visited the mother-plant in the Rare House and saw that it was so. Its great blooming had ended. The huge spathe that had clothed it had fallen, shrivelled, and its remaining vines lay grey, hung with the scent of fresh plant decay. What bulbous, unformed fruit still lay intact, Elle was uncertain would achieve form and maturity with their nourishment depleted and their pod-parents gone. The mother-plant was folded in upon itself, enclosed and sealed for its long sleep. She touched it, and wondered if it dreamed.

When she left the Rare House, the six recovering staff members were waiting outside, thin and wide-eyed, accompanied by the plant-people. Three round-faced maids stood, one of whom, the human, was leaner and more wane than her doppelgängers.

"Let us sit together," Elle said to the six. "We will retire to the orangery."

Behind the warm confines of the glass and under the pleasing scent of the trees, she gave the people oranges to eat—and to keep their nervous hands busy—while the plant-people stood about, silent and still, in their bare feet. One of the human gardeners began to speak. He was a tall, angular man, and Elle thought him a senior groundskeeper.

"We remember everything, Mrs Black," he said, his voice low and unsteady. "And we know what she felt...the mother-plant."

Elle nodded and peeled an orange.

"Inside her, we heard each other, somehow." His companions nodded in agreement. "And in that communion, we became aware of our...the world, the firmament, Our Lord. Life. It has been much to ponder. And now that she sleeps, our ties of thought fade. But it has left us with a familial bond, Mrs Black, one forged for our lifetimes." The others nodded again.

"How did this begin?" Elle asked.

"Well," he said softly. "I shall relate some of the very beginning, so that you might understand the circumstances of her feelings. Mother was taken from her home, as you know, and whilst on the ship, she knew that death came upon the atoll and her brethren. She heard them, when it happened."

"The earthquake," Elle said.

"Yes, that, Mrs Black. So when she was situated here, in the Rare House, I guess we could say that she felt a great sense of safety...and freedom. Because like a baby bird having discovered it had wings, she felt this need for testing her new surroundings.

"And she was curious," the gardener said with wide eyes, and the others smiled. "There were so many of us walking, talking, and moving. All so new to her. She called, but we didn't understand.

Then the gamekeeper's dog did answer, and she wrapped him up in a pod. In order to know the animal, you see. To learn. And then have a facsimile of it join our world with a bit o' her in it. In that way, she might be among us — if that makes sense, Mrs Black."

"It does," she said.

"But that Miss Devereux saw," the gardener said in a hushed voice. "She saw, and then terrible notions came to her."

Mrs Bunkley, Elle learned, was the first that the false Polly trapped in a pod. Since the matriarch had wanted her dismissed, Polly decided to act first. Then, while controlling Mrs Bunkley-plant with henbane, Polly forced more victims upon the plant.

"And Mother *had* to accept us, you see, because Miss Devereux threatened to kill us if Mother didn't. Mother had no choice." Elle nodded.

"A plant grows its fruit, its seed, in peace," the gardener continued. "But weather, animals, insects, disease…these things can make things seem wrong, and everything did go wrong. So much confusion and fear in poor mother, for the parts of her that were Mrs Bunkley and Miss Peasy — well, Miss Peasy became completely severed by the influence of henbane, and her mind, turned! Then there were too many of us to feed on the vine. We could only help the mother-plant by going dormant ourselves, and when some of us died, well. Then we slept more, saddened. Though." He paused. "Though when you know the world as she had shown us, perhaps we did not dwell on death with so great a sadness.

"She's such a fine plant," the gardener then said. "Really magnificent."

☠

The six assured Elle that they would work to keep the Living Fruit among them from being discovered. Such calm as she felt from them was like the communal spirit she'd sensed from religious cults, but theirs seemed a benign energy, for the time being. If Peasy had another house or parcel of land that could be set aside at Peaseflower, Elle thought it should be given to them. Peasy never stayed at the manor long enough for Elle to express the idea. Her hostess hid herself in the many conservatory houses until Elle gave up in trying to chase her out. Then, two days after the Unreal plant went to sleep and while Elle was overseeing the removal of ivy and decaying sweet pea, Peasy walked up the lawn with another on her arm. The older woman's loosened silver hair shone in the sunlight and she strolled with quiet dignity in her velvet and brocade dressing gown.

Elle watched the two approach and her mouth pursed. Mrs Bunkley gasped in happiness.

"You must be...little Eleanor Dunny! How you've grown! You are the very picture of your mother, Eleanor. I am so pleased to see you as a woman at last!"

Elle stared at Mrs Bunkley-plant and stiffly smiled.

The next morning, Elle banished Peasy to her conservatory work and spent the day with the new Mrs Bunkley. She watched the matriarch fall into the role of managing her staff and estate. Everything in her study was reviewed, put to order, and important matters swiftly addressed, including the writing of staff advertisements that Elle had struggled with. Mrs Bunkley-plant listened gravely as Elle shared her idea of the six survivors living apart of the main house with their fruit companions. Then Mrs Bunkley-plant's gaze sharpened.

"Elle," she said, her tone chastising. "Why do you ask this when you know better how we fruit people should be handled?"

Elle was taken aback. When Mrs Bunkley-plant's gaze continued to pin her, unwavering, Elle understood then how very similar the plant was to the human.

"You are correct," Elle said quietly.

"I would have expected more of Hayat's daughter," Mrs Bunkley-plant said severely. "Both you and Faedra have ignored our plant-selves threat to the security of the empire."

"You are correct again, Mrs Bunkley-plant." Elle took a deep breath and steeled herself.

She stood up. "How do you prefer to die?"

Mrs Bunkley-plant drew back. "Eleanor, I was referring to self-exile."

The Bunkleys, as it turned out, owned an isle in the Malay Archipelago, with an estate retreat ready to be settled. Mrs Bunkley-plant would retire to the retreat with the Unreal plant, fruit people, and their human counterparts. There, she would eventually perish out of sight of the Bunkleys' present society, relieving Peasy of the deception of a funeral.

"A formal death here will only involve a mortician," Mrs Bunkley-plant said. "Do you find this solution acceptable, Eleanor?"

For the first time since Faedra's departure, Elle felt true solutions would finally occur.

At dinner, with Peasy alternately weeping in silence and beaming at the sight of Mrs Bunkley-plant at the table (who ate nothing) Elle then wondered why she had allowed the fruit people to live and such an elaborate and possibly harmful sham to continue—the danger to England aside. Having been too recently and painfully reacquainted with loss, perhaps she had wanted Peasy to have her stolen time with a simulacrum of her mother.

Elle then became confused as to what the emotional harm might be in entertaining a false mother. She thought of Valentin, the one she thought she knew before the true creature revealed himself, and pondered what she would have done, faced with the prospect of his plant self right after his death. And then she thought of Faedra-plant and finally concluded that she could think no more on the morality or rationality of it.

☗

Faedra arrived the next Saturday to take Elle home. Elle waited outside Peaseflower's entryway to watch for the kites of her wife's Charvolant, and thought of her kitchen and garden. Peasy joined her, dressed in mourning black.

Elle looked at her and simply nodded. Returning staff were already propagating within the household and on the grounds, and at least one new botanist was due to arrive that day as well. Elle had already given her farewells to Mrs Bunkley-plant, who was interviewing a woman for the position of house steward. It was time to leave.

When Faedra brought her Charvolant to a stop before the manor and disembarked, Peasy surprised Elle by not flinging herself first into her wife's arms. Elle was in the midst of embracing Faedra when Mrs Bunkley-plant emerged from the house, her hands out in welcome.

"Faedra White," she exclaimed. "How beautiful you are."

Faedra looked at Elle.

☗

While Faedra spoke to Mrs Bunkley-plant, Peasy approached Elle.

"I shall miss you, terribly," Peasy said.

"Don't confuse yourself, Peasy, you will miss Faedra terribly. To alleviate your loneliness, you must socialise. Then, may you develop better flirtations."

"Flirt—what did my plant-self *do*? Did I flirt with you, Elle? What horror!"

"Peasy—! I need you to understand something. And *listen* to me, or I shall return in secret and throw salt upon everyone."

Peasy's eyes grew wide and she grabbed Elle's arm. "I'm listening, Elle. What is it?"

"You are isolated here, Peasy, with a version of your mother who may prove too accommodating—and who plans to retreat to your family's isle soon, leaving you to your destructive habits. You cannot remain here, working, forever working, in your perfect little realm. You must go out and meet true people and do so at least once a week, do you hear me, Peasy? Take one of your female scientists for chaperone. Go out, converse, dance, shop, travel!"

"But Elle, my Peaseflower Court. Now that I've eschewed the idea of providing amusements, I wish to focus on botanical tours, education, and the sharing of conservation's virtues. It shall require—"

"Peasy, what did I just tell you!"

"Yes, Elle! Yes, *yes*! I shall do all that you say."

"Write Faedra to report on your activities every week or I shall come and set everyone afire, and you will not know when or how I'll do it."

Peasy gulped and nodded. She gripped Elle once more.

"I shall come visit you," she said.

"Good heavens, Peasy!"

"Now I've reason to come to London! I shall do as you say, Elle, and commune and enjoy the company of humanity again! I will reopen our London home. Oh, we'll have such fun, Elle!"

Elle shrugged out of her grip, boarded the Charvolant with the aid of the footman, and bade Peasy a curt farewell.

☠

Elle watched Faedra handle the Charvolant's steering and then turned around to look at Peaseflower's blackthorn hedgerow diminish behind them. The white blossoms had already wilted and fallen.

"Is this wise?" Faedra said, but her tone held humour.

"Do you mean the entirety of this situation, or the greater possibility that Peasy will soon burden us with her ebullient spirit?"

"Something else concerns me more. I am very surprised to return and witness a simulacrum of Mrs Bunkley, alive, sharp of mind, and whole, and apparently managing Peaseflower again."

"I know, darling." Elle sighed. "Peasy somehow concealed that fruit while it was on the vine, and…I will explain the whole of that situation, and I hope you'll agree that the solution is satisfactory. For the moment. I was prepared to murder the creature, but I could no longer hurt Peasy more. She has lost too much, Faedy."

Faedra grasped Elle's hand as she drove, squeezing it.

"Perhaps the good of it outweighs any harm," she gently said.

"I dearly hope so. Peasy understands that the plant is not the same woman, and Mrs Bunkley-plant is fully aware of the situation. Perhaps a new relationship may grow, or the charade may prove its limits. Therefore, we may have to visit again."

"I'll make certain of it," Faedra said.

☠

On the train, Elle knitted, and Faedra read the paper. But Elle's mind could not calm. The farther they left Peaseflower behind, the more she felt that a thread to a world truer to the Earth than their own was fading. She and Faedra were returning to the chaos, strife, and struggles of London, the domain of the human species, and if she knew a plant, it was what she dug up from her own garden or purchased at market. Elle felt not only bereft, but also strangely alone. She laid her needles aside.

"Dearest, what happened to you inside the mother-plant?" she asked, and Faedra put her paper down.

"Well, I slept, for she was very tired, and there were many of us," Faedra answered. "But when I was aware, amid the jumble of pain, and confusion, and fear, I thought of you. And I asked the mother-plant to help keep you safe."

Elle moved to sit by Faedra's side and laid her head on her wife's shoulder. Faedra stopped reading and they watched the countryside roll by.

CHAPTER FOURTEEN

E lle's favourite Secret Commission agent had defeated the dreaded Defiler while Elle and Faedra had been at Pease-flower. Elle cautioned her wife to avoid his remaining taint in Whitechapel, though the Public Disinfectors had been brutally thorough in their duties. Rain came to London, and its populace seemed to exhale beneath rainfall's calm. What fears and angers had possessed the city collapsed in upon themselves, spent in their energies. Elle doubted such irrational conflict would ever fully dissipate. Human nature was adversarial, after all, among other complexities. She did note, when out to market, visiting her neighbours, or going about her volunteer work, that the trees and greenery of London maintained their silent exis-tence, oblivious to the activities of humankind, and she felt the need to thank them with equal silence for that stable, comforting presence.

Elle finished the unpacking from their Peaseflower stay, and also all the preparation, distribution, dehydration, cooking of preserves, and canning of even more bounty sent down by train as further expression of Peasy's gratitude. Included in the hay box had been star fruit.

At the sight of them, Elle had to close the box and breathe, memories of Peasy-plant and that night in the conservatory coming to the fore. When Elle had calmed, she resumed work again.

Sent along with the hay box were potted comfrey and chamomile, with instructions from Peasy that Elle plant them in her garden to help in soil enrichment and encouragement of pollinating insects. Peasy also gifted Elle with an elegant Wardian case, shaped like a small house, in which camellias in a bowl were already flourishing. Elle placed that on the sunny sill of one of the parlour's bay windows. And finally, Peasy bestowed upon them an elaborately decorated small picture frame, handcrafted by her, made of pinecones, beechnut bulls, and acorns. A photograph of Peasy was set in the frame.

Elle sighed, and placed the frame on the mantle, behind the red velvet clock. She then went into the kitchen.

That afternoon she'd gone to the butcher's and purchased rump steak and sheep's kidney. Lt Montague's chicken coop next door provided the eggs needed. With the meat cubed, liberally peppered, salted, and lining the pie dish, she whipped up flour, milk, and eggs, poured the batter over the meat and placed the dish within a fiercely heated oven. By the time Faedra returned home after her work day, Elle had a piping hot Toad-in-the-Hole ready for dinner, served with onion gravy, carrots, and buttered parsnips.

When they sat down to dinner, Elle was reminded of the grand table at Peaseflower, with its many seats and lavish centrepiece. She shook her head and smiled at the thought of having played "lady" for a brief hour, then served her hungry wife Toad-in-the-Hole.

"Your plant-self is now situated in the garden," Elle chose to say as they ate.

"Oh?" Faedra said. "And where was she placed?"

"I mixed her remains within the strawberry bed. I hope she might consider them good company."

Faedra cleared her throat. "I know you're fond of all parts of me, Elle, but...what if she grows again?"

"Into a fully grown woman? Before we exile her to the Bunkleys' isle, I would love for her to live with us a while. It's my fault she died so soon. Had she remained on the vine, perhaps the poisoning given her would have been cleansed and her faculties repaired. I'd picked her too early."

Faedra said nothing and frowned as she ate.

"Oh, now dear, what is the matter?" Elle asked gently.

"I don't know, Elle, I just...well, she's a *plant*."

"Yes?" Elle coaxed.

"She's a vegetable, Elle, and—I understood when you mourned as you did, for so much had happened to you, but I feel you are overly fond of her!"

"How so?" Elle asked, surprised.

"When we were both beneath the shower and she was being such a hindrance...how you stared!"

Elle gazed, innocent.

"At her!" Faedra said, her tone annoyed.

"Oh dearest, I was staring at both your wet bodies." She served Faedra more parsnips.

"Well, when I addressed you, Elle, I don't believe you heard a word I said."

"Faedy, place yourself in my situation. I had been struck by sudden, heavenly good fortune. *Two* Faedras." She sighed. "If she had not been so short-lived, the poor thing, I would have kept you both."

"Kept us? Like—well! Now I feel reduced to so much...cheap merchandise," Faedra muttered.

"Oh, dearest, I am horrible." Elle went to her side, hugged her, and kissed her. "Selfish and wicked." She kissed her again. "And having offended you, I am suitably chastened."

Faedra looked at her, amused. Elle took her seat again and resumed eating.

"When we're done with dinner," Elle added, "I'll confess to the vulgar notions that occurred to me, faced by your twin's temptation."

"You wicked woman! I've the perfect punishment for such a confession," Faedra said with cheer.

"Oh? Would that require your calling out my name repeatedly and begging for mercy?"

"*You*," Faedra said.

Elle dropped her napkin on her plate and departed swiftly from the table. She ran for the stairs, giggling.

Faedra jumped up and ran after her.

☠

Deep into the night, Elle woke with Faedra sound asleep by her side. She frowned, listening for what had disturbed her. A cat, a drip, an open window, a *telæsthesian* plant, calling? A shadow darkened the glass of the moonlit balcony doors. It was the shape of a person.

Elle rose silently, donned her dressing gown, and approached the doors. When she opened them, Valentin stood on her balcony in full evening dress, his glistening black hair rimmed by moonlight. He smiled, sardonic.

"I see that somehow we've a bond," Elle murmured, low. "Perhaps from your biting me when we were married. I don't like it."

"Elle," Valentin whispered, smiling. "I wanted to see if you were well."

"My tongue is quite fatigued, but all is well," Elle said.

A pistol's hammer cocked and Elle turned. Faedra stood nude, her silver Smith & Wesson aimed for the balcony outside.

"Fae'!" Elle exclaimed.

"I mean no harm," Valentin stated with calm from the balcony.

Elle hurriedly shut the doors and its curtains and turned to her wife.

"He's only being rude, as usual!" she hissed. "Get dressed, this instant!"

"You are not beguiled, then, and perhaps answering his seductive call to be his undead bride and so forth?" Faedra asked, her pistol still aimed towards the doors.

"If I were, the very sight of your perfection has broken such spells. Will you put on clothes!"

Faedra looked at her, took a deep breath, and then reluctantly turned to do as she was told.

"And there will be no more Gothic novels for you!" Elle called after her.

When she reopened the doors, Valentin's nose was raised in Faedra's general direction. He sniffed the air.

She took hold of the hairs of his moustache and tweaked it.

"*Ouch!*" Valentin cried.

"Lout!" Elle said.

"Elle," Valentin said peevishly behind the hand soothing his injured face.

"You disappeared entirely from Peaseflower. How were we to know if you weren't fertiliser in a basil pot? One I hadn't the chance to plant your head in?"

"I would have left a note," he said. "But—"

"Is this how you always are, coming in and out of a life as you please? Shall we blame your vampyre nature, or the rudeness that must come with preserving the secret of your species and its absurd longevity? You disappear like so much mist, and then reappear as you wish, time apparently having no consequence. You do nothing but inconvenience those you supposedly care for."

"You are a nag," Valentin muttered.

"I shall pull your ear."

"Don't." Valentin covered his ear. "May I speak now?"

"No," Elle said. Strain crept into her voice. "But if you must, let it not be in my house. In case I inadvertently destroy it."

☠

Elle and Faedra dressed and slipped out the garden gate. They walked in silence to the footbridge arcing over the canal, using the moon's bright surface to light their way. Faedra carried her fishing pole. She and Elle parted on the canal's bank, where Faedra took a spot and practiced casting, and Elle mounted the bridge to join Valentin.

"Is that false Polly now ash?" Elle asked when she reached his side.

"She is. I would have helped in destroying the plant-people but I'd need to...slumber."

"With all the cannabis in her blood, I don't doubt that. The plant-people still live. I only destroyed the one necessary."

"Elle," Valentin said. "The plants are dangerous."

"I had wanted to destroy all of them. But the alternative of exiling them to the Malay Archapelago presented itself, and for now, that is the plan. And to be more truthful, I'd killed enough. When I'd lost my good sense and had become mad again, I committed a terrible act, killing the Charvolant driver with my carelessness. Then I killed Peasy-plant deliberately, a death sentencing by my own hand. These are things I never want Faedra to have to commit."

"She is a grown woman, noble and courageous," Valentin said. "The decision to kill must be hers. And however she may change after that, you will be there for her. As she is for you."

They both gazed out upon the water.

"I have also weighed the responsibility of what to tell you," he said. "Just as you wish to protect your woman from having to decide, so now do I wish to protect you. But your continued activity as this psychic detective will only make you better known. You should be prepared—I should prepare you—for when that draws certain attention."

Elle looked at him. "When you arrived at the Punwicks' cottage, why did you first think that vampyres were involved?"

Valentin clenched the bridge railing and said nothing.

"What you must tell me is so hard for you to say." She watched his face in the dark. "You are personally invested; involved. Perhaps you are to blame."

"That intuition of yours." He grimaceed.

"I am only following the clues your body and behaviour give me, of what you say by saying nothing. We can stand here all night while I guess at your secret life's consequences until I've made a pile of coin. All I can determine is this: you think me in danger, and you are involved. Since I've done nothing, you've done something, and an enemy of yours may now be an enemy of mine."

"You are nearly to the truth. But the enemy was your father's, and now yours and mine."

Elle grabbed Valentin's arm and made him face her. He looked down and met her gaze, and though she could barely see his eyes, she felt his demeanour held the desire to communicate and have her know. He spoke low, his voice solemn.

"In Egypt, your father drew the wrath of an old vampyre, and your parents both thwarted it. But such creatures are patient. He was thorough in his vengeance."

Elle's heart turned cold.

Realisations rushed; thoughts of her mother—of being sent away to school. The happiness and utter relief that had seemed evident in her parents upon their return. She thought of the accident that ended them, right before her marriage to Valentin.

"Who killed them," she whispered. "Who killed Mama and Papa."

Valentin's hands rose to hold her. She turned away in his arms, seeking Faedra.

"Faedy!" she called

Faedra had already abandoned her pole and line and was hurrying to her. When Faedra reached them, Elle stepped from Valentin to enter Faedra's embrace. She hugged her wife and tried to gather her thoughts. She regarded Valentin.

"She must listen too. For you are telling me I've a longtime enemy."

"You do," he said.

"Tell us," Elle demanded.

"I'll not speak his name. As I'd said, he was an enemy of your parents, and his vengeance was to destroy them utterly."

"You were his instrument," Elle whispered. Valentin's face twisted, as wounded.

"He took one of mine," he whispered, "so that I would do his bidding: marry you. And your money I stole so that I could buy back the one taken.

"But you are correct. I was meant to be the instrument of your and Hector's ruin. Since I let myself be killed, I don't know what he had planned next for you. Perhaps he wanted you turned into one of us, or perhaps he wanted you...for himself. Whatever he wanted, I would have fought to my deaths. I still needed to save one of my own, but I could no longer do the creature's bidding."

"He murdered everyone I loved." Elle held fast to Faedra's hand. "But you say this thing is not yet aware I'm still living."

"Yes," Valentin said. The water stirred beneath them. A whirlpool formed, drawing leaves and debris. Wind began to whip their clothes.

"Then I've one word for it when I look upon its back," Elle whispered. "*Surprise.*"

More from Elizabeth:

The Dark Victorian: Risen Vol 1
The Dark Victorian: Bones Vol 2

Ice Demon: A Dark Victorian Penny Dread Vol 1
Medusa: A Dark Victorian Penny Dread Vol 2

Sundark: An Elle Black Penny Dread Vol 1
Poison Garden: An Elle Black Penny Dread Vol 2

Monster Stalker: A Darquepunk Novel Vol 1
Bloody Nike: A Darquepunk Novel Vol 2
Gunslinger: A Darquepunk Novel Vol 3

The Wrecking Faerie: A Charm School Novella Vol 1
Hot Roddin' To Hell: A Charm School Novella Vol 2
Body Chase: A Charm School Novella Vol 3

AUTHOR'S NOTES

Trains:
From what I've read of British rail history, train corridor carriages were not put into use until 1889. Before then, only an outside door accessed a first class compartment, and the compartment units ran the width of the carriage. Each compartment was entirely separate from another. A corridor carriage is what one sees in Agatha Christie movies (where the compartments are entered by a corridor running the length of the carriage) making for some splendid movement of characters. Since this is a Steampunk influenced train with an observation deck and dining car, I decided to put corridor carriages in.

Charvolants:
They do exist, and were invented by George Pocock and patented by him in 1826. I have no idea how the two kites avoided tangling, and my ability to describe the control lines (and my adding mechanised spools) leave something to be desired. Stunt kites (which I've flown) need two controls, and it looks like some kite buggies do too, so I tried giving the Charvolant those. https://en.wikipedia.org/wiki/George_ Pocock_%28inventor%29

"Pleasant and Delightful":

The English folk song Elle prompts the maids to sing is "Pleasant and Delightful", or "And the Larks They Sang Melodious". There are many renditions of this song on the net, so you can choose a favourite. Lyrics from:

http://mainlynorfolk.info/louis.killen/songs/pleasantanddelightful.html

It was pleasant and delightful on a midsummer's morn
And the green fields and the meadows were all covered in corn;
And the blackbirds and thrushes sang on every green spray
And the larks they sang melodious at the dawning of the day,
And the larks they sang melodious (3x) at the dawning of the day.

The true Polly Devereux's notebook:

Her fantastic paintings at the end of her notebook were inspired by the outsider art of Eugene Von Bruenchenhein: http://www.outsiderart.co.uk/eugene.html#

The rest of her notebook (without hallucinogenic influence), might have resembled work like Edith Holden's: *The Nature Notes of an Edwardian Lady 1905*, by Edith Holden, published by Little, Brown and Company, 1989.

Ergotism:

There are two kinds of conditions wrought by prolonged ingestion of ergot (via tainted rye bread) and I took the liberty of combining the gangrenous type and the convulsive one in Elle for the sake of dramatic effect. The gangrenous version has the symptoms of being on fire—the St Anthony's Fire, or Holy Fire (*The British Pharmaceutical Codex*, 1911. http://www.henriettes-herb.com/eclectic/bpc1911/index.html).

I also have a dangerous mix of ergot wine work swiftly to

gift Elle with extreme, physical agony and the hallucinogenic experience. LSD is derived from ergot ("The Discovery of LSD and Subsequent Investigations on Naturally Occurring Hallucinogens," by Albert Hofmann, PhD, Chapter 7 of *Discoveries in Biological Psychiatry*, Frank J. Ayd, Jr. & Barry Blackwell, eds., copyright J.B. Lippincott Company, 1970, http://www.psychedelic-library.org/hofmann.htm) but I highly doubt a true ergot poisoning would result in positive, mind-expanding manifestations.

Elle's hallucinogenic experience:

I've yet to be under the influence of an entheogen, though that may change. But I wanted Elle to have a particular kind of experience, one opposite the accepted Victorian understandings of psychedelic use (understandings which may even extend to present times).

Victorians (white, male, and upper class) appropriated the use of the peyote and other hallucinogenic plants from indigenous peoples and supplanted the entheogens' original religious purposes. They established certain assumptions based on racial and cultural superiority: while the white male intellectual was capable of receiving inspiration, mind expansion, and personal entertainment under the influence, the "lesser" races were assumed inclined to base, bodily experiences. ("Victorian Hallucinogens", by Susan Zieger, published in *Romanticsm and Victorianism on the Net*, Numéro 49, février 2008. http://www.erudit.org/revue/ravon/2008/v/n49/017857ar.html)

Women may also be included in those "lesser", as they were often depicted in illustrations and postcards, littering opium dens with their stupefied bodies. If the Victorian intellect under chemical influence was about proving control, the succumbing of the "inferior" races and the weaker sex to entheogens was perhaps about letting go.

Elle understood loss of self thanks to her time in the asylum.

I felt she would face her LSD experience with an openness that could allow revelation, communication, and commonality. These may be considered the three key goals of vision quest, in alignment with the original purpose of sacred entheogenic use.

Papers read:
"Hemlock Poisoning and the Death of Socrates: Did Plato Tell the Truth?" by Enid Bloch, published in *The Trial and Execution of Socrates*, edd. Thomas C Brickhouse and Nicholas D. Smith, Oxford University Press, 2001.
https://www3.nd.edu/~plato/bloch.htm

Books read:
Modern Cookery for Private Families, by Eliza Acton, 1845.
Mrs Beeton's Book of Household Management, by Isabella Beaton, 1861.
Bright Paradise, Victorian Scientific Travellers, by Peter Raby, published by Random House, 1996.
Sisters of the Extreme, Women Writing on the Drug Experience, edited by Cynthia Palmer and Michael Horowitz, published by Park Street Press, 1982.
King's American Dispensatory, by Harvey Wickes Felter, MD, and John Uri Lloyd, Phr, M, Ph, D, 1898. http://www.henriettes-herb.com/eclectic/kings/index.html

Reference watched:
Two Fat Ladies box set, published by Acorn Media, 2008.
Chemistry: A Volatile History series, BBC, 2010.

ELIZABETH WATASIN

The DARK
VICTORIAN

BONES

About The Author

Elizabeth Watasin is the author of the Gothic steampunk series The Dark Victorian, The Elle Black Penny Dreads, the paranormal sci-fi noir series, Darquepunk, and the creator/artist of the indie comics series Charm School. She is a winner of the 2015 Rainbow Award for Best Lesbian Fantasy and Romance Fantasy and a Gaylactic Spectrum Award nominee. A twenty year veteran of animation and comics, her screen credits include thirteen feature films, such as Beauty and the Beast, Aladdin, The Lion King, and The Princess and the Frog, and she's written for Disney Adventures magazine. She lives in Los Angeles with her black cat named Draw, busy bringing readers uncanny heroines in cyberpunk, historical fantasy, diesel fantasy, and paranormal thrillers.

Follow the news of her latest projects at A-Girl Studio.

www.a-girlstudio.com

Visit her online at:

https://www.facebook.com/groups/ElizabethWatasinsClubHecate

twitter.com/ewatasin